THE LINE

Jay Harlow

GW00601882

WILLOWBRIGHT

Published in Great Britain in 2020 by Willowbright

FIRST EDITION

niftyukeyahoo.co.uk

Copyright © Jay Harlow 2020

ISBN 978-1-8382262-0-6

Willowbright is pleased to support Seacourt (Planet Positive Printing)
in using the world's first waterless printing and LED drying process.
With FSC paper, VOC free inks and 100% renewable energy,
this book has been produced in a carbon positive factory
where zero waste is sent to landfill.

for all the good people

Change of Plan

'Prime Minister, as you are aware, I have always made a point of staying out of matters of state as far as possible….'

'Yes, indeed, Your Majesty, and I would like to say, once again, how very grateful my predecessors, and of course I myself, have been for this….'

'Yes, yes, quite. However, as you are also aware, I do take a keen interest in current affairs and I am kept abreast of the feelings of my subjects through their, very numerous, communications….'

'Of course, Your Majesty. I am sure they are all most honoured by the attention you bestow upon….'

'I have lived through too many wars, riots, strikes, various crises and periods of unrest to remain untouched by it all, despite residing, as it were, away from "the thick of it".'

The Queen indicated the opulent surroundings of the royal study with a wave of the hand and a wry smile. She strode over to gaze through one of the high windows that overlooks the palace forecourt, careful not to disturb the heavy brocade drape and thus raise the excitement of the tourists who were gathered, once again, along the railings below. Her own enormous, extravagant, unwanted prison, she had sometimes thought to herself.

It was hard to put into words everything she wanted to say, but the time had well and truly arrived. The Prime Minister stood silently, unaware of the bombshell that was about to rip through his

1

body. (Not literally, for the palace security had finally been tightened enough to make that fairly unlikely.)

The Queen moved over to an enormous, carved, antique oak chest and opened the lid to reveal its contents – hundreds of batches of neatly sorted letters, tied with ribbons of various colours. As the Queen explained how she dealt with and filed these letters personally, often according to the enclosed complaint about a particular political party, one of its policies or representatives, the Prime Minister could not help noticing that she was swinging a particularly large bundle from a blue ribbon. He adjusted his tie.

Looking him directly in the eye, the Queen continued, 'Prime Minister, can you guess the suggestion which I receive most regularly from all these good people who take the time to write to me?' She did not wait for a reply, which was fortunate for the Prime Minister, who, unaccustomed to playing guessing games with his sovereign, was imagining all the terrible fates his fellow countrymen (and women) may have suggested that he, personally, deserved to endure. 'Every one of these letters implies that virtually any ordinary member of the public could do a better job of running the country than its successive Prime Ministers and governments have done.'

And there it was. The end of the world as he knew it. Just when he thought things could not get any worse, just when he hoped that he, and the rest of the country, was emerging from the worst crisis that most could ever have imagined. The Prime Minister, veteran of studied public reactions to third world tragedies, ministerial indiscretions and strange public-school tortures, could not hide his shock. This was the Queen speaking. In all her years she had never rocked the political boat. Why did it have to be now, during his moment of power? Why me? he thought, as he suddenly and surely became that twelve year old boy again, being bullied in the dorm.

'Are you going to have a lottery for Prime Minister then?' he found himself blurting out.

The merest of twinkles fluttered in the Queen's eye. 'Well that does sound rather a good way to bring some fun back into everyone's lives, but I think we need to be a little more careful than that. I believe our beautiful country has enough problems at the moment without introducing quite such a measure. What I have decided is that I will, personally, interview the most suitable candidates for office, from amongst my chosen correspondents.'

The Prime Minister looked from the Queen to the letters, and back, several times.

'There is no room for discussion on this matter, Prime Minister, but clearly the changes will not be made overnight. I would request that your government agree to stay on for a changeover period of six months....'

With a foolhardy display of protocol-amnesia, the Prime Minister almost interrupted the Queen. 'But, Your Majesty, how can we continue to run the country in such circumstances?'

'Please note I did not use the phrase "run the country". During the settling in period of the new appointees, your government will act merely as advisers.' Realising the Prime Minister had reached his threshold for new information, the Queen abruptly drew the meeting to a close.

In that moment of defeat and desperation the Prime Minister asked, 'But Ma'am, who *will* be running the country for the next six months?'

The Queen indulged in a moment's light-heartedness, in celebration of finally making her stand. 'After all these years of appearing on coins, banknotes and postage stamps, none of which I ever use, and giving a rousing speech to the country on Christmas Day, I think it's about time I really ran it for a while.'

It was her final sentence that gave the Prime Minister the distant rumblings of a cunning plan. As soon as the double doors to the study closed firmly behind him, he reached for his phone. No longer the aggrieved schoolboy, but, once again, the astute, ruthless political animal still nursing a desperate need to prove himself and lay his demons to rest. 'Rupert?' he said, 'bit of a sensitive question this, but....' he lowered his voice to a stage whisper, 'how do I go about getting the Queen sectioned?'

The following day, the Queen had been rather surprised to receive a call from Edgar, the trusted family physician, suggesting a check-up. And somewhat bewildered, therefore, when he seemed to have little interest in her troublesome throat-clearing, but launched a rambling enquiry into her feelings and opinions. This would have been vaguely uncomfortable for the average person but for the not-so-average monarch, who had spent an entire lifetime striving to deny the existence of either, it was rather confronting.

'So,' said Edgar, eventually, 'a little bird tells me you've given the government their marching orders.'

A lightbulb went on in the Queen's head, just like in those cartoons she had so enjoyed watching with her beloved grandchildren, and now their offspring. 'What do you wish to know, Edgar?'

'Well,' he floundered a little, 'why would you make a decision like that without....' He caught her eye and continued awkwardly, 'um.... consulting the right people and going through the usual channels?'

'Because, Edgar, there are no "usual channels" for a move like this and, for your information, I have been consulting exactly the right individuals for some time now.' The Queen was attempting not to sound defensive but it infuriated her that she could be the Head of State of one of the most powerful nations on earth, for more years than she cared to remember, yet still become an unheard child when put on the spot. Fortunately, one of the few good things about her position was that it did not happen often, tradition dictating that there were very few people who felt at liberty to question anything she ever said or did.

Having determined that the Queen had not sought advice from any of those who briefed him on what to discuss with her, nor did she intend to do so, Edgar was running out of ideas.

'Have you considered Charles in all of this?' he ventured.

'My dear Edgar, Charles is right behind me, as always. He firmly believes, as do I, that it is high time the individual citizens of this country were given a real voice in the way it is run. If, for instance, they come to the conclusion that a republic is the best way forward for the British people, then Charles will be only too happy to be relieved of the burden that has hung over him his whole life, poor boy. It would be marvellous to see him able to commit fully to his passion for preserving architecture and organic gardening. And saving the world,' she added, as an afterthought.

'Well, what about William?'

'Ah, Wills. He would make a great king, would he not? But it would be so much pressure for him and it can take such a toll. I believe he should have the opportunity to build as normal a life as possible with his own young family, should he so wish.'

'Harry then?' asked Edgar, a little too desperately.

'Ah, Harry,' the Queen smiled, wistfully. 'I'm afraid that ship has well and truly sailed. Has it not?'

Edgar got up, creakily, from his chair and his face softened, 'Tell me Ma'am,' he enquired gently, 'how have you managed to remain so – stoic – through all the ups and downs over the years?'

Having elicited his promise not to breathe a word of it, if she told him, the Queen smiled back, knowing he would not last five minutes without passing it on. 'When I am really stuck, I sit quietly in the garden, near the fountain….'

Edgar leaned towards her, eagerly.

'….and I ask myself, "what would Diana do?" '

As Edgar was about to ponder this remark there was a timely yapping. Jasper, the least well-trained of the Queen's corgis, ran through the doorway and sank a mouthful of surprisingly sharp little teeth into Edgar's ankle.

Following his initial squeals and amidst assurances that he was fine, Edgar ushered himself out into the hall, pulling the phone from his waistcoat pocket. 'Edgar here.' Pause. 'Yes'. Pause. 'She's as sane as I am.'

'We're going to need more proof than that,' thought the person at the other end.

Memories

Feeling a little weary after her encounter with Edgar, the Queen sank gently onto a gold brocade chaise longue. Still as uncomfortable as ever, she thought wryly. Many times she had found herself trying to imagine the perfection of her life as it existed only in the minds of those who had not been born to live it. Deciding a short break was in order, she closed her eyes and drifted back to the days when she had found a way to experience other lives for herself....

Back in the seventies, as the country slowly crumbled around her, those usually preoccupied with the Queen's movements had become sidetracked by other, more pressing, matters. She knew it had been a tough and disturbing time for many, not alleviated by those hideous, garish clothes, but for the Queen it was a decade she remembered fondly. It was the time when she met Sky.

During the Queen's early morning constitutional around the palace grounds, she first heard those dulcet tones one autumn day. As she neared the stables the usual calm was interrupted, first by a faint muttering and grumbling and then by a rather amusing string of four letter words. Moving to investigate, the Queen silently crept around the corner into the block, just as a rather unkempt young woman stepped back from the horse she was trying to calm and into a large pile of (what was euphemistically termed in royal circles) his morning product. 'Shit,' the girl exclaimed, lifting her boot up for a sniff.

'I rather think so,' responded the Queen, with that imperceptible hint of amusement only noticeable to the well-trained eye of her closest associates.

Over the following dark winter months, in their almost daily encounters, the Queen had learned a lot about Sky and her view of the world. An electric fire had finally been provided for the junior stable staff in their tack/tea room. When the Superintendent of the Royal Mews had moved to terminate Sky's employment for her 'lack of etiquette and unacceptable attire', he had been quietly warned that this would not be advisable. However, he remained oblivious to the unlikely bond which had formed between the Queen and the lowliest of her employees, as did all the royal staff. This, of course, made the Queen relish it even more.

How she would have loved to be in Sky's position, she thought, at first. An ordinary girl, going home to an ordinary house in an ordinary part of the city, when the palace gate closed behind her. The Queen smiled at the simple and idealised fantasy she had of normal life, before she met someone honest enough to tell her what it was really like 'out there'. Thankfully, Sky's 'lack of etiquette' allowed her to speak to the Queen in a way no real commoner ever had before. Sometimes the Queen mused on whether it would be acceptable for Sky to address her by the name her other friends used, rather than stumbling over her formal title. It is a strange existence when hundreds of individuals' lives revolve around making life perfect for one at every moment of one's day, causing them untold and unnecessary anxiety, whilst one must also suffer the stress and disconnection of keeping those people at a suitable distance, so as not to offend the status quo. ('Not the band' as Harry would say.) Her thoughts jogged another memory of an early meeting with Sky and brought a more open smile.

'One, which one?' Sky had responded nervously to a comment the Queen had made about observing her work. Having been employed as part of a political move which aimed to demonstrate the growing connection between the Royal Family and their subjects, Sky had found it difficult to understand some of the terminology used in the royal household. When it had proved too hard for the Queen to explain why she was sometimes expected to refer to herself as 'one': in a very natural way, in her own stable block, surrounded by her beloved horses and their product, the Queen had finally made a vow to herself to substitute the word 'I' as often as possible. At once she had felt normal. (Well 'normalish' as the boys would say.) As normal as any woman with a collection of palaces, castles, luxury cars, planes, trains, yachts and racehorses, plus the constant attention of the world, could feel.

From that moment, the Queen's longing for ever increasing contact with her ordinary subjects, and to experience the everyday lives they lived, grew daily. When the most notorious palace intrusion occurred and a young man was removed from her bedroom, following a surprisingly genial conversation, she was quietly amused that no-one seemed to have considered how easy it would be for her to sneak out, when it had proved relatively easy for others to sneak in. In fact, once she had become familiar with the schedules of the palace staff, it had been pure simplicity to avoid them, she remembered with relish.

Her first desired port of call, obviously, had been Sky's home. Understandably, the poor girl had been devastated when the Queen first mooted the idea. In fact she had turned a rather weird shade, not unlike clotted cream, but her numerous and increasingly desperate excuses fell on deaf ears. Although Her Majesty secretly prided herself on her 'common touch', it did not extend to accepting the word no. And, of course, Sky could not have been more proud to plan the visit of such an illustrious guest, once she had recovered from the initial shock.

Sky's mother, Maureen, was more vocal in her protestations, not having the additional pressure of Her Majesty's presence when Sky nervously informed her of the plan. Sometimes Sky was not sure which of the women made her the most anxious but, at that moment, she had decided it was definitely her mum. Not her ma'am. Despite the amount of time it had taken Sky to remember it rhymed with jam, not farm. Whereas 'mum' simply rhymed with bum, which appropriately was the body part Maureen predicted she would be working off to prepare her house for a visit from the Queen. In fact the ranting continued for some time before she finally relented. It was going to cause her a hell of a lot of stress but it really was not something she could turn down. Having fully convinced Sky of her total displeasure and left the lounge in one of her famous huffs, it was as she lay down in bed that a sly look of pleasure spread across Maureen's face. Talk about keeping up with the Joneses. This was really going to put paid to the neighbours' boasting about their new wall-to-wall carpet. With a grin, she turned out the light.

Perhaps the hardest part of the visit for Sky was persuading Maureen that she absolutely must not tell anyone anything at all about it, neither before nor after. The big day was to involve Maureen finding a good enough excuse to cancel her shift at the pub, having previously requested as much overtime as possible in order to pay for all the necessary cleaning products to make the house smell sweet enough for the royal visit. Plus a fancy array of boxed cakes and various exotic goodies fit for, well, a queen.

Alby was another recruit who had been employed under the same scheme that had brought Sky to the palace. Although perhaps a little unfair, the Queen was happy to assume that these young people were particularly appreciative of the special chance they had been given and would, therefore, do anything to ensure their good luck would continue. Their age would also make them more likely to be open to a little adventure and to welcome a break from the usual stuffiness of palace protocol. So it was Alby who escorted her to the Isle of Dogs one early spring morning in the late 70s. He had taken his life in his hands by asking his dad for the use of his precious Ford Capri, but a sizeable donation of beer money had swung the deal. Mr. Wright had been concerned that Alby was planning something dodgy and took some convincing that he was not 'up to no good' and intending to 'do the business' with some 'bit of crumpet' on the back seat. He also worried that Alby was skiving off from the best opportunity he was ever going to get. Oh, the joy Alby would have felt from setting him straight.

As the Daimler pulled silently to the kerb in a quiet back street, the Queen concealed her dismay at the replacement she was about to climb into. Bright yellow was not the colour best suited to avoiding unwanted attention but she appreciated Alby borrowing the car for this special outing. Unfortunately, despite spending most of the night polishing and spraying, there had been no way for him to fully conceal the smell of the curry, chips and fags which comprised his father's regular diet. As the Queen caught the glimmer of shame in his eyes she put on her most diplomatic expression and complimented Alby on how the car shone. His eyes lit up and she was happy already. What a relief it was to have a few hours off from the role she had to play at the palace. How lucky the ordinary people were.

The street was empty as the Capri turned away from the docks. If anything was likely to have given the game away, it would have been the way the Queen turned her head rapidly from side to side as if in the royal box at Wimbledon, wanting to take in every bit of this new landscape. It made her a little sad to realise she had seen the wonders of the world but knew so little of these humdrum streets so close to her own residence. It never seemed quite right to think of the palace as home, when she had dreamed of an ordinary house like these since childhood.

All too soon they were pulling up in the centre of the terrace and Maureen's net curtains were twitching. Sky had told her, in no uncertain terms, that she was positively not allowed to pace around outside in anticipation, so Maureen flung the front door open with as much restraint as she could manage. She accidentally started to do a small curtsey but Sky surreptitiously kicked her and she backed off. At the Queen's request, the visit was to be enacted exactly as it might be with a close friend and Maureen intended to stick to this instruction. Without the chipped crockery, the grubby apron and the swearing. And the fags, probably.

The visit got off to an uneasy start, with the Queen and Maureen equally unsure about how to behave and anxious not to cause offence. After a while, with a little screeching all round, the stand-off was abruptly broken by the sudden arrival of a large black and white cat on the Queen's chest. Horrified looks were quickly followed by Maureen yelling what sounded like, 'William, get off 'er now.' As her mother chased the cat outside, Sky apologised profusely and explained that, when he was not launching himself on the other cats in the area, he had a habit of sitting stock still on a shelf for hours on end, so they completely forgot about him until he took the opportunity to pounce on any unsuspecting guest. The drama over, the uneasiness resumed. No matter how the Queen ached to have an everyday conversation, she realised her status had isolated her once again, despite her best efforts. The women managed to make polite, rather stilted yet mildly interesting conversation for around an hour until, with some relief, Sky noted that Alby had returned to the car. In this particular area it would have looked too suspicious for him to sit in the driver's seat for long, so the Queen had suggested he take a walk.

Following courteous goodbyes, the Queen approached the car, pausing briefly before realising she had instructed Alby not to open the door for her. She thought about sitting beside him in the front, as she had toyed with asking to look round Maureen's house. It was no problem for her to discuss complicated political situations with the Prime Minister, nor to greet the heads of state of every nation on earth, but some challenges were beyond consideration. In response to Alby's enquiry as to whether the Queen had enjoyed her visit, she mentioned that the 'rather lively' cat seemed to be called William, and was that not an unusual name for a pet? It was fortunate she was looking out of the window when Alby responded carefully, having heard certain stories from Sky, 'I believe that might be rhyming slang Ma'am,' with a twinkle of amusement in his eye.

Meanwhile, Maureen had collapsed onto the couch in her best film star pose, fanning herself with the Radio Times and declaring, 'Never again.' Sky shushed her, as though the Queen's powers stretched to superhuman hearing, the car being several streets away by then. Maureen continued, 'I mean, she's a lovely lady and it was a real honour and I'll never forget it. But what am I going to do with all these bloody cakes? She hardly touched a thing.'

Emboldened by her venture into the outside world the Queen made a private commitment to herself, promising she would meet as many of her ordinary subjects as possible, incognito. There were no repercussions from her first foray so she took great pleasure in fantasising elaborate plans for her next escape, during the many boring state functions she was obliged to host. Visiting dignitaries were honoured by the enthusiasm she showed for their irrigation plans and new factories, whilst she secretly imagined her sojourn among the homeless on Oxford Street.

And so it was that the Queen came to find herself huddled in a shop doorway one night. It had taken all her powers of persuasion this time but Alby had finally relented. It was hard for him to refuse, since a rather generous pay rise had enabled him to buy a car of his own. He was a bright and good looking lad who rather reminded the Queen of her own young sons. What fun it would have been for the whole family to camp out on the streets together, but she could hardly bring them along. It took enough planning for one member to escape.

Wrapped up in a sleeping bag, on fresh but unironed newspapers, and attired in drab but rather too clean layers of simple clothing, the Queen wondered for a moment what the attraction was. It was not too cold or wet that evening but the boredom was a killer.

Nobody would have suspected the identity of the new arrival and those who slept regularly in the area were used to drifters who appeared and disappeared unannounced. The youngsters sometimes larked about and wandered off to score something to help them tolerate the boredom, the memories and their current circumstances. The older ones mainly kept to themselves, sniffing and drinking and staring into space. There were no more thoughts for them to have. They were no longer waiting to be discovered, rescued or helped. Many of them could not remember why or how they had ended up there in the first place.

Alby was not so much suffering from boredom as the fear of what would happen to him if something happened to Her Majesty. He could see the front pages of the tabloids now. He would never work again. He would have to leave the country. He had been sorely tempted to advise James, the Queen's head bodyguard, of the plan. It would have given him peace of mind to know that James was around but if he had broken the Queen's confidence then he would never work again and he would probably have to leave the country. It was not the sort of dilemma he was used to, being more familiar with choosing 'beans or peas', 'telly or pub'.

It was getting later and darker and no-one would be suspicious at the palace, it being past the Queen's regular bedtime. Alby felt very alone. He was glad he did not have to do this every night. He, of course, was not at liberty to even try and sleep. It was hard to stay close enough to watch for any potential danger, let alone doing so for hours on end without arousing suspicion. He wandered up and down, looked in shop windows, then wandered up and down again. A few times he even walked round the block but that made him afraid of what might happen in his brief absence. He had to admit he was also afraid for himself, feeling intimidated by an area which was so vibrant, bright and busy during the day but transformed into a place of dark corners and menacing noises at night. Few people passed and those who did were the worse for wear or distressed at missing their last bus, with no way of getting home to the suburbs. Except for the ones with enough cash to hire a taxi; the only vehicles which sailed past at night, the inhabitants oblivious to the suffering going on so close by but so far from their thoughts.

Returning from his last parade round the block, Alby was alarmed to see that a scuffle had broken out too close for comfort to the Queen. It appeared that some elderly drunks were fighting over a bottle but, on closer inspection, he realised a young girl was involved. He was also surprised to note that one of the men at the heart of the skirmish was of a smart appearance, younger and clean shaven. As Alby stood, momentarily rooted to the spot, he realised everyone was ignoring the Queen, who was relatively safely shrinking into her corner, trying to make herself invisible.

The fight was turning nasty. There did not seem to be any weapons involved but the smart man was being aggressively persuasive, trying to force the girl to go with him. Her long fair hair flew out around her as she wept and fought ineffectively. A part of her seemed resigned to the outcome.

At that moment one of the men in the doorway came back to life, summoning the will to extricate himself from his smelly old blanket and struggle awkwardly to his feet. One of his blackest memories had been triggered and there was no way on God's earth he was going to let that slimy git force the girl to go anywhere. With a tremendous surge forward, he leapt at the smart man and smashed a bottle over his head. Unfortunately, as he swung his arm back, the broken bottle made contact with not one but two of the other men, who had been woken from their slumber by the drama taking place in what was, to all intents and purposes, their bedroom. Justifiably angry, they fumed at their unintentional assailant, beating him with their fists and shouting things that made no sense to anyone but themselves. Then came the moment Alby had been dreading, as one of them stumbled backwards towards the Queen.

In an instant, from nowhere, a dark figure appeared from the shadows. In one swift movement, he swept the Queen up and into the night and was gone.

Alby could not have been more distraught. What had he been thinking, agreeing to help her with this mad idea? What could he do now? He looked around manically, despairingly. He was dumbfounded. How had he let this happen?

In a blind panic, Alby did all he could do. He started to pace the street again, obsessively going through potential plans of action. Would the police believe his story? Would his dad believe it? Who could possibly help him out of this nightmare? And what about the Queen - what was going to happen to her? He was actually quite fond of her; also acutely aware that he would never work again and would probably have to leave the country if she came to even the slightest harm. He looked around for a phone box, he knew he had spotted one earlier.

Pulling open the heavy door, Alby wondered how a little old lady would manage to get in to make a call. His mind returned to the Queen and her predicament. Not one about phone boxes, that most probably had never been an issue for her. Overwhelmed by the smell of stale wee and the pornographic graffiti, Alby lifted the receiver. What was that nasty muck on the mouthpiece? Was there a very faint dialling tone? Who the bloody hell was he going to call anyway? The police? Come off it, what sort of a cock and bull story would it sound to them? He'd be labelled a junkie and slapped in a cell faster than he could say 'but I don't take drugs, officer'. Everyone at the palace would probably be in bed. Also unlikely to know who he was and extremely unlikely to believe anything he might tell them about the evening's events. He replaced the receiver. There was nothing to do except to continue pacing. At least he would escape the smell. Small mercies and all that.

He did not get very far this time.

Silently a car approached and the driver's window rolled down beside Alby. 'You stupid, stupid little tosser,' the driver hissed quietly, 'get in.'

James was fuming. He fumed as he drove his two passengers through the palace gates and he fumed as he wished Her Majesty goodnight. He could not fume directly at her so, once she had headed for bed, he let Alby feel the force of his wrath. It had to go somewhere. James had been through too much, security threats and otherwise, to contain his fury indefinitely. And an important part of his training was to remember that he was never truly off duty. Particularly when his employer was clearly making ludicrous plans which severely compromised her safety.

Finally at home in his bed, Alby had never felt so exhausted. Physically, mentally and in every other way. Anxious thoughts competed for attention until he finally drifted off, only to jolt upright as the most immediately disturbing thought struck him. As they had pulled away from the scene of the fight, most of the drunks seemed to have settled back down in the doorway, but there was no sign of the smart man. Nor, more importantly, the distressed girl.

The Inner Circle

Bringing herself reluctantly back to the present, the Queen let out a brief sigh. She had always loved coming up with ideas but she was used to them being thwarted by her advisers, more often than not. So she was well aware that her current plan was going to need every bit of the strength and fortitude she had accumulated over the years. In fact, she had a feeling that this was the very purpose for which she had been saving her strength. The country had been running into the ground for so long, whilst she had felt compelled to keep quiet and not intervene as government after government piled on the problems through their petty squabbles, poor decisions and self-serving bureaucracy. When she had no choice but to watch her subjects, no - her countryfolk - die in their thousands, she had known she could no longer sit back whilst her people continued to suffer.

Having ensured she was alone, the Queen made the call she had been putting off. The one which would change everything. She summoned those she had begun to regard as her own temporary cabinet; the chosen few she had been carefully putting together in her mind for some years, unbeknownst to its members. Her Inner Circle. Made up only of those she knew she could really trust, or so she had hoped.

Next day the tabloids were full of supposed plans for 'Strictly P.M. Factor', as one of them had dubbed the reported search for someone to replace the current Prime Minister or, possibly, the entire government. Having no solid facts to go on had never stopped them from going ahead with breaking important news before, and they were not going to change at such an exciting time. Whilst the articles varied in their level of ridiculousness, there was one thing which had been made clear to the Queen. It was the reason she had called the brief meeting and the reason why she had said nothing substantial during it. Sadly, it was because she had already been aware that there was a possible traitor in her little group.

When the occasion demanded, the Queen could be disarmingly ruthless and now she knew she was acting for the future of her country. Her under secretary had barely entered the room and looked around for the tea tray which had accompanied their cosy chats until now. The Queen was still standing, fixing her intent gaze on the other woman. 'Gillian, it's time for you to leave,' she said. Gillian looked confused and glanced around the room, about to say that she had only just arrived, when the realisation struck her. There was no more to say. She knew how shrewd the Queen could be, so why had Gillian been tempted to betray her trust? What on earth had she thought she would get out of it? No matter, it was over. The friendship, her career, her life really.

After the initial hiccup with Gillian, the Queen's plans ran more smoothly. She thanked her lucky stars for the continued loyalty of James, who knew everything there was to know about security and would do his utmost to ensure there would be no more nasty surprises, so long as he was around. Tall, strong and steadfast, a good man to have on side in any encounter, she thought with a quiet smile.

At the first real meeting of the Inner Circle, things started to move forward apace. Individuals were assigned urgent tasks; firstly to pull out the most positive and constructive ideas from amongst the letters which had not previously made it into the, now famous, wooden chest, plus the additional missives which continued to stream in each day. With her team around her, the Queen's enthusiasm and optimism really started to grow. It was a new lease of life for her. Though she could not help thinking she had left it a little late, her increasing age merely served to encourage her determination to make her mark on history a truly significant one. Never lacking in her commitment to upholding tradition, she had come to believe that the way forward had to be different. There were many aspects of the past which were to be admired, even resurrected in some cases, but her belief in the changes needed to resolve certain issues was growing stronger by the hour.

For days on end the Queen closeted herself away, reading through the latest letters which had been chosen for her perusal. If only she had time to read through everything herself but that was not feasible, nor had it ever been. It was disconcerting to know that somewhere in a huge pile of papers there may be the answer to all her wishes but she had to trust her loyal staff to know her desires as well as she did. In some cases, they had proved they knew better. She had been quite miffed, at first, when a lady-in-waiting encouraged her to try some of the brighter clothes from the designer batches which seemed to arrive almost constantly. However, when she could not help but notice the ubiquitous photo spreads in magazines, she was often rather pleased to see herself smiling from under the brim of an attention-grabbing hat. Particularly the bright yellow one. Since the day in the Capri, she had always had a fondness for the colour. When she once let a comment slip, in a moment of reminiscence, the dressmaker assumed the Queen was referring to some luxurious cruise to Italy, so her secret remained safe.

It was hard to keep her attention on track when there was so much to get through as quickly as possible. If she gave herself too much time to stop and think she would remember what inauspicious times she was living in. How even she may not be indispensable should she say or do too much to upset the wrong people. The greatest difficulty, she admitted to herself wryly, was not knowing who the wrong people truly were.

A few words were beginning to fit together and draw the Queen back to the page in front of her; 'I am begging you, Your Majesty. I am desperate and there is nowhere left for me to turn. My life has fallen apart again over the last few years and it has taken all my strength just to keep going. I know you are a busy woman, who does not have the time to listen to my traumas, but I am honestly at the end of my tether. There have been headlines, dramas and documentaries about how life has become impossible for the ordinary people in this country but nothing changes. Ever. More huge buildings go up and big businesses make massive profits but somehow there is never enough money to help the sick, homeless and jobless. People are dying because the ones at the top are not listening. I'm afraid I'm going to be next. Life is too hard and I just need a break. Please can you help me get a proper roof over my head? I'm too tired to try anymore.'

The Queen's heart wanted to go out to the sender but there was no address, nor contact details. Why would there be? He or she had said they were homeless and desperate. It was so hard to deal with, so hard to bear, until she looked around and reminded herself that all she had to do was read it, not live it. What the country needs more than anything is compassion, she thought to herself. Had some of the people in power really made it so hard for others intentionally? She may not be able to help this individual immediately, nor directly, but maybe she could do something about the system that seemed to be causing so much anguish to the masses, many of whom genuinely loved her and her family and, from the increasing amount of messages she was receiving, would agree with this correspondent that they had nowhere else left to turn.

'Alison,' the Queen called gently into the next room, 'please come through. I have an urgent press release for you.' Her secretary looked a little taken aback, this had never happened before. She picked up her laptop and joined the Queen in what had become the mail room; moved a pile of papers from the spare chair, making room for her to sit, and prepared to type whatever the Queen was about to say. Smiling softly, the Queen made an unusual remark, 'You're going to remember this.'

The statement seemed to write itself; 'Her Majesty the Queen has announced today that she shares the concerns of the many compatriots who have written to inform her of their views on the state of the nation. Her Majesty wishes to express her intent to take a more active role in resolving the numerous serious issues facing the United Kingdom today, and to pledge her continued support for all those who reside here. More information will follow, in due course.'

Leaving no time for discussion, or change of heart, the Queen brought the meeting to an end by saying, 'Now please send the message to all the usual recipients, then take yourself home for a good rest. I have a feeling we are going to have a rather busy day tomorrow'.

Always a master of understatement, thought Alison as she pressed 'send' and grabbed her coat.

Reactions

'Her Majesty Speaks Out', 'Thank You, Ma'am', 'Our Saviour' and 'Are These The World's Biggest Bazookas?' were just a few of the headlines the next morning. Naturally the latter did not refer to the Queen but editors have differing opinions on the news items that will attract the most readers. Editors are a law unto themselves, much like an increasing number of groups seem to be, reflected Her Majesty as she flicked through the pages. It never failed to astound her how a few sentences could be manufactured into a dozen pages, by asking the opinion of various perceived experts, members of the public, psychologists and, sometimes, through using enough 'artistic licence' to embellish the most simple phrase. She could put off the day no longer and strode purposefully from her private quarters to face the music.

Ironically, as the Queen entered Alison's office, the old tune Burning Down The House sang out from the radio. It was quickly turned off, but not before a passing thought struck the Queen; that maybe Guy Fawkes could have saved us all a lot of trouble. It was sometimes a good thing no-one could read her mind.

As she had expected, the media had gone straight into frenzy mode and were clamouring to set up a live press conference at the palace - yesterday, if not sooner. However, they had been less of a problem to Alison than the Queen's official advisors, each of whom had been insistent upon a private audience 'at the earliest possible opportunity'. Which, to a less illustrious family, would be equivalent to kicking in the bedroom door to get her attention. Aware that she had not fully thought her actions through, she now had to deal with the repercussions. But no amount of thinking could sort out the tangle the country was now in, so it was time for action. High time for action, in fact.

The Queen had to stop and remind herself that she was under no obligation to do as the media demanded. If she could feel intimidated by their intrusion, it crossed her mind how unnerving it must be for a more ordinary person to come under the spotlight. Often at times of distress, when they needed peace and support more than anything. She mused briefly on whether it was preferable to have a team of legal and medical experts (plus those from every other conceivable field) at your beck and call night and day, but to be unsure if all were totally trustworthy, or to be on your own in times of crisis.

'As you know, Alison, I have long been a fan of ingenuity, creativity and "thinking outside the box", as it is now known. I believe it has fallen on me to encourage these attributes in our citizens and I have decided to lead by example. None of us must be allowed to be used as pawns by the media, nor to feel that control of our lives has been taken away by some faceless organisation or government department. My liberties, in many ways, are so much greater than those of most, but I also lack the freedom which I might have desired. In such time as I have remaining, it is my wholehearted intention to bring about a truly fair society in our own nation, which I sincerely hope will have a positive influence around the world.'

The Queen, who had been speaking whilst gazing out of the window at the gloomy London weather, turned to see Alison's mouth hanging open. She righted this quickly and cleared her throat, still looking somewhat shocked.

The Queen felt a little perturbed by the reaction of her loyal colleague. 'Do you think I'm being too presumptuous?' she enquired, with a rather endearing hint of nervousness.

'Not at all, Ma'am. I was just thinking that's your next speech right there!'

As if on cue, the sun came out and flooded the room. The Queen turned back to the window and indulged in a small, contented smile.

'How many times have I said? You never need to call me Ma'am.' Her smile continued as she gazed across the city with renewed enthusiasm.

The Queen's Speech

Starting as she meant to go on, the Queen arranged for James to broadcast her announcement. She wondered why she had, for so long, let television companies and her advisors dictate the setting and manner of dress to be used on these occasions. It now struck her that the unnatural formality which tended to be the result had served to create more distance between her subjects and the Queen herself. Perhaps that had been the intention? It was hard to be sure of anyone's motives these days. Her plan was to encourage her compatriots to become more caring and thoughtful towards others and she owed far more to James than she did to the media. He was unlikely to say anything but she imagined this would be a small source of pride for him, knowing of his passion for film and photography. Things were starting to look so much clearer. To bring a little happiness to someone was so much more important than the optimum lighting or starched suit. She would love to have a hair out of place but she knew that really would be pushing things.

As Alison had suggested, the main body of the speech was formed from the words spoken to her in private by the Queen. She continued, 'There was a time when speech writers would have me say something akin to my being proud to be head of the greatest nation on earth and, I must admit, I took a little quiet pride in that, in those days. But egotism never really was The British Way. And, in recent years, it has been harder to make such statements on behalf of this, or indeed any other, country. The world really is in a bit of a mess, is it not?'

As the Queen paused, millions of viewers around the country (and the world) looked at each other with incredulity and secret hope.

'Our home, the United Kingdom, has welcomed people of all nationalities, races and faiths for so many years now, that ours can no longer be considered solely a Christian society. My belief is that this time of troubles is the right moment for those of all faiths, or none, to commit to working together and to following the main teachings which surely we all share – to love and respect our fellow beings as equals.

For some time I have been aware that a significant number of you feel ostracised by the many initiatives which have been introduced in the name of helping particular sectors of society, no doubt with the best intentions. However, by offering certain non-essential advantages or opportunities to only those with a specific disability, of a particular age, gender, race, religion or sexual preference, this immediately excludes others from those benefits. "Positive discrimination" seems to me to have the ring of an oxymoron and I believe our country will benefit most from an inclusive policy of cohesion rather than division. To pigeonhole numerous sections of society as potential victims of "hate crimes", for instance, is to create further distance between us. When individuals feel connected to their compatriots by means of fair treatment for all, then their natural inclination will surely be to work together to create an atmosphere of peace and harmony. There will be no reason for unrest or aggression when there are true equal rights for everyone.

It has come to my attention that many of you feel unable to cope with our current systems; to live positively and productively with the proliferation of complicated rules and convoluted procedures which have been introduced in recent years, rendering what should be the most simple tasks overwhelming in many cases. Everyone is expected to be a master of technology, without the training, funding, support or choice of whether they wish to live their lives in a virtual way, increasingly disconnected from other human beings and, for some, interacting only through the robotic computer systems which replaced their jobs. We are losing touch with nature and we are losing touch with each other, in a personal sense. Collectively we seem to have almost lost sight of what we can do to improve our planet and what is truly most important. I doubt any of us would wish to see a Third World War started over the strength of our broadband connections.

I understand you have a need for independence and control over your own lives and that many of you feel these rights have been taken from you. Today I give you my personal assurance that I will do all I can to return those rights and to put the "Great" back into Britain.'

Beaming smiles, a little hesitant clapping and even a few whoops of glee ensued as the Queen finished her speech and James turned the camera off. It had been a risk to insist on broadcasting live but it seemed the only way to ensure her message would be viewed in its entirety and that no salient points would end up, accidentally or otherwise, on a cutting room floor. As it were, or used to be. The Queen had taken the measure of insisting that all electronic devices, save those necessary for the broadcast, be left outside the room. What a relief it was to have some breathing space to relax a little and discuss the next move, rather than accept the current demand for constant contact and knee-jerk reactions. The phrase 'Tone Down Technology – Bring Back Humanity' had introduced itself into her dreams the night before. New ideas kept coming to her, unbidden, these days. As Harry would have said, she really was 'on a roll'.

Of course, peace did not reign long in the palace that momentous day. There was no stopping some people and a particular group from the Old Guard of advisors reacted in a surprisingly politically incorrect way to Her Majesty's speech. Suffice to say there may have been calls to resurrect the old law which decreed the death penalty for high treason, if some of their comments had been heard outside the room in which they were secreted.

'My God, I don't believe it, the Queen has turned into a hippy!' raged Bertie Barrington-Smythe, a senior member of the group, twiddling his impressive whiskers in frustration as he stormed off to the Queen's quarters. He was not allowed in.

An Old Chum

The next day's headlines were no surprise, though some publications seemed intent on excluding the most important elements of the announcement. One seemed to focus on the alliteration of a particular sentence, with 'Are you taking the P, Your Majesty?' It reminded her of a time, many years before, when the press were similarly excited; declaring 'The Queen and "I" - Yes, you heard it right, Her Majesty DID refer to herself in the first person during her latest speech!!!' The Queen could not decide whether to sigh or chuckle at the madness of it all. As usual, the best thing to do was to take it all with a bucket of salt. In her position, a pinch had never been enough.

Reluctantly the Queen admitted to herself that she could avoid her official aides no longer. She was well aware that, so far as each one may feel able to push their boundaries, she stood firmly in the firing line now. Pushing himself forward, as ever, to represent the unhappy contingent, Mr. Barrington-Smythe knocked on the door imperiously. The Queen had always wondered how he managed that. Even she had never found an imperious way to knock on a door. Then again she hardly ever had reason to knock on a door, because everywhere was open to her. Officially, at least.

'Good morning Bertie, what a beautiful day,' the Queen began, noting his faced looked like thunder, beneath a thin veneer of superficial subservience. He was a little taken aback by the lightness of her remark, and floundered momentarily before launching the gentle and carefully worded attack which he and his cronies had spent the night preparing, to sound as though it were a few casual comments from an old chum. None of it was unexpected and the Queen maintained her customary expression of calm throughout, much to his annoyance.

Satisfied that Bertie had finished, the Queen set out to explain one of the main aims of her plan for the future of the country. 'What we really need now is a comprehensive health and welfare service that is free and easy for everyone to access.'

Bertie responded with a raised, perfectly coiffed and quizzical eyebrow, plus the merest hint of schoolboy sarcasm, 'You mean like the NHS Ma'am?'

'Oh for goodness sake, Bertie, there is no real National Health Service anymore. Much as the dedicated workers on the front line are, so rightly, lauded by the people, there are not nearly enough of them and nowhere near enough resources, equipment or back-up support to keep them safe and working to the best of their abilities. Our poor old NHS had been systematically decimated and gradually moving into the hands of mercenary, multinational tycoons for years, way before the latest crisis. It's time for us to help our own people in the way they deserve.' Bertie opened his mouth slightly but the Queen continued, 'And yes, Bertie, by "our own people" I really do include those of every colour, creed and sexual persuasion. At least, all those who desire to live a peaceful life and show kindness to their fellow man.'

There followed a slight, nonplussed, pause before he responded, rather petulantly, 'and woman.'

'Yes Bertie, "and woman", and transsexual, transgender, birds, bees and corgis. But it's time to end all this rhetoric and political correctness. My personal wish is to put an end to the pedantic semantics of the past and to ensure a happier future for everyone, as simply as possible.'

'With respect, Ma'am,' Bertie started, without respect, 'what about the "Irish Situation"? ....the "Scottish Situation"? ....the "Welsh Situation"?'

'With equal respect, Bertie, the only "situations" which exist are those which have been manipulated into existence by the governments of the day and the media moguls whose priority seems to have moved from providing information to causing devastation. Too much power in the wrong hands has almost brought this country to its knees and I'm not prepared to watch it fall even further. Everything is going to change. The Empire is in the past – the proud days and the warmongering days. Our country is going to become the most peaceable, neutral nation on earth.'

'You mean we're…. going to be….'

'Yes, Bertie?'

'….the new Switzerland?'

Stifling a twitch of amusement the Queen replied, 'If you like.' She paused, then added, with a wry smile, 'But perhaps without the bunkers. I hear that fracking has already caused quite enough problems underground.' She moved to her desk, sat down and shuffled her papers. Bertie knew it was the accepted signal for him to leave. He stood rigid, fixed to the spot, as if he was thinking what to say. He could not think of anything to say. The Queen shuffled the papers again. Bertie nodded and left.

The Queen permitted herself a proper, joyful grin. It really was about to hit the fan now.

The Chosen Few

The next morning, at the Queen's meeting with the Inner Circle, much time was devoted to the need to ensure the privacy of every discussion between the members. There were some quite amusing suggestions regarding the use of code names, encompassing a system of vague references to popular television shows, until it was pointed out that complicating everything unnecessarily had played a large part in the current state of the country. After that it was unanimously agreed that all interaction, other than face to face, would take place using the basic, 'old-fashioned' mobile phones which James had sourced and made safe, specifically for contact between the members of this elite group.

'So, are we all agreed that our primary focus is to increase the wellbeing of every one of our citizens, as soon as we possibly can?' The Queen looked around the room rather pointlessly, as if anyone would say no to this (or her) at such a crucial stage. 'And are we all clear, as far as we can be, about each of our immediate, personal tasks?' The cautiously eager reception belied the palpably nervous undercurrent emanating from this well-meaning group of individuals who were only too aware they were about to throw themselves to the wolves. But rather than making her anxious, their obvious apprehension further endeared the chosen few to the Queen. She had always hoped the meek really would inherit the earth. Maybe 'on her watch' they could.

So it was that work began in earnest and connections were made.

One of the first letter writers to be invited to the palace was approached due to her interest in different therapeutic methods and her desire to see the country 'restored to full health'. Sal Jenkins had trained in several modalities but had been keen to emphasise that she was not the kind of reiki master/NLP practitioner/life coach/ psychotherapist/fishmonger who seemed to have enjoyed such popularity over recent years. Indeed she equated the combination of such roles with the previously ridiculed singer/dancer/actress/ model.

A woman with spirit, the Queen had thought, when she read Sal's letter. She had always admired the type; being one herself, on the quiet.

Put very mildly, Sal had been gobsmacked to be invited to meet the Queen. If Sal had been fortunate enough to have close friends to share the news with, she imagined they would have taken the mick unmercifully. It would have appeared obvious, to her imaginary friends, that there had been some sort of mix-up or that one of those 'candid camera' type tv crews were playing a strange and elaborate joke on her. Still, reasoning with herself that she had nothing to lose, Sal called the number at the top of the page and managed to confirm that she was, indeed, invited to attend what sounded strangely like some sort of interview, the following week. Pushing back her hair, as she looked in the mirror, she realised there was much to be done. Starting with her roots.

Tom Newman was the sort of person who took everything in his stride and did not see an unexpected invitation to Buckingham Palace as a reason to change. He vaguely remembered sending off a letter some time ago but he regularly approached various organisations, societies and individuals in the hope of securing support for the ideas and inventions which presented themselves to him in a seemingly never-ending stream. Feet firmly on the ground, Tom chose to see this as an interesting opportunity rather than a cause for excitement. Not like the rest of his family. Katie had been happily sticking ballgowns on the princesses in her latest 'must have, 50 collectable weekly editions' kiddiezine, when Tom casually mentioned where he would be going next Tuesday. You could have heard a pin drop but what Tom actually heard was the clattering of the baking tray falling to the kitchen floor, scattering the vegetables which Jess had been about to dish up. Her open-mouthed look of shock had also spread around the room, with even Billy looking as if he were about to swallow a goldfish.

Of the letter writers at the top of the list, probably the one most likely to be known to the general public was Brett Pearce, a Labour backbencher who was no stranger to voicing strong and controversial opinions. His own party found it hard to get behind him, realising his views made him more suited to a greener seat, should they be possible to secure. With a prominent human rights lawyer for a father and ancestors born into slavery, Brett was a man who would not be easily dissuaded from a cause.

As Sam Jarvis had told the Queen, in his missive, he was sick of a lot of things in this country. Sick of the unfairness, the stupid rules and the complications involved in trying to survive, let alone live a fulfilling life. Yes, he came across as an angry (not quite so young anymore) man, who sounded quite depressed, but there was no escaping the passion in his words. To give him the chance to air his views would be to offer a helping hand to one individual, if not millions. Being naturally instinctive and astute in her ability to sum up a writer from just a page or two, the Queen had a hunch that this man's anarchistic views could be tempered sufficiently to offer the breath of fresh air which she was looking to bring to her suffocating nation. It would be hard to ascertain whether it were she or he who was most intrigued as to what might be the outcome of their meeting.

A proven young businesswoman with admirable ethics, Ms Sandeep had to be on the list. In fact the Queen had been made aware of her existence following an awards show the previous year. Andrina's family had provided the supportive background necessary to instil in her the strength and fortitude to fight for what she believed in. It was clear she also had the skill and ability to win over the most unlikely people. The Queen was really looking forward to working with her.

It was important to ensure that men and women were now given truly equal opportunities and it would be pleasing to see more prominent female roles in all arenas. The more she thought about it, the happier the Queen felt about her decision to start rocking the boat after all her time on the throne. She could not help but feel wistful, knowing there was another woman who really should be here now, to be a part of this brave new world.

Isle of Dogs

After so many years, finding himself back on that same terraced street (now one of the few remaining untouched by developers on the Isle of Dogs) brought back mixed emotions for Alby. He was proud to be one of a handful of staff who had proved his loyalty to the Queen for so long, and he liked to think he was as close as one could get to friendship with someone in such an elevated position.

Of course there was nobody else who could have undertaken this particular task. As far as Alby was aware, there was still no other member of staff who knew about that far off day when he had dropped Her Majesty off for tea. Had all that time really flown by so fast? Had the world really changed so much? As he lost himself in his musings, the door opened and an unexpected face appeared. Older and wiser but still blonde and beautiful. He could tell at first glance that Sky had not lost her spirit either. Always an expert at masking her emotions, her eyes showed no sign of shock at the sight of Alby and, as ever, a hastily conceived quip came to her lips.

'You really must stop stalking me you know,' was Sky's opening line, her eyes twinkling and her accent touched with a slight hint of the antipodean.

Immediately wanting to kick himself for regressing to a tongue-tied young man, Alby could not help but reply that he had not been stalking her, before remembering Sky's default setting had always been to send him up gently as soon as she set eyes on him. Even after decades, it seemed.

Alby could not believe how easy it had been to locate Sky. Of course it would have taken the guesswork away if he could have involved other people but Alby still liked to do things the old-fashioned way, personal and private, whenever possible. And when the Queen had told him of this secret mission it had set his heart racing, just a little bit. He had better watch that at his age.

It had seemed highly unlikely that Maureen would still be at the house to provide helpful tips on where to find her daughter, let alone that the girl herself would be there to greet him. Funny how he had still thought of Sky as a girl yet recognised the woman she now was, as soon as those clear blue eyes had settled on him. Fortunately, his instructions left little time for small talk. He was merely to ask that Sky contact the Queen's office and speak with Alison, to arrange a visit to the palace as soon as possible, if she would be so kind.

Alby was touched by the way the Queen's face lit up when he informed her that he had actually spoken to Sky and given her the message in person. He had never really known the details of Sky's sudden departure from the palace but it had not been unusual for an outspoken or indiscreet member of staff to disappear without notice. It would have surprised him to learn that the Queen had been as much in the dark as he had.

Catching Up

Sitting close to her old friend, the Queen was relieved to finally learn that Sky had not walked out of her job in the stables on a whim, without saying goodbye, whilst simultaneously furious to hear how she had been unceremoniously removed by the faceless powers-that-be. How many times must that have happened? It now struck the Queen that any time she had shown the slightest indication she may have a fondness for a member of staff, that person suddenly disappeared. Had she been aware of these subtle acts of subversion at the time, the Tower could have been as full as an 'affordable housing' waiting list by now.

All those lost years melted away, with Sky being gracious enough to say it must have been meant that she did not get to keep her job with the Queen, because her life had been amazing. She had 'been there, done that', as they used to say, back in the day. It reminded the Queen how Sky had always liked to use little catchphrases and colloquialisms. How lovely it was to hear them again. The two women chatted away until Sky eventually brought up the pertinent question of why the Queen had looked her up after all this time.

The Queen was only too aware of her proclivity for procrastination. She would be embarrassed to admit just how long some of her plans had been on the boil. Which was why this one, the biggest of them all, really must pay off for her, the country and the world in general. No pressure there then.

Without further ado, she thought, she really had to get things moving. So like her ordinary subjects in some ways, it may have surprised them to know she would also hover over a cup of tea and another biscuit, rather than go through that intimidating pile of paperwork. Rather take a long walk with her dogs than make arrangements for that pressing function she was obliged to host. The list could go on but she was digressing again and the clock seemed to tick faster every day.

Alison had been on tenterhooks as to how the next stage of this transition period would be arranged, knowing she would carry a good deal of responsibility for ensuring things ran smoothly. So it was with a mixture of relief, trepidation and excitement that she greeted the Queen's instructions. Always having been a fan of the personal touch, the Queen had realised this was the time for her to really put that belief into practise. It had struck her that the surprise invitations she had sent out would be intimidating enough, without possibly creating further unease for those individuals whom she truly hoped would be the answer to her prayers. It followed that the arrangements she made for her guests' first visits to the palace were to be as low-key as possible. Alison was not the only one who was excited.

New Ministers

Following a week of intensive meetings with the letter writers, during which the Queen had spent a full day with each individual on a one to one basis, save for the quiet presence of Alison discreetly sitting in a corner taking salient notes, there had followed a further week of in-depth discussions between the Queen and her Inner Circle. This culminated in some unique and unrepeatable job offers and called for some important introductions.

Being aware of the daunting effect the most opulent rooms tended to have on visitors, the Queen had opted to hold the introductory get-together of the letter writers in one of her private drawing rooms. This had rarely happened with members of the public but she already had the strong feeling that these notable individuals were about to become far more than that to her and to each other.

Ushering everyone in with her brightest smile, Alison suddenly had the most immense feeling of pride, with the realisation she may well be about to play a small but not insignificant part in changing world history. She fervently hoped it would be so, as did the others now seated around the room. Indeed it was why they were all there. Including, particularly, the Queen herself. Having greeted everyone warmly as they arrived, she also took a seat, in the interests of informality. Momentarily slightly choked by the importance of this seemingly casual event, the Queen took a deep breath. Such a simple action, such a valuable tip from her once dear nanny. No, no, stay in the present, she told herself, looking around the room with growing affection and gratitude.

'Thank you all so much for coming,' she beamed. 'As you will be aware from our individual meetings, I was particularly impressed by the ideals and ideas demonstrated in all of your personal letters to me, as I have now been by the thoughts expressed by each one of you in our comprehensive discussions. And so, today, I have asked you here to meet together as a very special group of individuals whom I believe are about to make a most rewarding contribution to our collective future. Being satisfied, as I now am, that we share the same values and goals for ourselves, our country and our fellow citizens.

The world has changed so much, in my now considerably long lifetime, and I have followed those changes with great interest. However, in recent years that interest has moved towards disillusionment and sometimes, quite frankly, veers toward dismay. I do not wish my children, grandchildren or great-grandchildren, nor yours, to inherit a ship that is sinking. Our generations have endowed this planet with the greatest creations and the most horrifying methods of damage and destruction. Fortunately we still have a limited, though admittedly uncertain, amount of time in which we may attempt to right the very serious wrongs which have been committed, particularly against the environment. This immense task is certainly daunting but I have been most encouraged by the work of the numerous altruistic groups which have already sprung up around the country, especially the newer ones which are helping so many people deal with the wider repercussions of the health crisis.

I have given a considerable amount of thought to the subject of climate change and it has not been easy to break down all the other pressing issues which face us now. However, it seemed essential to start as we mean to go on, by simplifying our objectives to ensure that everyone in our United Kingdom is able to understand the motivation behind the unprecedented step I have taken, by introducing the new roles which you have kindly agreed to accept. Therefore, taking into account our discussions and associated research, I propose that each of you focus primarily on one particular aspect of this "campaign", for want of a better word, whilst working together and combining your efforts as needed. You will be given the autonomy to work as you choose and to employ those whom you feel will most benefit each cause. What will be different about your roles, compared to those held by some of the individuals previously entrusted with the power to make important decisions for our country, is that they will be founded on your concern for the world and all its inhabitants. There is no longer any place for egotism, greed, anger or blame. Please believe I am under no illusion about the great level of responsibility you have each agreed to accept. I have faith in you all and I thank you most sincerely for placing your trust in my vision.'

As the Queen turned to introduce him, Sam let out a small, slow breath and smiled imperceptibly. He could not remember if or when he had ever felt the positive glimmer of pride which he felt at that moment. 'Mr Jarvis has agreed to head one of our teams and the title we have chosen together, for the moment and for ease of understanding, is Backtrack Bureaucracy Minister. In times to come, another term may prove more suitable but it is important in the current climate not to present our citizens, our current political and business leaders or our unpredictable media with more complicated information than they may be able to absorb. Ladies and gentlemen, may I present Mr. Sam Jarvis....'

Polite murmurs of appreciation followed, along with a few uncertain claps, as everyone felt their way around this unique situation.

Sam stood up nervously, feeling overwhelmingly out of place in his ancient suit. A little rough around the edges, him and the suit. He had never expected to receive a reply to the rambling, ranting letter which had been the result of his frustrations with his former workplace and the system which had denied him the opportunity to help his clients in ways which were so obvious to him. What was he doing here? He had always railed against the establishment. He had presented every possible obstacle to the Queen and posed the sort of questions which had seen him fired on the spot more than once. Maybe his mum had been right, maybe he was his own worst enemy. As a final challenge, during their private discussions, Sam had declared that his belief in true equality for everyone meant he would be unable to adopt any of the accepted terms of respect for Her Majesty. Not that he had called her by this title, of course. What a very interesting young man, had been the Queen's immediate thought. Followed swiftly by the assertion that he was just the sort of person she needed to assist her in shaking things up.

'Thank you,' responded Sam, to the Queen and his new colleagues. If anyone perceived a lack of respect towards the Queen, it was not apparent to Sam. There were so many emotions flowing through him at that moment, it was a challenge to string a few sentences together. Let alone decide how he actually felt. 'I'm very pleased to meet you all and to be given this opportunity to do whatever I can to change things for the better. I've seen the damage done by the current obsession with demanding personal data and "ticking the right boxes". I've known men and women, black and white, break down over being treated like criminals for not having a good enough excuse to be walking down a certain street. Having their benefits cut off because their review was conducted by someone with no relevant medical knowledge, then being expected to live for months with no income. I've seen people with learning disabilities forced to fill out tax returns when they've never earned enough to pay tax. And I've seen people kill themselves because there's nowhere for them to get help with their traumas, their break-ups, breakdowns or abuse....'

Sam paused, suddenly realising where he was and unsure of what to say next. He had never acknowledged how his forthright manner could be disarming, or even appear threatening, to many who heard him open up about his opinions. He always caught their attention though. It was a pity he hated public speaking, it meant he had never realised his capacity for it.

There was a slightly awkward silence before anyone felt it right to speak. Being the closest to the Queen, if only through their very recent re-acquaintance, it had to be Sky. 'What's your job, Sam?' she asked, her face open with compassion and genuine interest.

Sam looked over to her, gratefully. He was back in the room, feet on the floor again. 'Was,' he replied, 'I was in Mental Health. "Support Work" they called it,' he laughed, shortly and with clearly intended irony. Sky could feel his pain and she hoped the others could too. Sam was the sort of person who had started off misunderstood and never found a way to overcome that. Sky had a certain empathy with that feeling and she could tell he needed encouragement to continue, so she gave him a smile and a nod and set him on track to his new future.

Sam raised his head and spoke with confidence, a new air of enthusiasm in his tone, 'I want to make a decent life accessible to everyone - I want to give everyone the same opportunities, rich or poor. If you're in a violent marriage, you need to be able to pick up a free, simple form that will get you a hassle-free divorce; if you're isolated and depressed you need free access to all the entertainment and information that most people get via the tv licence we all resent paying. Nobody should be afraid to go to hospital in an emergency because they might get a ticket for parking in the wrong zone or staying too long while they wait to be seen, or just because some dodgy contractors control all the car parks. We need to make life simple again, remove all the unnecessary stressors. We need to completely overturn the benefits system, the legal system and all the other systems that have been fu - messing up everyone's lives for so long. We need to take the power away from social media and the tech giants and all the faceless oligarchs who control our lives....'

Sam paused again, realising he was getting a little carried away. He would never know just how much respect his passionate outburst had generated in the small group, nor how he had grown in their eyes. Still not quite as tall as most men aspire to be, but it was almost as though his untidy brown hair had been combed and his suit silently pressed by an invisible hand, such was the perceived change in him.

'Thank you, Sam,' interjected the Queen swiftly, feeling it might be a long afternoon if she did not. 'Next we're going to hear a little from Sal Jenkins. Welcome....'

'Thank you Ma'am,' replied Sal, moving to curtsey, then stumbling slightly as she remembered the Queen had told her it was not necessary. 'I'm not honestly sure what I'm doing here and I'm sure you're all more qualified to be here than I am,' Sal continued, biting her lip involuntarily. Her lack of confidence was a picture and the Queen silently nursed her fears that Sal may not be able to overcome it enough to instil faith in others. It was a gamble but she had also been privy to the astute, determined and well-informed woman who lurked behind this timid mask. Perhaps the Queen could enlist Alison's help in bringing out the lion which roared quietly inside Sal's currently rather mousey exterior. The two women were less than a decade apart in age, and outward appearances were deceptive, but Sal did not seem to have had the motivation or encouragement to make the most of herself in the way that Alison always did, in public at least. Then again, Sal was not the Queen's personal secretary, nor had she ever aspired to be. Each to their own and all that, the Queen thought. Perhaps she had already spent too long talking to Sky.

Her mind back from its brief stroll, the Queen was pleased to note that Sal had indeed got into her stride and the others in the room were listening intently to her words. 'So, we couldn't really decide if my title should be Health For All Minister or Health Yourself Minister. The latter has a nice ring to it but perhaps lays itself open to parody. The point I really want to make is that it's equally important good healthcare is available to everyone and that we're all given the freedom to take responsibility for choosing the best remedies and treatments for ourselves, at prices that are affordable, or without charge wherever possible. To my mind, that includes those decisions which are made from the start of life right through to the end of life. We're all individuals so my mind and body don't necessarily need the same medications or nutrients as yours, whatever certain campaigns would have us believe.

We must strive to ensure that clear and accurate information is provided with regard to common health risks. For instance, the risks involved in flying and using mobile phones haven't disappeared because those seeking to expose them have been silenced. And in the interests of encouraging healthy eating in a more effective way, we'll be working towards a blanket ban on all refined sugar. It's the root cause of so many serious illnesses, yet continues to be added unnecessarily to virtually everything, even products found only in health stores. I would also like to see further taxes introduced on anything which may lead to ill health, but that's probably not part of my remit so I'll leave the thought with you. Thank you.' Sal smiled and sat down, relief washing over her as she silently congratulated herself on not completely messing up her big chance.

The running order had been of some concern to the Queen and she hoped no-one would feel less important because of it. Someone had to speak last and she had decided to give the first spots to the two who appeared to need the extra boost. It felt a little as though she were organising a talent show, as some members of the press had suggested, rather than something so much more. And she sincerely hoped those contending with the most difficult pasts would be as popular as similar entrants were on the tv talent shows.

Brett Pearce was not lacking a professional background, a good family or a public profile. Young, dynamic, attractive and apparently assured, his thoughtful and caring qualities tended to be overlooked. Perhaps due to the oft-quoted assertion that 'you can't have it all' or the common envy which causes less appealing individuals to believe that good-looking people are all vain and selfish, or a bit thick. Brett was none of those. In many ways he seemed too good to be true, but the Queen trusted her judgment. She had been rather flattered to receive correspondence from one of the rising stars of the House of Commons and this young man, of mixed race, really deserved his important new role, purely on merit. The Queen wanted him to realise that. She believed the politically correct policies of engaging candidates for any other reason had caused more harm than good in society and created further division. How demeaning it must be to realise you had not been the most suitable applicant for the position you were awarded and how unfair it must seem to the person who was.

As the Queen had expected, Brett's brief speech was strong, motivating and polished. He was going to be very effective in his main role as Jobs For All Minister and she was sure this would soon stretch to encompass other important duties. She had hoped the others would not be too intimidated and was pleased to note the assembled party were already behaving in the cohesive way which she had aspired they might, some time in the future. There was an energy in the room which she did not remember experiencing before. Certainly not around politicians, of any flavour. 'OMG', as her granddaughters might have said, the feeling was one of genuine support and the 'we're all in this together' attitude of the Blitz. Happy Days.

Three speakers down and three to go, it was time for a welcome tea break. She wished she did not think this way about such an important event but the Queen could not shake off the almost daily experience of gritting her teeth through interminable presentations, state visits and garden parties. They were enough to try the patience of....

Just then there was a startling clatter as a young footman dropped a silver platter full of biscuits onto the heavy oak sideboard in the tea room, causing the doors to spring open and the royal Tupperware collection to spill onto the thinning carpet. 'Bollocks!' he exclaimed.

Bets could have been taken on whether the guests were more shocked by the expletive, the unearthly crimson shade which spread across the footman's face or the reaction of the Queen. All eyes went to her as the entire room envisaged the young man collecting his things and never darkening the royal doorstep again. The Queen thought otherwise, however. There and then she vowed she would never allow another free-spirited member of her staff to be expelled as Sky had. 'Thank you Jeremy, that will be all,' she said, intending to save him any further embarrassment.

As Jeremy bowed out, literally, the assembled party looked silently at the Queen. And the Tupperware. The Queen looked back at them and realised what they must be thinking. How disappointed Sky must be.

'Oh dear, no. Alison, please catch up with Jeremy and reassure him that I am quite happy with his work - and his amusing turn of phrase. He has absolutely nothing to worry about.' There were a few open smiles and some barely audible sighs of relief and the Queen paused. 'We all make mistakes,' she added, hoping most sincerely that she had not and would not.

Next up, after the break, was the Homes For All Minister. The Queen enjoyed the simplicity of the temporary job titles and the positive message they carried. For she knew little would be simple about the challenges to come and she was determined to relish whatever pleasure she could get, whenever she could. Purely in legal and respectful ways, of course.

The Queen said a few words about the plans they had discussed, then introduced Tom Newman. He stood up, calm and confident. A happy, family man, comfortable in his own skin. His fairly ordinary looks were overshadowed by his infectious manner and his easy authority. A builder by trade, he had become increasingly committed to matching his occupation to the plight of the homeless and his intention to ensure that the environment was a primary concern when planning new buildings, renovating or rescuing older ones. He hated to see perfectly good structures standing empty and unused, or even being demolished, while thousands lived on the streets. If he had been of a different temperament it would have made his blood boil.

'It's great to be here and I can tell you're all as excited about this opportunity as I am. For years I've been looking for a substantial way in which I could truly make a difference and I believe this might just be it, for all of us. I have so many ideas I sometimes find it hard to rein them in and I'm really looking forward to working with all of you, to sharing our knowledge and supporting each other. In this Age of Waste, we all need to commit ourselves to using the world's resources in the most economic, effective and sympathetic way. Inventions and innovations are a real passion of mine and, ultimately, I would love to see a variety of new communities set up around the country, where groups of individuals with a particular connection can live an ethical lifestyle with like-minded people. Currently millions live alone and it's not really the best use of our residential properties when it's obvious things are going to be a struggle for many of us for some time yet, whatever our circumstances. I believe it'll go a long way towards improving the health of the population and the economy if we strive towards providing better accommodation for everyone who lives here. That is, the UK, not the palace.' Tom looked around the room with a winning smile, and added, 'I can't wait to get started.' Short and sweet and surprisingly powerful. And there was no doubting the sincerity of his words. The Queen could see him on television now.

Fittingly, the next person to be introduced by the Queen was a young woman with an expansive knowledge of communications and information technology.

'Good afternoon everyone, my name is Andrina Sandeep. I do not expect you to have heard of me but I trust you will have heard of the products and services my company promotes and, hopefully, used some of them.' For a brief moment the listening members of the group felt a little let down. They all had such altruistic ideals and the Queen seemed to have brought a mercenary businesswoman into their midst.

The moment did not last. 'As you can see, my family did not originate in the UK but I am third generation British and I come from a proud tradition of hard-working shopkeepers. My parents taught me to be respectful and tolerant and to treat everyone as equals but I received less positive messages from some of the publications sold in our shop and from the attitude of some of the customers. All these experiences made me stronger and gave me the idea for the business which I run now. I am pleased and proud to be the owner of a prominent yet fully ethical advertising agency, which supports only the most carefully chosen and deserving clients, and I am looking forward to assisting each of you to promote your projects, whilst also overseeing the greening of the media industry in this country.

I am passionate about ensuring that we address all forms of discrimination, bullying and victimisation. In the new media which my team will be introducing, we will be doing all we can to stamp out loaded terms such as 'whistleblower', which are as blatantly intended to create negative views of the individual they are aimed at, as were the old racist and sexist terms which used to be so popular. It must no longer be acceptable to judge someone for speaking out against wrongdoing or dishonesty, nor to mock an individual for being different in any way. Despite my own heritage, I am not blind to the fact that white people can also be victims of racism, as men can experience sexism. I could cite several examples of gay male and middle-aged female comedians who have got cheap laughs for what amounts to sexual harassment of young men, on prime time television. And it may be the good looking, slim girl or guy who gets bullied by larger and less attractive acquaintances. This is all equally unfair and equally wrong. There is no excuse for intentionally causing pain or distress, whoever the victim is and whatever the role of the bully.'

Andrina's strength of character, and opinion, were clear to see. It was reassuring to know they would all be able to call on her support and technology skills. She would be an essential part of the team, in her role as New Media Minister.

Glances began to fix upon Sky, the only one in attendance who had not yet been introduced. She felt like a teenager again, being lectured by that grumpy stable manager then 'let go' by the white haired stranger in the expensive suit. But she would not let the tears of that day spoil this momentous occasion. Now in her late fifties, she knew she could be a match for anyone in the room, as she was finally about to be given the chance to prove what she could do. What a funny old life it was, she could never have seen this coming, not in a million years.

'Last, but by no means least,' the Queen gave Sky the most warm and genuine smile, 'I am very pleased to present to you an old friend of mine. Someone with whom I lost touch for many years, due to circumstances sadly beyond the control of either party. I must say, we struggled to decide on a job title and description which would encompass all the issues arising from the general misfortune and malaise which sadly beset so many of our compatriots today, in addition to the major issues already addressed by the roles assigned so far. But this is not going to be a gloomy post. It is an important and uplifting one, which will comprise a multitude of diverse tasks, for which life experience is the essential qualification. Indeed this role is ideally suited to someone who has lived many lives in one, succeeded in retaining her compassionate nature and her sense of humour. I would like you all to meet Sky Finch....'

'Hi everyone,' Sky opened, with a big smile that reached into the corners of the room. 'Well your job descriptions all seem pretty clear and I guess mine is harder to explain, rather like the strange chain of events which has led me back to the palace today. But, enough of that for now - I'm grateful for the opportunity to be a part of this experience, project or whatever we're calling it.' She smiled at the Queen and her eyes twinkled back. 'Seriously, I was inspired by all of you and I'll do my best to give you the support you need in your roles, as well as coming up with my own ideas and plans.

If I were applying for a tv show, I suppose I'd be saying my life has been a bit of a rollercoaster, but it seems to have given me some insight into how the world works. Jobs, homes and health - plus redesigning the media and backtracking bureaucracy - are all of vital importance and my experience has led me to believe that another crucial factor in creating a happy life is to have a sense of real value. Before anyone can fully start living, or find their true vocation, they need to feel loved, supported, heard and appreciated. I believe our society has been making a critical mistake in assuming that everyone starts off in such a way, when the reality appears to be very different for a lot of us. To be honest, it took me many years to realise how much I had been held back by my early experiences and I wonder what I might have achieved sooner, if things had been different. Anyway, I'm here with you now and, like the rest of you, I'm eager to do what I can to improve life for everyone. I quite fancied being The Happiness Minister, but that seemed a bit naff....'

The Queen smiled and shook her head slightly, amused again by Sky's choice of words. Sky continued '....so I'm here as The People's Minister and my goal is not only to support all of you, but with your assistance, to set up whatever centres, groups and websites are needed to help people overcome their traumas and difficulties. And to ensure that hidden loneliness, feelings of worthlessness and desperation are consigned to the past. Too many needs have been unaddressed for too long and, together, we're about to change all that, permanently.' She smiled confidently, then, as an afterthought, added 'fingers crossed!'

Reflections

Amongst a less enlightened group there may have been some who would have questioned how the Queen had chosen her final minister. In fact, compared to the way most official systems have been run since time immemorial, her choices had been made far more fairly. In this case, using her common sense (she loved that term) the Queen had simply decided who she felt would be the best people to take charge of the tasks ahead. She firmly believed these individuals must be independent thinkers who had lived largely outside the currently archaic systems which control everyone's lives.

Alone in her private quarters the Queen pondered over the situation. The Old Guard would have a field day over all this, but then most of their days were field days. Despite the hefty salaries afforded to the 'grey area' positions held by those with the silent power to run the country (until now), they generally spent most of their time in muddy fields harassing some unfortunate form of wildlife in one way or another.

Less than half a mile away, in one of those old London pubs where the red flock wallpaper still holds the faint aroma of the smoking days and frosted glass separates the private booths where confidential discussions can remain that way, a small party had re-grouped. Without the personal and business responsibilities of the other three New Ministers, Sam, Sal and Sky were keen to launch themselves into their roles as soon as possible. This opportunity had been a long time coming for Sky and it had already made her feel twenty years younger, at least. She could hardly contain her excitement about what lay ahead, which was fortunate for there would be some work involved in bringing out similar enthusiasm in the other two.

Sal had slipped back into self-doubt and it was proving an interesting test for Sky to list all the reasons why Sal was right for the job. Serendipitously, those reasons coincided pretty well with her own skills and Sam's.

'I'm sure the Queen really does want to change things completely and that's why she's picked a group like us. We don't pretend to be perfect but we care about others, we've seen a lot of life and we're all sort of "champing at the bit", wanting to do what we can to change the world. If that doesn't sound too grandiose.' Sky took a breath and Sam was ready with a response,

'You know, "grandiose" is one of those patronising terms which psych workers use to make themselves appear qualified to pass judgment on their clients. There's a whole raft of them, words like that. What always bugged me was getting pulled up for saying that someone was depressed, angry or disturbed.'

Sal frowned, 'But surely most people who are seeking help for their mental health are depressed, angry or disturbed. Or all three. Did they expect you to use more specific terms?'

'No, we were expected to say they "presented" as depressed, angry or disturbed. To me, that term implies that the client is putting on some sort of act and not being honest. It encourages suspicion and mistrust all round. I remember when one worker floundered, trying to choose the most acceptable term, then summed the guy up as being "just mad". It brought the house down and she wasn't fired for lack of political correctness because it was a long time back. I've been given my marching orders for a lot less than that.'

'I bet you have, I think you've got the same syndrome as me....' remarked Sky, with a straight face. The others looked at her quizzically and she continued '....foot in mouth.' They all smiled and relaxed. There was clearly a rapport between them but it was too early in the relationship to share all of their foibles.

Meanwhile, Brett was doing what he did best. Exercising his admirable brain by coming up with ideas on the tube, during the short walk home, whilst eating his dinner and taking a shower. By bedtime he could have run the country single-handed but he checked himself. His father had always been a good example of humility and Brett sincerely wished to emulate that. Most of the time.

Andrina was at her desk, pouring over her meticulously laid out plans and making a few changes here and there. Not too many though, for she was a woman who knew her own mind. Yes, she was ambitious, but in a good way. At least she hoped her new colleagues would also see it like that.

At Tom's house, as usual, there was no time to think about anything except new ways to cajole the kids into going to bed before midnight. Six and four but going on sixteen and fourteen sometimes, they could tie their parents in knots with the greatest of ease. 'But Why?' was the favoured phrase of the moment. Tom and Jess prided themselves on being fair and responsible parents, who restricted artificial additives and tv time, but it did not stop them from sometimes wishing they could ring the little darlings' necks.

As they finally slumped in front of the telly themselves, Jess turned to Tom and asked, 'Do you know what I was thinking?' Tom raised a questioning, slightly hopeful, eyebrow. 'You've got to be kidding,' she continued, 'on a school night?' Tom looked rueful and gave a slight shrug. 'Well, you're going to be working for the Queen, right?'

'I don't know if I'll actually be working directly for the Queen, we haven't really thrashed out all the details yet.'

'Ok, but basically you're going to be working for the Queen, right?'

'Er, yes, I suppose so....' he replied, uncertain where this was leading.

'So what are we going to do about the kids' names?'

'What's wrong with Billy and Katie? It took us ages to find two we could agree on.'

'I know but.... William and Kate! We're going to look like the two biggest suck-ups ever. People might even think that's why you got the job!'

'Oh come on, it wasn't quite as simple as that,' Tom said, without much conviction, wondering why he really had been given the job.

'So what are we going to do about their names?'

'Do you think it's too late to change them?'

Further Information

It had been weeks since the Queen dropped her bombshell on the Prime Minister and the media had become increasingly frustrated by the lack of further information. There was only so much they could blatantly produce from thin air and imaginations were drying up. All the usual 'talking heads' ('not the band' the Queen thought to herself) had been interviewed, ad infinitum, on every chat show and current affairs programme. Tempers were fraying and malicious remarks were increasing in all circles. Except, the Queen was increasingly relieved to acknowledge, amongst her loyal Inner Circle and newly chosen ministers.

When the Queen finally relented and a press conference was arranged, Andrina took to the podium like a duck to water, a picture of self-assurance. She had wondered how she would get the attention of the audience but something about her presence commanded instant hush amongst the assembled crowd. Brett felt a pang of jealousy coming on, but choked it back when he thought of his father.

As Andrina began to speak, 'We are gathered here today....' Sal was reminded of her stints as a marriage celebrant and slightly bemused by the choice of words '....to celebrate the launch of a union between every individual in our nation. Her Majesty the Queen has asked me to speak to you on her behalf, and as a member of the small group of ministers who have pledged to bring life to her vision.

We truly hope all of you will receive this information with open minds, for we are well aware that you have been promised much in the past and that many of you feel those promises have not been met. Her Majesty would like to take the unprecedented step of sincerely apologising for any responsibility which may be hers, in choosing to adhere to past protocol rather than interfere with the decisions of her successive governments. She now realises, as many of you already had, that these decisions have sometimes been rather unhelpful.' There had been quite a discussion about the precise wording of the speech, with some preferring the addition of 'to say the least' at this point.

'But this is not a time for blame or recriminations. Today it is all about the future of our country, an open invitation to all of you to help us improve it and to stand together as an example to the rest of the world. From now on we will be keeping things simple and positive. Anyone who wishes to put forward ideas which meet those two requirements, will be very welcome to do so. You will, of course, be able to send us your thoughts by email but Her Majesty has asked me, most particularly, to make it known she is no fan of social media. As always, real letters will be most acceptable, in supporting our essential postal service, and, to conform to our vision, we request these be written on recycled paper. If you feel strongly that you have a unique ability to help this country move forward, please read the manifesto which is being made widely available as I speak. My new colleagues and I, acting as ministers temporarily appointed by Her Majesty, look forward to hearing from you.'

Prior to the announcement, it had been made clear to the assembled media that no questions would be permitted. The Queen knew this decision would be unwelcome but she had formulated her plan carefully and there was no room for more pointless discussion or the inevitable negativity which would ensue from opening the floor to some of the people who had helped drag the country to its current state. She had great faith in her ordinary compatriots and believed the vast majority of them would be right behind her once they had become familiar with the details of the manifesto. She had not been completely happy with that term but she was no longer young enough to have the luxury of staring into space for hours until the right word eventually popped into her mind, so she had taken action and hoped for the best.

The Morning After

'MANIFESTO? One of the first words uttered about her Brave New World shows the Queen is more out of touch than ever. Is there anyone else in the country who would still deem it acceptable to use such a blatantly chauvinistic term?' ranted the column of a notoriously sexist former member of parliament, who had personally been removed from office following several complaints of harassment by young female members of his staff.

'MINISTERS? Are they not the very people who got us into this mess in the first place? What on earth is she thinking?' was the offering from another.

'MAJIFESTO more like! Has the Queen finally lost the royal marbles? Surely no-one else in this great country of ours can agree with her self-indulgent flight of fancy?'

On and on the headlines went, to the Queen's abject dismay. She was truly horrified and yes, a little fearful. Over the years, various comedians, writers and social commentators had risked being increasingly cheeky but, for the most part, the ribbing was tongue-in-cheek and in good humour. This time she had to admit it was not. This time the attacks were personal and they were attacks. Several powerful editors openly questioned her sanity, whilst others took issue with the motivation behind her plans. It seemed she really had misread the situation and even her husband could not console her.

For several hours the Queen remained locked in her room, alone, whilst her New Ministers and her Inner Circle held intense and urgent discussions.

By mid-afternoon, she had summoned her wartime spirit, donned her well-rehearsed mask of blank responsibility and requested a meeting with all her supporters. As the door was opened onto the assembled group, the room went quiet. It was Charles who stepped forward,

'Mummy, you were right. The people really are behind you. Just look....' Charles indicated the large, heavily laden trolley being wheeled in. 'These are just some of the letters delivered since yesterday. We were going to print out all the emails too, but somehow that did not seem to sit happily with our new "green" approach.' Charles was positively beaming by now and his smile spread around the room.

'You're really onto something, my love. I'm so very proud of you,' uttered Philip, quietly taking his wife's hand. It was a great moment for everyone to see and it meant more to the Queen than anything. Nobody could stop her now.

Time was of the essence and her new staff worked all the hours they could manage, despite the Queen's constant insistence that they should go home, eat, sleep and spend time with their families, at least. She was surprised to learn that some of them had no-one to go home to and more surprised by the amount of letters which echoed this situation. Fortunately the issue of combatting loneliness was already high on her list. However, after a fairly brief discussion, it was decided that the term conjured up a sad and negative image which few would be pleased to associate themselves with. Encouraging togetherness had a happier feel and it suddenly seemed so obvious and so easy to acknowledge that improving lives really could be quite simple, with a new way of thinking. The Queen was rather enjoying what the press had termed 'getting in touch with her inner hippy'.

It was exhilarating for everyone involved to discover the wealth of innovative ideas which could be initiated by a simple invitation for the general public to share their thoughts, and it confirmed what had been on a lot of minds for some time. That those at the top of the tree had been hanging by a tenuous thread and the country was overdue for some big changes.

With the health and happiness of all citizens now accepted as being of paramount importance, there were certain projects which involved several ministers, plus their steadily increasing staff. Whilst the intention was to keep numbers to a manageable level, which allowed for personal interaction and the family atmosphere which the Queen had pledged to restore throughout the country, nobody doubted what a monumental task they were taking on, together.

Rollercoaster

So many projects took off so quickly, with so many people involved, that it was hard for anyone to grasp the enormity of what was happening. The Queen hoped it would be the last, most successful and significant period to be referred to as a rollercoaster. She quite enjoyed a good cliché but there are limits to everything.

One early project elicited great enthusiasm, because it was easy to see how almost everyone in the country could play their part. And so the Pubsidy was born, in conjunction with the Empty Properties Rule. Many people had echoed Tom's ideas with regard to the amount of perfectly good, usable buildings which they had seen standing empty, either temporarily or much longer-term, whilst unfortunate individuals made their beds and their homes on the street, sometimes even in the doorways of those properties. Others walked the streets alone, with nowhere to belong, homeless or not.

After many pubs were forced to close, some innovative communities had already acted on the bright idea of clubbing together to buy their local, but the majority of them sat empty. Before the pandemic many had blamed the greedy breweries and gastropub chains which had monopolised the industry, or the licensing laws and the long hours which publicans were forced to work to have any chance of success. Letters which suggested a reversal of the smoking ban were assigned to the bin.

It was time for those who had caused problems to pay for them to be fixed. Moves were put in place to ensure that a generous percentage of the vast profits which had previously filled the pockets of the major players would now be used to subsidise the re-establishment and re-invention of the humble local pub, an institution which had been an essential feature of almost every British community until recent years. However, it would not be acceptable for any of the new style pubs to turn a blind eye to any form of addiction, whether the substance in question was consumed in the bar or snorted from the lid of the cistern in the toilet. They would not be the sort of places for losing all your money on a card game, nor watching strippers.

It reminded Sam of the old joke about giving up sex, booze and drugs, living a lot longer but not wanting to. Or something like that. He was rubbish at remembering jokes, plus he was a 'new man' now, so he would not be doing those things anyway. Shame about the sex but somehow that opportunity seemed to have slipped away some time ago, long before the brief and ill-advised ban that had featured as one of the many ludicrously unenforceable and ever-changing rules introduced at the original peak of the virus.

The intention was to re-open every possible public house or, in fact, any building which was sitting idle and would be a suitable venue in which to reinvigorate the local area and bring people together, in a SAFE (Something Appropriate for Everyone) and safe way. This time around, past lessons - triumphant or disastrous - would be used to highlight the best way forward. The emphasis would be on serving and supporting everyone. Subject to local preferences, the buildings could reopen as pubs, clubs, hubs, or perhaps havens. So long as they were true community centres - not the type that were dull, hidden away and always closed or empty.

There may still be evenings when a pub would be full of loud football fans swearing at the telly, but these might be followed the next day by the LGBT+ Ecobrick Circle or a cream tea for the Companion Animal Owners Bereavement Group. The aim being that every individual in the area would feel welcome at their local, at least once a week.

Brett was keen to incorporate one of his own major tasks into the nationwide Pubsidy Project, realising that many builders, tradespeople, decorators and labourers had fallen victim to zero hours contracts or more natural disasters, such as the Great British Weather. The scheme would provide skilled and unskilled work for these people ('outdoors if fine and indoors if wet', as seen on posters for village fêtes) in addition to catering staff, cleaners and anyone who fancied running some sort of free class, workshop, group or, indeed, community centre. Sometimes wages may even be available.

The Queen was delighted that some valuable workers were able to provide their services gratis. With her vast fortune, she knew she would never be able to voice her belief that the best things in life really are free. But acknowledging aloud that she was occasionally teased in the press, and the palace, for her surprising frugality, she mentioned how she had decided long ago that the saying, 'you get what you pay for' is - what was that term again?

A crock of shit, Sam had thought, but not said, obviously. The question had been treated as rhetorical but Sam and the other New Ministers quickly agreed that charity shops were the way forward and freebies were not to be sniffed at. There was no end of amusement when the Queen admitted her secret desire to visit a few charity shops herself, if she could get away with it.

Another interesting situation arose, with regard to the Empty Properties Rule, after many people wrote to say how they had looked into buying a mobile home, as their only opportunity to own property in the current climate. On finding that some of these, more appropriately, static caravans were sometimes available for very low prices, the prospective purchasers would get their hopes up and briefly envision their dreams of independence coming true, only to fall at the small print. Their current rent was often less than the monthly outgoings required to maintain a place on the type of park where the caravans were almost invariably located. The ground rent contract might also insist they be tied to specific utility and service companies but the real sticking point was the golden rule which stated the caravan must not be used as the owner's main residence. Therefore, once you had purchased your new home, you would be expected to find somewhere else to live for up to five months per year.

Maybe this obscure licensing law was intended to ensure that Great Britain's less affluent citizens would avoid the 'trailer trash' label of our transatlantic cousins, maybe some huge company was making money out of it or maybe it was the invention of some little jobsworth in the government who did not like poor people. Whatever the reasoning behind the rules, the result was they closed another door in the face of hopeful homeowners. It also meant that thousands of decent, well-maintained homes were sitting empty throughout the coldest months of the year.

Whilst the law would remain in place for the moment, a new rule was brought in which would again favour ordinary citizens over businesses. Compulsory Purchase Orders had generally worked against the little people in the past but Compulsory Rental Orders were set to do the opposite, starting immediately. These gave the temporary ministers, acting on behalf of the Queen herself, the control of all out of season holiday homes and little used second homes, plus any other buildings which were not being put to good use. Thus providing instant accommodation for the homeless, those currently living in emergency housing and the 'hidden homeless' who survived by sofa-surfing until they outstayed their welcome and lost their friends. Part of this agreement would see the properties maintained by the local authority, at far less expense than they had previously incurred for placing desperate families in small hotel rooms, whilst penalties would be charged to the temporary tenants for any wilful or neglectful damage done to the properties. It was time for a return to respecting other people and their property, whilst simultaneously improving one's own self-esteem. Tom had been in great favour of the move, as it seemed like a win-win situation for everyone. Put simply, those who made their living from summer rentals would now also have an income in the winter, whilst those who might have died on the streets could now stay alive.

Where small companies or individuals had run out of money to complete a building or renovation project, various easy-to-access schemes were to be set up, enabling work to go ahead to provide the extra accommodation so desperately needed by the ever-increasing population. Many of these schemes would be supported by the proliferation of home improvement shows which dominated tv screens throughout the day, with further backing from various DIY centres and building goods suppliers. In turn, more jobs would be created and rising unemployment figures would only be acceptable when referring to robots, now the intention was to return real job roles to real people.

One exception stood out, with regard to the support on offer - none would be available to anyone intending to demolish a perfectly safe building. Several of the Queen's new associates had expressed their dismay at seeing a beautifully constructed old family home reduced to rubble, only to be replaced by a group of jerry-built, generic red-brick blocks with tiny windows and no personality. Or, perhaps worse, a building with less character yet almost identical to the original, which was now just a huge mound of good quality waste materials destined for landfill. You might think someone was making a profit out of all this wanton destruction.

Health Concerns

Sal was all in favour of anything which improved the housing and job markets, but she was really itching to get her teeth into all the health projects which had been the subject of many in-depth discussions with her new team. Another conversation with the Queen had led to Sal adopting the title of Health For All Minister, having decided that Health Yourself sounded just a little bit too aggressive. Sal felt it best to avoid any touch of negativity if possible, though utopia was some way off yet. Not that it had stopped some of the tabloids indulging in a little 'witty' wordplay, such as 'Utopia? More like UKope 'ere if you can!' These sad little attempts to ridicule more hopeful headlines and make light of the current dire situation had merely convinced the Queen she was on the right track. Particularly considering the amount of correspondence which confirmed the view that it was going to be a damn sight easier to cope once all the new plans were put into practise.

Health Yourself, as a public project, had been toned down to Autonomous Health, which Sal saw as a good compromise between the former idea and the terms 'alternative health' or 'complementary health', which seemed to confuse people. Soon everyone would be enabled to personally access all the resources they wished to investigate with regards to maintaining their health and addressing any well-being issues; whether physical, mental, emotional or, more commonly, a mixture of all three. And the natural medications which humans had been using for hundreds, or thousands, of years would no longer be disdainfully pronounced 'alternative', although Sal was well aware how powerfully the pharmaceutical giants could influence terminology, given half a chance. She reckoned she could fill all the new community pubs in the country with speakers on health and ethics, all day, every day. But that would be greedy. And food issues were just one topic amongst many, as she found when she called round to have a chat with Tom one day.

As Billy ran round the kitchen manically, Sal was reminded of the time when a friend's kitten had lapped up a spilt puddle of wine and spent the next half hour tearing up and down the curtains. 'Er, is he often like this?' she ventured to Tom.

A little flustered and somewhat embarrassed, but mainly bemused about how to handle his son, Tom replied, 'Only most days,' with a resigned, halfhearted smile.

Sal had spent many years toeing the line and trying to be diplomatic. She had finally decided life is too short not to be honest and that it is best to just say what you think, so she went for it and waded straight in with her questions and ideas. It was no surprise to hear that Billy had just returned from a birthday party, having not only observed his behaviour but also the smears of lurid blue icing on his school shirt. Sal had seen many children behave like this and she hoped Tom would take on board a few useful suggestions before Billy got labelled, classed as 'on the spectrum' or, Non-Denominational Deity forbid, medicated. Tom seemed a classic example of how someone can be so practically gifted in so many ways but completely at a loss when it came to understanding their own child. Many parents get so weary from the tears and outbursts they lose sight of identifying the real cause. Mum and Dad start fighting, specialists and agencies get involved and, the further down the line it gets, the tinier the light at the end of the tunnel becomes, until sometimes it is completely extinguished. 'What have you tried so far?' Sal asked.

'Everything,' Tom replied, sadly. He cast his eyes down and let out a small breath. Fortunately Jess was not around. She did not like him discussing their family problems with anyone else, especially as she did not like to admit to having any. Tom reckoned that her family was half their problem and he was probably right. As his family was the other half.

'Have you looked at his diet?' Obvious as it seemed to Sal, who could never understand how sensible people knew not to put diesel in a car designed to run on petrol, yet would constantly feed their kids on synthetic junk and then wonder why they got hyper. But she was not perfect either and she liked Tom, so she summoned up a little of her old diplomacy when Tom frowned at her with some confusion and mumbled something about trying to avoid artificial additives.

'You know how we've had the official campaigns telling us we should eat five portions of fruit and veg a day, or seven or whatever it's gone up to now?' He nodded. 'And you know how we're told to avoid sugar, but we can't because it's in virtually everything?' Tom nodded again. 'Well they're good places to start and I might introduce a slogan to get the public on board too - perhaps "Keep things sweet, don't add sugar"?' The confused look on Tom's face suggested this might not catch on, so Sal focussed back on the issue at hand, 'The problem is that sugar's been used as a cheap filler for a long time and most people are probably addicted to it at some level. It was easy to sell it to a generation who had felt deprived of their sweeties during the war, so then they happily fed it to their kids as a treat. But because kids have more trouble controlling their emotions, their reactions can be quite dramatic. And often that's the issue. A simple reaction, either to sugar or virtually anything else. And it's not so simple to diagnose or address because the substance they're reacting to may be in everything they're eating, or they're reacting to any number of different things, or a particular combination of foods, so it plays hell with the emotions. Or the body. Or both. Many people find it easier to get into a cycle of frustration, annoyance and blame than to inconvenience themselves by working out a healthier diet. The sad thing is that anyone's system can get completely overwhelmed, or even messed up for life, if they keep eating things which don't suit them.'

'So what can we do? It sounds like it's too hard to give up the worst things and even harder to work out which they are.' Tom sighed again, imagining a complicated life looming ahead.

'It's not necessarily easy but it's well worth it to set you all up for a healthier future. First you need to work out what the issue is, so it would be a good idea for all of you to go on an exclusion diet for at least a week or two, to give your systems time to detox. It'll help the whole family learn about the foods which are best for each of you and it won't seem to Billy that you're being unfair to him. Your GP should be able to explain diets and fasts to you but they often have fixed ideas from their training and they're unlikely to have time for discussions on preventative healthcare these days, so look for some reliable websites or books or a good nutritionist to help you work things out for yourselves. Learning to trust your own instincts will be an important lesson for the kids too. Your health really is about the most valuable thing you've got, you know. And the secret is not to feel you're depriving yourself by leaving things out of your diet but to work out which healthy foods you enjoy, then plan balanced meals and snacks around them.' Sal was pleased to help Tom by talking about her favourite subject, but also a touch frustrated. 'If only I was a bit further along with my plans I could put you straight on to the right person, or website, for some more suggestions....'

Tom had brightened up a little anyway, 'Queenie picked the right job for you, didn't she?'

'Are you saying I'm obsessive?' Sal smiled back. 'And for NDD's sake, don't refer to her as Queenie or I'll accidentally say it to her!'

Tom looked a little confused again but decided he could wait for another time to find out who or what NDD was. At least he had got it when Sal said the best way to give up a problem food might be to go 'cold tofu'. He knew she would rather think of a turkey as a rather ugly bird than a foodstuff.

Safebook

Andrina had invited Sky to her apartment, to give them both a change of scenery. Not quite grand enough to be called a penthouse, it still demonstrated her success and personality. There were few unnecessary ornaments on show, but numerous business documents and more technology than you could shake a stick at.

'Fantastic view,' admired Sky, surveying the outline of the city, 'how long have you lived here?'

'It's been a few years now. Buying my own place was the first thing I did when the business started to take off. My parents weren't too happy but I eventually managed to convince them I needed my own space.' Not one for small talk, Andrina veered the conversation around to a more comfortable topic, 'So, it sounds like you've got a lot of ideas to discuss....'

'Too many - I don't know where to begin. But you're the media person and I've got great faith in you getting all our ideas out there. How are things going with the new online paper?'

Andrina's dark eyes lit up, 'It's early days but the public seem to be taking to it,' she said modestly, without revealing the site had noted millions of hits in its first week. 'They seem ready for some positive and encouraging news and the chance to interact with us.'

'Ah yes, about that. I'm a bit of a technophobe myself.'

'That's fine, I pride myself on being a bit of a nerd and, weirdly, I love picking apart the meaning of small print, media law and things like that. We're all here for different reasons but to share our skills where we can. So which project you would like to start with?'

'Well, as you know, I'm particularly keen on the idea of promoting togetherness. Most of us have been lonely at some point but nobody wants to sound like a sad git and admit to it. Something I'd really like to set up, as soon as possible, is a free and easy access friendship website which does not demand personal information, even for administrative use - I'm sure you know of a way in which to flag up any unsuitable content and block anyone who's trying to abuse the site, or other users, without infringing on the privacy of decent folk.' Andrina nodded thoughtfully, contemplating the options, and Sky continued, 'One of the big companies had a great friends section, years ago - it was popular and got good results but they closed it down despite all the pleas they received. I guess it was a business decision and they'd been made an offer they couldn't refuse, probably by one of the big dating websites. But it left a huge gap in the market, for people who were only looking for friends - and did not want to pay for them.

Our site needs to be as simple as possible, to enable everyone to use it. It'll be entirely up to each individual how many or how few details they want to include about themselves. People have been made fearful by scaremongering about the dangers of meeting online, but I wouldn't be surprised if that was partly generated by companies with a vested interest in getting clients to pay them a higher fee for an enhanced service, with the implication that it'll be safer to use. One of the things we all agreed on was that it's important to return personal responsibility to the individual and to get rid of the "nanny state" image. It's a shame social media has decreed us to be suspicious weirdos if we don't want to cover the web with loads of photos and all our relationship details, and I'd really like to turn that around too.' Sky noticed that Andrina was not quite biting her lip but rolling them around a little bit. 'Sorry, I know you're really into all this and I know that someone like you can use all these things in a positive way, so I'm sure you can set a good example to all those who don't. It's all about keeping things simple, so there can be some basic suggestions about what information users might like to include and an individual page set up which can be filled out in a few minutes, with space to add a couple of photos if they wish. Plus a box where they can put what they're looking for, like "walking buddy", "fellow pebble enthusiast" or whatever. A classified section would also be good - where someone can just write a basic line or two, if they prefer.

It needs to be different from other sites in its emphasis on honesty, empathy and inclusion. The users should be encouraged to think about the true amount of time they have available to spend with a potential new buddy and I definitely don't want to encourage "competitive friendship", so please don't include the option to "like" anything or give ratings. I want this website to be absolutely about using the internet as a tool to find real-life connections, not virtual ones. I'd like a few separate sections for specific intentions too. For those trying to trace family members or people who are without family but looking to form a surrogate one, for instance.'

This was an alien concept to Andrina, having a massive family which she had trouble escaping for just a few days, but her mind was opening to the fact that not everyone was in her position. 'What would you like to call this new site?'

'I was toying with the idea of Safebook - I rather like it and it sort of sums up how I'd like it to be presented, but I decided we'd probably get sued to hell. So, I think we'd better go with my other thought - it's funny, because it's based around a term which has bugged me in the past, when I've been alone and it's been trotted out everywhere, seemingly to rub my nose in it.... but I think I'd like to go for "Free Friends and Family". And there's a particular name I've had in mind for ages, to use for one of the most important sections - "N.I.F.T.Y. - No Immediate Family To You". It'll be interesting to find out how many really are in that situation, as distinct from the vast number who are estranged from their family, or just can't stand them.'

Sky had expected there to be a lot more discussion involved but now she saw how Andrina worked and she was impressed. Andrina had noticed Sky's handwritten notes and asked to look at them. Glancing through, she could tell a great deal of thought had gone into the ideas and they certainly had not been thrown together since meeting up with the Queen again. These were the outline of a plan which had been brewing for some time and it clearly meant a lot to Sky. It was also a plan which would truly enrich a lot of lives and it was exactly the sort of thing which they had all agreed to prioritise. 'Leave it with me,' Andrina said. She already had in mind a very keen new assistant, an IT whizz who was born for this task.

Job Fair

The Prime Minister had been kept at a distance until the Queen diplomatically invited him to support Brett at the National Job Fair, which had been hastily arranged as a high profile way of introducing the new schemes he had been working on. As with all her New

Ministers, the Queen had taken great pleasure in working closely with Brett and meeting members of his new team. Indeed the roles already created by the ministers were a shining example of the range of opportunities they planned to offer all jobseekers.

Brett was pleasantly surprised to observe the large crowd outside the Exhibition Centre, and particularly to note the diversity in ages, colours and sexes. All of this suggested to Brett that the Queen and her new team had successfully captured the imagination of the country in general.

As the crowds filtered in to the event, Brett and the Prime Minister took up their places on the main stage. Heeding Andrina's advice, Brett had arranged for the lectern to be moved aside. He saw what she meant about it creating a physical barrier between him and the public and he understood how important it was for people to see the New Ministers as being more approachable than their predecessors, and more on the same level. He still was not sure what to do with his hands, with no papers to shuffle, so he decided to straighten his tie. Then, on a whim, he decided to remove it completely. It seemed like a pretty wild move to him.

'Welcome to the fair everyone,' announced Brett to the assembled masses. The little devil on his shoulder popped up momentarily and pointed out that this would be a good time for a deranged government sympathiser to pull out a gun and shoot him on the spot. Without missing a beat, he fixed his mind back on track and continued, in good spirits, 'Thank you all for coming along at such short notice. I'm pleased to see that you're as keen as we are to get your careers back on track. I won't keep you long because I know many of you are impatient to find out what's on offer here today. Our new team have been working night and day to put this event together and we sincerely hope there will be something to attract your interest. Particularly, we invite you to apply for any jobs which appeal to you - not only ones in which you've got a background or qualifications. Passion and enthusiasm can still be just as valuable, to the right employer. This is a real Job Fair, so that is what we are offering you today. Whatever your skills, education, experience or lack of any of these, we ask that you do as we are doing and see things in a new light, with an open mind.

You have, no doubt, seen the public notices encouraging potential employers to also view things in a new light. Or, perhaps, an old light. For many of you have let us know your preference for the days when an applicant's suitability for a role was judged more on personality and aptitude, at a face to face interview, than the ability to email a comprehensive CV in advance and produce an impressive amount of certificates.

Maybe your background is in administration but you would like to try catering. Perhaps you have always worked in construction and fancy a go at computers, or vice versa. Today you have the opportunity to peruse vacancies from all around the country, so don't restrict yourselves to what you've already done or to the area you currently live in. Don't be afraid to try something new. We're here to encourage you to take on a new challenge, as we have done. And, please remember, we are all living a new normal now, so don't hold back on seeking the right job and the right life for you. You can check out our website for an in-depth quiz to help you decide on the best industries and the most suitable roles for you, the ideal parts of the country and even the sort of personalities most suited to being your boss, your friend or your future partner. So we really are doing all we can to help you move forward.'

Brett looked around for the Prime Minister and realised he had chosen to stand behind the lectern, which had been pushed to the back of the stage. Brett was about to summon up some sort of introduction when, without warning, the stage curtains descended rapidly, in front of the erstwhile leader of the country. There were quite a few giggles from the crowd, muffled and not so muffled, then people started to shuffle their feet and wander off.

Brett's little devil kicked him for using the word 'peruse'. His common touch still needed some work but he had not done too badly and his countryfolk would probably forgive him if he really managed to provide the sort of jobs they wanted. As he exited, stage left, he noticed Andrina in conversation with the Prime Minister. 'I can assure you it was not intentional. We are most keen to ensure a good working relationship with you and the former government. Everybody understands how important it is to treat each other with respect during this period of transition and....' Andrina's words faded into the background as Brett observed Sam, a little way off, smirking broadly.

Around the vast hall, many visitors were taking an interest in the large screen versions of the new Jobs For All website, which they learned could be accessed anywhere, from that day. The new community pubs would all have free computers available for public use and assistants would be on hand for those unable to use a computer, for whatever reason, so the Job Fair also served to remind the public of another major new initiative.

Perhaps the most attractive aspect of the new website was that it was intended to list every single job available anywhere in the United Kingdom. Again using the 'free and easy' model, it would be so simple and beneficial for prospective employers to advertise to jobseekers that most were bound to post their vacancies on the site. If the response was overwhelming, it would also be easy to remove the ad and replace it with a polite notice to inform interested parties the post had been filled and, if they were likely to be seeking further staff, when to re-apply.

'Certainly, I can try to explain a little more,' replied Brett, to the disgruntled and unshaven man who had cornered him. 'Obviously it won't all happen overnight but we'll be doing our best to encourage anyone who has a legitimate vacancy of any sort, literally anywhere in the UK, to post it online. It won't cost them anything and the ad will be live almost immediately.' He was interrupted again by the man, who appeared to be quite drunk, despite the fact it was not yet lunchtime.

'So, if a lighthouse keeper needs someone to walk his dog round his little island one afternoon a week, he could post that?' he sneered, then hiccuped.

'In theory, yes,' Brett replied carefully. The man closed his eyes a little and wobbled uneasily. 'But I think you'll find all the lighthouse keepers were replaced last century. However, my colleague, the Backtrack Bureaucracy Minister, has some thoughts on reintroducing that particular role, so he may be able to assist you. He's very keen to reverse the effect of jobs being lost to technology.' Brett caught Sam's eye and beckoned him over, making his own escape as he did so.

His next assailant was more welcome, being young, attractive and female. Brett wondered whether it was ok for him to notice any of that, now that political correctness was going to be toned down to a sensible level. Despite some of the quite lurid suggestions he received from his political groupies, Brett was not clear if it was even acceptable to fancy someone anymore. Did finding a woman attractive constitute harassment? What if he actually told someone he found them attractive? It was a minefield. No wonder so many more people stayed single these days.

The girl ignored Brett's blank look and repeated her question, 'I've just picked up a form about your new "Shop For A Week" scheme and I wondered what it actually involves.' She really was pretty and he hoped she was not going to suggest something unethical.

'What did you have in mind?' he enquired, wondering immediately if he should have phrased the question in a different way.

'I just wanted to check if I can really get paid to go shopping.'

Brett frowned, 'I'm sorry, I'm not quite with you.'

'Well is it like "Mystery Shopping" or something?'

"Mystery Shopping"?

'You know - where the Mystery Shopper buys things at a store then reports on the service and that sort of thing.'

'Oh.' Brett was confused. Was that really a job or was it a job he had not heard of? Did that mean he was in the wrong job? Something about this girl was interfering with his thought patterns but he pulled himself together quickly. 'No. Actually it's an opportunity for anyone to run their own shop for a week, in premises that would otherwise be standing empty; selling their own creations, their skills or belongings they no longer need. It would also work for groups of people who each have a few items to sell or perhaps they have adjoining allotments and surplus vegetables to dispose of, or they want to raise money for a specific charity event. We want everyone to use their imagination to think of alternative ways to increase their income.' He could not stop double meanings coming into his head. He hoped she could not read his mind, she looked as though she might.

'Ok, I see, thanks for that. I'll have a think about it.'

Brett could not help feeling a little disappointed when their exchange ended so abruptly. Maybe she was not his future wife after all.

Boris Annoys Sam

After his little bit of fun at the Job Fair, 'lighthouse-man' notwithstanding, Sam returned home to continue his work on rewriting history. Or, at least, rewriting as many unhelpful, official public documents as he could.

His experience had taught him that a large number of benefit claimants gave up at the first hurdle of trying to complete confusing forms, thereby losing their entitlement to the money they needed. Particularly since so many more people had been excluded when some bright spark had decided that all applications must now be made online. Once Sam had dealt with that, he was eager to get onto tv licences (i.e. eradicate them) and private parking charges (i.e. have the people who issue them shot. Or, at least, get the companies closed down) and whatever other little bureaucratic annoyances he could wipe out, to make people's lives easier. It was going to be a long night.....

Sam was surprised to hear a knock at the door and his dog promptly started tearing round the room in circles, barking wildly. Unexpectedly, Tom stood on the doorstep, hopping around restlessly.

'Hi mate, good to see you. What can I do for you?' Sam waved his arm towards the living room, inviting Tom in.

'You know we were talking about that Fair Tax scheme you want to introduce?' started Tom, breathlessly, 'Well I've had some ideas and I thought I'd drop in and run them by you while they're fresh - I was telling Jess about it but she said she was busy and she wasn't the one to talk to and I should just come straight over here and....'

The scruffy little mixed breed terrier was now chasing his tail, loudly, round and round the room at great speed. 'Stop it Boris,' commanded Sam, then turned back to Tom, his irritation barely concealed, 'You sound like you've been at the same thing as him! What's going on?'

'What? What d'you mean?' Tom replied edgily, his eyes darting around the room.

'I mean you seem a bit, what shall we say? "Not yourself" this evening. What've you been up to?'

'I was at the Job Fair but everyone seemed really busy and I had stuff to do at the yard and then I had to collect the kids from school and I told Jess I'd make dinner but she was in a mood and she said I needed to get out, for some reason, so here I am. What shall we sort out first? I'm raring to go....'

'So I see. Bit confused though, you being the wholesome family man and all that. What exactly are you on?'

'Me? Nothing. What are you on about? I've just got loads more energy on this new diet Sal suggested. I feel great.'

Fortuitously, the phone rang just at that moment. Sal, being a bit psychic, might have picked up on the conversation. Or it could have been a coincidence. It turned out Jess had given her a call.

After a few words, Sam handed the phone to Tom, 'How did you know I was here?' He listened to Sal speak for a while, then replied, 'No, no coffee, that's what you said. Yes, that's right. Yes, they are a bit quieter. And sleeping better.' He listened to her for a few more minutes, 'Ok, I will. Thank you.' Tom replaced the receiver and Sam looked at him.

'Sal reckons the detox is working. She reckons this is the coffee withdrawal kicking in, firing me up a bit.'

'Just a bit,' Sam grinned, relieved. He genuinely wanted to help people but he had seen too much to have a great deal of patience left for those whose addictions ruined others' lives, as well as their own. As he wondered how best to deal with Tom's current level of enthusiasm, he noticed snoring from the sofa and realised Tom had suddenly gone out like a light. In a whispered phone call from his kitchen, Sam was amused at how relieved Jess was to hear Tom had settled down and she might get some sleep tonight. When he found little Boris crashed out on Tom's feet, Sam treated himself to a really broad grin, while no-one was looking. Maybe one day he could afford to drop the grumpy, aggrieved attitude, but not quite yet.

Happy Days

Sky had been quite excited by the Job Fair. She sometimes imagined she was back in her twenties - thirty years younger and searching around the globe for casual vacancies. It would have been great, back then, to be able to pick out a job you fancied and go anywhere. She hoped the new website might eventually show worldwide vacancies, but had to remind herself she might have moved on a bit from fruit-picking and casual labouring. Anyway, she had done those things back then and was happy to relegate them to ITP (In The Past), as she liked to call it. When she missed someone or something it was a good place to leave those thoughts. A handy cut-off. Nowadays it was easiest to relegate nagging memories to the ITP box, whether good or bad. Who would have thought she would finally start living a worthwhile life, at her age?

With Andrina's assistant putting in the hours on the Free Friends and Family website, Sky was able to get started on her next project for People Together, the umbrella term she was currently using to envelop all her plans. She still could not believe the Queen knew her so well and thought so highly of her, after all this time. It had really turned her life around to find that someone she thought had banished her had been as upset at the loss of contact as she had. Especially as that person was THE QUEEN!

Her train of thought took Sky back to that day in the 70s when she was shown the very formal notice in the Jobcentre, advertising 'A special opportunity for a select group of disadvantaged young people'. At the time, Sky had been going through her teenage rebellion stage and had convinced herself she was quite happy dossing around and getting drunk on cheap cider. However, the seemingly ambitious Jobcentre assistant had actually been put on a rather dubious incentive scheme (to get people off the dole or sign on for it herself) and was most insistent that Sky should apply for one of the positions. Maureen was not often around and Sky would definitely not be telling her mum she had been labelled disadvantaged. Maureen was a proud woman who would take that as a personal slur. And the odds were favourable that she would have made Sky look a lot more disadvantaged by causing a scene at the Jobcentre and baying for the manager's blood or something. So Sky had not told anyone about the job offer. It was hardly likely to impress her drinking buddies and she could not say she had any real friends, when she thought about it. Anyway, all ITP now.

Although Sky guessed Sal was a few years younger than her, they had similar ethics and aspirations for the good they would be able to achieve in their roles and, in spirit, they were both still in their twenties. So it seemed they would get on like a house on fire, once they both relinquished a few unwitting layers of self-protection. Words were not needed for each to realise that neither of them had experienced the best start or the most positive situations. And both secretly hoped that, in their new lives, they may have finally found the best friend they had always hoped for. So it was fortunate that numerous projects would see them working together.

The Happy Groups would be fun to organise and they did not need to wait for the reopening of all the community pubs, to be able to get the idea up and running. Neither Sky nor Sal could understand why there was not already such a group established in every current pub, cafe, community centre, library and pretty much any other public meeting place they could think of. It would not take long to put together some draft notices to post online, for interested parties to print or copy out. Piles of free printed notices would soon appear in many places too. The Queen's enthusiasm for the project had been a reward in itself, feeling as she did that, 'I'm sure most people consider happiness to come automatically in my position, so I think it only fair that I personally finance the setting up of these groups.' It was the thought that counted, it would not really have to cost a lot - motivation and encouragement are free, when you find caring people with the right attitude to offer them.

Instead of turning a simple subject into something to be analysed and complicated, as had tended to happen in the past, the plan for the Happy Groups was to bring together all sorts of individuals: to watch comedies, talk about what makes them happy, listen to uplifting tunes, play games (cohesive, not competitive) and generally to chat and make friends. There would, of course, be eating and drinking involved and, being a subject close to both their hearts, Sky and Sal intended to gradually increase the healthiness of the fare on offer. One step at a time though.

When Sal had suggested it might be good to run groups on a Monday, because some found that a miserable day, Sky naturally put forward the idea of calling it 'Happy Mondays'. They had both been bemused when the Queen automatically piped up 'not the band' with a smile. She really must speak to Harry more often, she had thought to herself. It's so good to chat with someone who really shares your sense of humour, whoever and wherever they are.

Getting Serious

Enjoyable as it was to come up with the fun ideas, Sky and Sal each had a more serious side which clamoured to have its needs addressed.

'It really bugs me that there have been all these initiatives to encourage everyone to live more healthy lives but the food and drink industries aren't buying into it and the governments haven't forced the businesses to change,' began Sal. 'We really need someone to get through to the manufacturers but who's in charge of things like that?'

'Good point, I'm not sure. You're "health" and I'm "people", so I suppose we can make a start on it. I'm sure Sam will be happy to lean on big businesses and Brett can approach it from the employee satisfaction point of view. Imagine how much happier people would be in their jobs if they knew they were producing things that would make everyone healthier. And you know what we really should do? Tax the hell out of any business that's doing the wrong thing. Hit them where it really hurts. Like you said at our first meeting.'

'Oh, right - yes, I suppose I did. Thanks for noticing! It can extend to all sorts of businesses too, not just the food and drink industries. Maybe we should get the guys involved, sooner rather than later?'

Sky nodded and reached for her mobile, with a smile. 'No time like the present.' It was great to be around others who had the same vision and her procrastination was a thing of the past.

As luck would have it, Brett and Sam were both in their palace offices and were at the door within minutes. The two women shared their thoughts and it was promptly decided that the tax system needed to support the new priorities which the Queen seemed to have been selling to the nation rather effectively. Sam and Brett were quick to agree that, whilst any industry or product which was harmful still existed, the taxes involved would be pretty extortionate, whereas there would be generous tax benefits for those able to sponsor ethical businesses, particularly promising new startups. All providing the general public agreed with their ideas. Sky found herself adding, 'And I was wondering if we could start using the term Occupassion instead of occupation or job or whatever.'

'Where did that come from?' asked Sam.

'Dunno, it just came to me then. Is it too naff? Or twee? Or something like that?'

'Yes, probably, but you know.... I quite like it. And it's the sort of buzzword that people will laugh at, or cringe at, so it could catch on,' Sam replied. 'What do you two think?' Brett and Sal smiled and nodded. Things moved quickly these days. 'It could work well when we roll out the new wage structure guide that Brett and I have been working on. That's going to cause quite a lot of flak.'

'To say the least,' interrupted Brett. 'Telling the major players in the richest companies that they're going to be forced to take massive pay cuts. Rather you than me, Sam.'

'I thought you were going to make the announcement? You're the jobs guy.'

'Yes, but you're the one who's in charge of turning back time and doing all the bolshie stuff. Maybe if we tie it to the Rich Enough scheme, we can get Andrina to release the information,' Brett suggested hopefully. Realising Sky and Sal were not up to speed on the current conversation, he gave them a quick rundown. 'You remember our initial group discussions about the most requested changes? That wages should be paid at a rate which reflects the value the public place on each particular job? Well, it's going to be happening sooner than we thought. Her Majesty really is taking the bull by the horns now.'

'Go on,' Sal replied, eager to hear more.

'I don't suppose you've seen the "chart positions for wage entitlement", have you?' asked Sam. The two women shook their heads and he continued, 'It makes for interesting reading - I'll bring the list up on my phone.' He reached into his pocket.

'So, where did you get this list?' asked Sky.

'A couple of my assistants compiled it from official surveys, online data and extracts from all the correspondence we've received on the subject, I think you're going to enjoy this,' Brett replied, nodding at Sam to read it out.

An engaging smirk appeared on Sam's face and remained whilst he completed his task. 'So, who do you think is at the top of the list?'

'It's got to be the emergency workers, hasn't it?' suggested Sal, 'ambulance, police and fire crews.'

'And all the regular doctors and nurses,' added Sky.

'Right. So, where do you think refuse workers, cleaners and shop staff would go?'

The women looked at each other and Sky nodded in agreement, as Sal replied, 'A while back I'd have assumed they'd be near the bottom of the list, I suppose, but now....'

Sky caught her eye and finished her sentence '....Now they're probably right up there - after all the medics.'

'Absolutely. And it turns out they were always more highly valued than we might have thought. People who don't do those jobs really appreciate the fact that someone else is willing to. Do you want to have a guess at the occupations trailing at the bottom of the list?' he asked, impatient to let the cat out of the bag.

'I don't know, probably solicitors or estate agents, insurance company bosses and people like that?' suggested Sal, thinking of a few personal choices.

'They're getting down there, who else?'

'Oh, of course, it must be politicians!' announced Sky.

'Well, pretty close. They're right down there, just below drug dealers but just above lab animal testers and crisis profiteers.'

Sal looked thoughtful, 'I'm not sure it's going to be easy to control the earnings of dealers and profiteers - we'll have to catch them first. And they're not exactly official careers, are they? That still leaves the animal testers and I'm quite happy for us to give them a hard time anyway.' It was unusual to see a bit of a wicked grin on Sal's face but it rather suited her.

'That's a point, which of us ministers is overseeing crime?' enquired Sky.

Brett and Sam looked at each other and Sam jumped in quickly, 'As it is a sort of occupation, I reckon it must be part of Brett's remit.'

'I don't know, I think it fits better with your role. You're rewriting all the official papers and legal documents.'

'Well you're still a sort of part-time politician, so I reckon I win,' replied Sam, sort of jokingly.

'Does that mean you win the chance to be responsible for dealing with crime?' asked Brett, hopefully. Sam shook his head.

'Thought not. Any other surprises you'd like to tell them about?' asked Brett, suddenly struck by the thought that he was about to be master of his own downfall, still being a sort of part-time politician and now, apparently, Minister for Crime. For some reason he looked even more awkward when Sam informed them that anyone who could be loosely classed as a celebrity was also pretty far down the list. With the current amount of reality tv and panel shows, that included about half the country.

Sky looked thoughtful, 'Interesting. So, what's the Rich Enough scheme and how does it tie in with the revised wage structure guide?'

'The Rich Enough scheme is going to be another rude shock to the current elite,' Sam replied, with barely concealed glee. 'Again, it's all about valuing the "little people" and giving opportunities to those who have not yet had their time, instead of allowing our television and computer screens, airwaves and sports fields to be monopolised by the relatively small number who were fortunate enough to get the right break at the right time. We've got nothing against anyone succeeding in life but fair's fair. When there are so many talented people out of work, who've never had a break, is it right to keep paying vast amounts of money to hear the same dozen or so presenters trot out the same gags ad infinitum? And are we really dumb enough to believe that someone who won a suspiciously engineered talent show is the best singer in the world? What's the chance that the most talented footballers never get past playing on a bit of tarmac in some inner city or on scrubland in the middle of nowhere?'

Sal looked a bit confused, 'Is it all about famous people who earn too much then? What about all the big business leaders, particularly the less ethical ones?'

'Of course, absolutely they're included. Anyone who has reached a certain level of income will be expected to retire, at whatever age, and to pass their job or their business on.'

Sky exchanged glances with Sal, then asked, 'How's that going to work? Why would ridiculously rich and maybe high profile people agree to that?'

'Because they won't have a choice,' Brett interjected. Then, toning it down, 'and, if they're that fond of show business or whatever business it is, they can remain connected to their industry by passing their skills on to newcomers for free. There are too many people on this planet to restrict the jobs which are most lucrative, or most rewarding in other ways, to an exclusive few and give them a meal ticket for life. And, more than money, it's about everyone having the opportunity to succeed in their chosen field, not giving up before they start because the market has been taken over by a few people and there's no room left for new talent.'

'This is all getting a bit overwhelming and I don't know how we're going to carry it out. We've digressed a bit from what Sal and I called you in to discuss but I can see we're all "singing from the same hymn sheet"....'

'As well as any bunch of atheists can,' Sam felt obliged to add. He was not sure the others were atheists but he would be a bit worried if any of them were big supporters of any religion, believing as he did that it was the root of all evil. Not to put it too strongly.

The others were learning to see through Sam's gruff persona and knew his heart was in the right place. They were all getting used to each other and pussyfooting around the big issues had not worked out too well for governments so far, so they appreciated each new colleague being true to themselves.

'It would be good to take the best bits of each religion and find a way for them all to work together,' ruminated Sal, ever the idealist. 'I like the Dalai Lama quote, "My religion is kindness". He keeps it nice and simple.'

'Hallelujah to that,' said Sky, lightening the mood and turning to the two men. 'What we want your help with is bringing together all the schemes; to improve ethics across the board, in all companies, businesses and organisations. Sal and I believe it'll benefit everyone if workers can feel proud and happy about the goods they're producing or the services they're providing, whatever they are.'

'Particularly starting with the food and drink industry,' added Sal. 'How can workers be happy knowing that what they produce is contributing to ill health, on a massive scale? We need to end this hypocrisy of telling the public what they should be consuming, whilst making it impossible to follow the rules without trekking to the ends of the earth and spending a small fortune. It shouldn't cost less to buy some unhealthy muck in layers of plastic packaging, which has been shipped - or flown - from the other side of the world, than it costs to buy a local apple. And don't get me started on working conditions or....'

'No, quite right, we wouldn't want to get you started,' smiled Sky, knowing they were all of the same opinion on these points. All that was needed was to bring the rest of the country in line asap....

Celebration

To keep everyone's spirits up and promote further cohesion, the Queen had decided she would host regular get-togethers at which the new Inner Circle (including the New Ministers) could celebrate their achievements so far.

Ever since William and Harry had both been 'spoken for', the media had become increasingly desperate to find prominent new eligible bachelors to harass and, not too surprisingly, since his arrival in the palace Brett was an obvious target. Perhaps to deflect attention from himself, Brett chose the first of the get-togethers to introduce a couple of unexpected guests. And it was certainly a surprise to the others to be presented with two celebrities of the 'gameshow/ quizshow/jungleadventure/iceskating/competitivedancing/cooking challenge type tv show' that was anathema to the New Ministers and all they stood for. To be fair, these two attractive young people also had legitimate jobs, albeit as a premier league footballer and fashion model.

Hearing Nathan and Jolie speak was the real shock, for they had come along to announce their voluntary retirement 'at the top of their game', to step forward as good examples/guinea pigs for the Rich Enough scheme. Although both successful, they had not reached the outrageous earnings of those at the very top of the Rich List, but then many of those who had would not be recognisable to the general public, nor engender the media coverage that Nathan and Jolie's imminent public announcement would ensure.

The Golden Couple bowed out gracefully, to allow the meeting to continue in private, and someone asked if they were indeed a couple. Someone else asked how on earth Brett had swung a coup like this.

Informing the assembled group that, 'No, they are most definitely not an item,' it was a matter of moments before Brett resigned himself to answering the second, more pressing question. There was no getting away from it now. 'They're my brother and sister.'

Who would have known that doing the right thing would suddenly become so attractive? And so fashionable.

One Downmanship

No sooner than the papers dropped and the social media sites jammed in response to Nathan and Jolie's news, sportspeople and celebrities of every ilk gratefully took the opportunity to take early retirement, with a large helping of brownie points. Big business leaders were a little slower to follow suit and it turned out some of them had been nursing a bit of a grudge about being completely unknown, yet rich enough to buy a couple of small third world countries before breakfast. Calling a press conference to announce their retirement would be a rewarding way of becoming famous at last.

The ministers took to starting their mornings with a quick meeting to swap stories on the latest 'celebrity retirees'. It put them all in good humour for the day ahead and no-one, especially Brett, could believe how smoothly the scheme had taken off. But he found the praise it brought him and his family rather pleasant.

Within a matter of weeks, there were new angles to what the press had now begun to term 'one downmanship'. One formerly famous model, who had craved a return to the limelight for years, came up with a great idea for shameless self-promotion which would not jeopardise her standing on the celebrity retirees list. As the point of the scheme was to free up coveted jobs for new talent, it was not acceptable for those who had already enjoyed more than their fair share of success to profit financially from their retirement, so Lauren Hargreaves resurrected an old idea. The jumble sale. High end auction houses had long made a fortune in commission on selling the clothes of the elite. Now Lauren was offering hers to the public, in local community centres, for 10p an item (25p for evening dresses). A lot of well-coiffed/manicured/pedicured/surgically enhanced VIPs attempted to raise an eyebrow at her audacity. But the public loved her and she finally realised that is what she had craved all along. It turned out she was not really that bothered about the trappings of wealth, so it was a few short steps to donating her art collection and sports convertibles to charity, then riding off into the sunset with a taxi driver from Lambeth.

Back in the real world, Lauren quickly found she had more in common with a dodgy hedge-fund manager from Hampstead, who could keep her in the manner to which she was still accustomed really.

But once the ball had started rolling, it was impossible to stop. Formerly ubiquitous 'legends in their own lunchtime' started a trend for being reclusive and 'reclaiming their privacy'. Begun as another way of gaining the attention of the media, by the time the first hundred or so celebrities had sold their Garbo-esque 'I Want to be Alone' stories, even the paparazzi were tiring of playing the same old game and chasing the same old story. As the former celebrities were gradually left alone, many of them rediscovered the simple joy of buying a bag of chips without the accompaniment of fifty flashguns or walking on the beach and not catching the glint of sunlight on that massive zoom lens a couple of miles away.

Some celebrities chose to misunderstand the new rules and concentrated only on reducing their earnings, to the point where charities could expect them to outbid each other when paying for the honour of opening a new respite centre or animal sanctuary. Sometimes no other fundraising was necessary, if two or more major ex-stars really coveted a particular appearance. It was not quite what the ministers had in mind but it did free up the real jobs for unknown, talented newcomers, so everyone was happy.

Real Reality

Meanwhile, Andrina had been occupied with building up Positive Media. She had received some really innovative suggestions from the general public and there was a vast selection available when it came to choosing enthusiastic new assistants. Andrina had loved watching television as a child, when her parents strictly limited and regulated viewing times, so the opportunity to plan exciting new programmes was a source of great enjoyment for her, in addition to the pleasure she intended to bring the viewers.

One of Andrina's new assistants had told of the horror she felt at the turn of the century when she heard the prediction that reality television would be taking over. Somehow she had known this was going to come true and had found it a gloomy prospect. She was sad for the younger generation, who would not be able to spot a good drama if it got up and bit them. Maggie had seemed the ideal person to take on a research role for one of Andrina's favourite projects, but the offer was not received well.

'Are you taking the mick, Andrina?' asked Maggie, more confused than annoyed. 'Real Reality tv?' She clearly thought her complaints about vacuous, plastic bimbos had fallen on deaf ears. A 'no-nonsense northener', as she frequently reminded everyone, Maggie was one of the few people who seemed she might give Andrina a run for her money in the confidence stakes. She could certainly take her in a fight, being the polar opposite of Andrina's slim physique. Hopefully it would not come to that.

'No, no, hang on a minute, you've got me wrong. The title, if it's going to be that, is a send-up of how things have been in the past. We hope viewers will choose to watch whether they love reality tv, love the idea of sending it up or would like to watch interesting real people, rather than not-very-interesting people pretending to be real. Without being too preachy or "message orientated", we want to offer ordinary people the chance to tell their story.'

'Ordinary?'

'Well, ok, not too ordinary. But there are millions of people out there with very interesting stories to tell. Some of them may be happy to be on screen themselves and some of them may prefer to have an actor tell their story, if it's a delicate subject for instance.'

'Or if it shows them to be sectionable or arrestable or something?'

Fortunately, Andrina had already learned to tell when Maggie's outward mix of cynicism and down-to-earth wit meant she was secretly very interested. Indeed, she took to the role as enthusiastically as she took to the doughnuts that featured regularly on her desk. Sometimes it was hard to make her leave the office in the evening, if she had more calls to follow up to potential new 'stars'. For that, in a way, was how she saw them. Coming from a line of hardworking souls who never got the recognition she believed they deserved, Maggie felt deeply rewarded to finally have the chance to make a difference and to be able to offer these opportunities to anyone searching for their chance to be heard. It was exciting that no subject was off limits, with the strict proviso that programmes must not advocate any type of harm or gratuitously cause distress. In the pseudo health and safety conscious world, where everyone's real concern had been to protect their employers from being sued and to ensure their own job security, complying with that regulation would have been a nightmare. But times were changing, so it was easier for Andrina's team to agree on what might legitimately upset viewers, without an endless and pointless debate in which the players endeavoured to outwit each other with their state of the art level of political correctness. They were able to concur that nothing and nobody is truly black or white, despite all the past effort invested in squeezing the whole population into neat little boxes.

'So have you found us any good swots yet?' another of Andrina's newbie assistants asked Maggie one day.

Maggie could not help but feel a little affronted. The project had become her baby; an emotional investment for her, and she was starting to feel quite attached to the individuals she had contacted to discuss their stories for potential broadcast. 'They're not all braniacs or anything, there's going to be a real mixture,' she said, carefully biting her tongue.

'Oh, no, that's not what I meant. We can all see what an effort you're putting in and someone said they wondered who the new stars were going to be. Then someone else said they're just going to be interesting ordinary people and we had a bit of a discussion about a new term. Then I said we needed an acronym but that I.O.P. didn't really trip off the tongue. Anyway....' he noticed Maggie's attention wandering and cut to the chase, 'we decided swots would work best.' Maggie gave him her most benign smile and raised an eyebrow in query. 'S.W.O.T.' he spelled out, 'someone who's on telly.'

Maggie had always secretly fancied having a rose or something named after her but she guessed an acronym for the stars of her first tv project would just have to do. Quite nicely, really. Her family would be proud.

The swots were building up quite well, to the extent that another new show had arisen as an offshoot. One of the team had made a remark about the amount of money that must have been spent on following already wealthy and well-known people around the world, helping them to trace their ancestors for a popular and long-running programme. 'Some actor or tv chef or whatever visits a historian who shows them a certificate and tells them their ancestor was born in Barbados. So the celebrity says, "Are you saying I need to go to Barbados then?" and the expert says, "I think you do," and all the tv crew rub their hands together and run home to pack for their free holiday. How many of us have thought, "That's not bloody fair, he could pay for all that himself"?'

A few hands had gone up, nods were exchanged and a discussion ensued, which led to the birth of Who Do I Think I Am? A new show which would level the playing field by offering those with less money, and a lower profile (but the strong hint of a promising backstory), the same access to the top experts. The owner of the last hand in the air wanted to check if he could still volunteer to accompany a swot to Barbados for the new series 'now they've dumped the Queen'.

In the pilot episode of WDITIA, viewers would be shown how they could find a good deal of genealogy information for free for themselves, on their own computer or in a library, with help if necessary. Maggie was not sure which of the ministers was responsible for institutions like libraries and museums but she had always been a big fan and she had been welcomed into an environment where she was encouraged to make suggestions, so she was confident that a little plug for them would be acceptable.

Following the pilot there would need to be a few weeks gap, to allow viewers to do their own research, as it seemed likely there would be a great deal of interest in the new show. The first series would contain the stories of those who already had a fairly complete family history chart but were stuck on a particular piece of missing information. Maybe regarding a member who would turn out to be 'the black sheep of the family' or an interesting character who would shed light on family patterns and enable positive changes to resolve long-standing issues for future generations. Maggie realised she might never need to watch a detective series again, once she started researching her own history. She also believed it could save people a lot of money on shrinks.

Rubbish

Once Tom's energy had diminished to a controllable level, following a few more changes to his diet, there had still been no stopping him. He was looking good, feeling great and in high spirits for the filming of his first community information film.

'By now I trust you will all have heard about the Just One Thing scheme,' he said to the camera, which was reversing away from him as he sauntered from an area of wasteland into the adjoining recycling centre. 'And I'd like you to picture one of my old favourites, Detective Columbo, turning as he walked towards the door, raising an eyebrow and saying the immortal line, "Just one more thing...." ' Unwittingly, Tom stooped to pick up a stray can which had caught his eye, and tossed it casually into the nearest bin. 'It's as easy as that,' he smiled.

'Except that's the wrong bloody bin,' shouted the director, pointing at the large sign which read PAPER and CARDBOARD. 'Cut. Go again....'

The camera operator and crew repositioned themselves and Tom, slightly red-faced, went again. He was starting to feel that his insistence on ad-libbing, to appear more natural, may not have done him any favours. Fortunately he was not distracted by any stray waste this time and the scene ran to plan. 'When Columbo said that line, it was to strike fear into the guilty party but we know you're all lovely people with nothing to feel bad about....' winning smile to camera, 'so we're just asking you to turn to yourselves as you reach your front door and, wherever you're heading for, remind yourself to pick up at least one piece of litter on the way. If everyone does this from now on then we won't have a litter problem anymore. How simple is that?'

The camera panned around to reveal a large, basic, rather eclectic-looking building with a hastily painted 'SHOP' sign over the door. 'Some of you may already be familiar with the concept of tips and recycling centres including a small store. We like the idea so much that we plan to expand on it to the extent that every facility which is responsible for dealing with waste, will attempt first to sell or donate items to be used in their current state, before sending them for "re-manufacturing". Our aim is to never destroy items which might have a further purpose for someone, somewhere. Despite the argument which has been made for turning waste into fuel, we must all be aware that burning vast amounts of mixed materials and thus creating further pollution isn't the best way to treat our environment, our waste or our economy.'

One of the hardest ongoing challenges for the New Ministers was to find less dry ways to present important issues, to a public who were sick of trying to do their best whilst having the wastefulness of the big boys thrown in their faces. Why would any hard-pressed individual, rushing off to work for the minimum wage, be inclined to pick up a few crisp bags and put them in a bin, whilst walking past backstreet factories pumping out strange vapours or being passed by huge 4x4s, barely controlled by drivers who gave them withering looks as they picked up Just One Thing? Because Her Majesty was about to get involved, that's why.

Tom selected an item from the 'SHOP', placed it on the counter and enquired about the price. 'You've got a friendly face, young man,' came the rather chummy reply, 'so we'll call it a pound.' The refined voice seemed out of place, as, indeed, it was. When the camera panned around to reveal the Queen behind the counter, wearing an overall and holding her hand out for the money, whilst smiling broadly, it was hoped the effect would be immediate....

....as, indeed, it was. If the Queen was willing to, literally, get her hands (ie her protective gloves) dirty, then how could anyone of lesser importance (ie anyone), raise a reasonable objection to these new initiatives? Those who tried would simply succeed in looking pompous or misguided.

There had been quite a few high-fives on the day of the shoot and a lot of happy faces after the broadcast. Particularly when Brett announced how many new jobs would be available at the recycling centres. Being a rubbish inspector suddenly held a certain prestige, yet people with no qualifications were being particularly encouraged to apply for the positions. It seemed rubbish was the key to a whole new world.

Buy Back

Right at the top of the list of issues which the ministers were addressing was the NHS Buy Back scheme. Seen as the real biggie, it had been agreed that the responsibility was too much for one person to take on and that it should be viewed as a joint venture. Consequently, they all felt equally lumbered.

Considering the public had been overwhelmingly duped into turning a blind eye to the gradual disappearance of reliable and extensive medical services over quite a lot of years, great fortitude was going to be needed to deal with this one. But 'strength in numbers' and all that.

A sickening amount of money and insane levels of misdirected power had been used to support the establishment of the new networks of healthcare trusts, laboratories and clinics, plus the legal and administrative departments necessary to produce the documents which justified their operational procedures. Fortunately for the powers-that-be, in the past, many of the old school continued to believe anything they were told, so long as enough 'facts and figures' were included, no matter how dubiously collected. Anything which questioned the status quo ('not the band') was easily dispelled as the musings of an uneducated person or a conspiracy theorist. The invention of that derogatory term had been a master stroke in silencing anyone whose opinions threatened the hierarchy. It had worked like bromide in the nation's tea, removing the natural inclination for free people to speak out and ask questions if they were not happy. It was much easier to keep quiet and go under with everyone else than to be labelled a nutter.

But the evidence could be denied no longer. Although not easy to find, thanks to those faceless powers, people were gradually discovering the documentaries which spelled out the reasons for the collapse of the universally revered National Health Service, and other (previously) sacrosanct institutions. The situation had gone too far and many had been too weary to protest any more, had died waiting for operations or doctors' appointments. Perhaps because a specialist referral had been sent to the wrong address, due to a glitch in the computer system that had been deemed essential for the transfer of everyone's personal information. Sometimes it was impossible just to find your way round a hospital in an emergency. Brave nurses, doctors, consultants and surgeons had spoken out and been ignored, bullied or worse. Apathy was everywhere. Life was too hard. It really was a lot for anyone to take on. But someone had to. The virus had changed everything and surely the public were ready to hear what the New Ministers had to say.

It was inevitable that contentious issues would continue to raise their heads and one of the most disputed was that of Compulsory Purchase Orders. They generally have a negative connotation amongst ordinary folk, for whom the term conjures up the image of handing over their family home to a major building firm, to be flattened and used as the base for another block of luxury flats or a motorway. It was a tall order to turn this image around but, if anyone could do it, Andrina was that person. She hoped. After all, this time it was not about forcing people out of their homes. She looked around the room, at the New Ministers and their hopeful faces. 'Obviously we will be providing our own take on the situation, through the website and community information broadcasts, but we need a way of getting the regular media on side....'

'Buttering them up?' Sam offered.

'Yes, if you like,' Andrina smiled, grateful for a little light-heartedness to soften the gravity of the task.

'You know how certain papers love to consider themselves "the voice of the people" and to hook readers in with hard luck stories that tug at the old heartstrings?' Sky mused aloud, unsure herself where she was heading. The others waited, hoping she was about to come up with the sort of helpful suggestion that was eluding them. 'Well let's give them that, in buckets. Let's open up the call to anyone and everyone who has been affected in any way by the diminished service of the NHS over recent years. Get the emails and letters flooding in from patients and their relatives, bereaved families, doctors and nurses, ambulance crew and maintenance staff....'

Andrina went a little pale. 'I'm not really sure we could handle that amount of messages, Sky. It would take all of us to deal with it - all our staff and volunteers, maybe even the Queen and her family....'

'Yes, it would generate a hell of a lot of contact. And that's the beauty of it.' Everyone in the room regarded Sky a little more intently. 'Because they're all going to be directed to the newspaper of the writer's choice. I'll bet each paper will be flooded and overwhelmed - we've already experienced the power of letters ourselves. The papers won't even bother reading many of them but....'

'....It won't matter because virtually all the writers will be on our side! And the papers won't be able to ignore public opinion anymore,' interjected Sam.

Sky was not bothered about the interruption, when Sam had obviously got the point and was looking so happy about his realisation. It seemed clear that none of the newspapers, nor their owners, would be able to ignore such a tidal wave of feeling, even if they just picked a random few readers' stories to tell on their pages. So it should not be long before (almost) everyone in the country would have a revised and positive view of the Compulsory Purchase Order, now that a very important one would return the NHS and all its properties to its rightful owners, the Great British Public. Once it was clear how many hospitals had been siphoned off and were now in private, non-British hands, the instigators and supporters of those moves would finally be called into question, along with their motives.

Bloody British

Ready for a brief snooze, after discussing the Buy Back, Sky and Sal retired to the private drawing room, as they liked to call it. The comfortable little room, with soft furnishings in every relaxing shade of pink and heavy on the brocade, was another perk of their recently acquired status and Sky appreciated the setting, along with the irony.

'Is it an age thing, d'you reckon?' asked Sky, as she kicked off her shoes with a flourish and settled into the cushions. Sal raised her eyebrows, in lieu of a question, and Sky continued, 'I mean I was a proper tomboy, bit of a drinker in the old days, had some pretty crazy times around the world and look at me now....' Sending herself up gently, she gave a shrug and opened her arms wide to best indicate their surroundings and her pleasure in them, '....precious in pink.'

'Maybe it is an age thing. I was never a "pink person" myself,' smiled Sal, sinking back into her chair. There was an unusual moment's silence between them, which felt pleasingly comfortable. It was not just their room but for the moment it was.

A few minutes later their dozing was rudely interrupted by Tom, who burst in, as usual, with a burgeoning plan. 'The lads are right behind me,' he blurted.

Startled awake, Sal asked sharply, 'What? Right behind you about what?' Immediately on the defensive, as programmed by past events which were her business alone.

'No, I mean they're actually right behind me,' at which point Brett and Sam appeared at the door in a rush. They were all clearly excited about something and the peaceful interlude was over.

'I guess this NHS thing has fired us up,' continued Tom. We all had the same thought about how it's time to really get our teeth into the Fair Tax scheme too. We may as well have it hitting the fan from all angles.'

'Not that we want to hide one issue behind another. That would be too much like old times, politically,' Brett worried.

'Calm down mate, we're really on the side of the people. Don't use that as a quote though - also too much like old times,' added Sam, with his trademark wry smile.

'Ok,' said Sky, shaking the cobwebs from her mind, 'stick the kettle on and let's hear your ideas.'

'How very British,' commented Andrina, from the doorway. 'Would there ever have been a solution to anything without tea?'

'You had it first,' quipped Sam. The silence was deafening, as everyone stressed about how they should feel. Such an innocent remark. Or was it? Political correctness could be almost as hard to finish off as the NHS.

Andrina smiled at Sam, 'For goodness sake, stop worrying so much, all of you. That's so bloody British too! And so am I. I'm British and Indian and I don't know which part of me is the one that prefers coffee. But I do.'

A silent thought passed around the room. 'Sorry Andrina,' said Sam, closely followed by sorrys from the others, straight-faced.

Andrina narrowed her eyes and surveyed them, one at a time. 'Don't take the mick, it's so....'

'Bloody British?' asked Sam in good humour, feigning innocence. 'What is - taking the mick or saying sorry?'

'Both!' Andrina blurted, with mock indignation and a grin. She accepted her black coffee from Brett and they all decided, individually, not to make a joke about that.

Sal could not help worrying that Andrina may have been offended by the banter and she took the opportunity to have a quiet word when they stretched their legs in the corridor later, during a quick break from the serious discussion they were all now engaged in. Andrina already seemed to have forgotten the incident, which bemused Sal; who had to remind herself, not for the first time, that most people were not as sensitive as she was. Andrina, rather sweetly, put her hand on Sal's arm and told her the world could do with more sensitive souls. 'Fortunately, or unfortunately perhaps, I'm not one of them,' Andrina said, finishing her sentence and her coffee. Abruptly, Sal thought. NDD, it was hard being her sometimes.

It had been quite a day for big decisions. Every adult in the country was to be given individual control over how their taxes were to be used, and their choices would be the clearest indicator yet of the issues and services which were really of most importance to British citizens. As a prime example, if the public did not favour donating a decent percentage of their income to healthcare then the NHS Buy Back scheme would fail.

As obviously counter-intuitive as it may have seemed to hand over the most monumental decisions to the people, the whole reason this group of individuals were now in this small room in Buckingham Palace was that they had been given an opportunity millions desired. Through being open and honest and treating the general public as grown-ups who knew their own minds, they had the chance to change the future of the world.

'Well, everything's a right cock-up at the moment, isn't it?' Sam had observed, in his own, inimitable style. Brett, in his own (public school) way, found that very refreshing.

Specialist Subject

As she waited, briefly, outside the Queen's office, Sky could not help feeling she was back at her old comprehensive, awaiting another telling off from the headmistress. There was no reason for the Queen to be displeased with her but then she never knew why the headmistress had taken a dislike to her. School can set you up, or put you down, for life, sometimes at the whim of one bully; pupil or teacher. It was one of those things Sky had never truly got over and the education system was one which she hoped to lend a hand in overhauling.

'Good morning, my dear, I trust all is well in your corner of the palace?' was the Queen's greeting. Sky was a little taken aback by this unusual familiarity and the Queen's guard went back up to mirror hers. 'That is, I'm wondering how you are getting on in your new role. Are you quite happy with how everything is going? Do you need another assistant or anything?'

'Has there been a complaint?' Sky responded, without thinking. It was hard to know who looked more perturbed by this sudden window into the soul. Try as she might, she could not always stop her real self from peeking out and there was a deeply wounded side to that self which even she did not fully understand or acknowledge.

The Queen's eyes softened again, 'Of course not. Why on earth would you think that?' she said with concern. But they both knew why and Sky just shrugged, like the teenager she had regressed to. You can take the girl out of the palace but you can't take the palace out of the girl - or something like that, Sky thought to herself. Sometimes she was good at getting out of awkward situations with a pertinent quip, but this was not one of those times. 'My dear, you have no idea how pleased I was when young Alby found you so quickly.' Funny how she still called him that; he must be pushing sixty now, Sky found herself thinking. Not sensing a positive response, the Queen tried harder to make her smile. 'Do you know, when Philip and I used to watch Mastermind, he once asked me what my specialist subject would be....' Sky frowned slightly, confused about where this was heading. 'And, after you disappeared, a thought came to me. You were my special subject, Sky. You were the person I might have been without all these trappings and I enjoyed hearing about your life. I admired your spirit and I missed your presence.'

Sky was happy the Queen had not made the mistake of saying she had merely left the palace. She had known that would have been an inaccurate and loaded term for Sky. 'What did you tell Prince Philip?'

'About what?' The Queen looked puzzled.

'What did you tell him your specialist subject would be?'

'Oh, I don't know. Probably corgis or something.' The Queen smiled and they both relaxed. 'And so to business, of sorts. I know you are aware of my discomfit with the pervading obsession with the class system in this country and my desire for a rather more egalitarian society, so I was wondering if you have any thoughts on how we may go about changing things for the better?'

As politicians are so fond of saying, while struggling for an answer that will gain the most brownie points from the voters, 'it was a good question' to ask Sky. As the Queen suspected, there were few people in the country who thought an issue through as deeply as the two of them.

'Funny you should ask....' began Sky.

Sleepless in London

As she lay in bed that night, unable to sleep, Sky was quite content. She could not help but feel, following her long and in-depth discussion with the Queen, that she, Sky Finch, was about to be responsible for revolutionising one of the most revered education systems in the world.

Meanwhile, the Queen revelled in the fact that she would not have to take full responsibility for finally dissecting the very foundations of the Empire which her family had overseen for hundreds of years. Sky had been right in stating that one of the earliest indicators by which a child could gauge their place in society was by their parents' choice of school. The more advantageously placed in the class system a family were, the more likely it would be that their children's education was fully mapped out before they were even conceived. Once the Queen and Sky had both thought about it, the more clear it was to see how early one recognises one's worth, or lack of it. A subconscious realisation, perhaps, and all the more potentially damaging.

If she and Sky had taken the system for granted until now, the Queen could only assume that the general population must have unwittingly done the same. She suddenly came to realise why all those who were not cursed by a proclivity to think too much simply accepted their lot and made the most of it. How she had wished she could swap places with someone who worked in a shop, went to the cinema on Fridays and married the boy next door. But she knew it was not meant to be. The same, presumably, as all those people working in shops may have dreamt of being monarch but accepted they never would.

Despite her occasional yearning for a more ordinary life, it was only now that the Queen was struck by the realisation that the majority of citizens have little choice in changing the path of their lives, which was likely to have been determined generations ago. Some wealthier, more fortuitous or bolshier members of society would, no doubt, disagree but there would be no convincing the Queen, now she had seen the light. This brought her to another train of thought which she had been pushing to the back of her mind for a long time. It clearly was not going to be a good night for sleeping. The niggling thoughts concerned a major aspect of the Queen's life which, being Defender of the Faith, she had never felt at liberty to question. The role of Christianity in modern society. Purely by upholding her decreed role, she was aware that she, personally, was ostracising many of her current subjects. With great trepidation, she was compelled to decide that changes must be made, very soon.

All Work and No Play

Andrina finally took a few hours off, to walk in the sunshine and appreciate the simple joy of being outside, surrounded by the greenery of the park. As a true Londoner, born and bred, she had long been able to block out the ambient noise of horns sounding, sirens blaring and the incessant chatter of a thousand busy folk.

Time off for Andrina consisted of moving to a different location to think about work. Her parents, great advocates of the 'do as I say and not as I do' approach, had often reprimanded her for not making time for herself. This had all changed when Andrina was awarded her current position; their pride had reached bursting point and they no longer pushed her to come round for the traditional Sunday lunch. Traditional curry, that is; the Sandeeps were quite happy to mix their traditions as they saw fit.

Andrina's mind turned to the Queen's latest missive. On religion, no less. It was going to be a hell of a task to take on, so Andrina was grateful for her ever-expanding group of new colleagues and assistants. As she absentmindedly gazed at a couple of squirrels doing something she had not often seen while eating her sandwiches, Andrina mulled over bigger issues. She really must get out more. Not just out of the office.

Brett was also in danger of falling prey to the old adage 'all work and no play'. He comforted himself with the thought that if ever there was a legitimate time to obsess over work then that time had arrived. His task felt monumental, so it was a great relief to sense a palpable change in the air, with regard to the general attitude to employment. He had tried not to sniff at the use of the term 'occupassion' and it seemed to have struck a cord in the hearts of the population. The newspapers and social media were full of positive comments from those who felt a new sense of enthusiasm at the chance of a potentially fulfilling career. Those small employers and individuals who could offer a little money for a few hours regular work, or a simple, one-off task, now found it straightforward to post their requirements and deal with responses personally. Particularly touching were the messages from those who were housebound and had found there were plenty of good cooks, cleaners and handypeople willing to help them out, now it was being made easier for them to do so. Naturally the site included clear guidelines to protect users, strongly advising them to check out references or potential employers before making contact, and enforcing strict penalties should anyone violate the new system. For those unable to pay for work to be done, particularly due to a disability, they could always contact one of the voluntary Odd Job Squads that were springing up at many of the community pubs.

Brett was adamant that no-one should be penalised for accidentally flouting the plethora of ridiculous clauses which had made the most law-abiding citizen terrified of putting a foot wrong, or being sanctioned when they had simply made an honest mistake on their application for benefits. He discovered mistakes were actually made far more often by the government departments and it was easy to see the current system was shooting itself in the foot. By making it so hard for people to obtain a little money when they were desperate, and tying them in knots about how their income would be affected if they had the opportunity to take on some casual work, the system ensured that claimants felt compelled to hang on to their benefits like grim death. Simplifying the benefit system and the way job applications were dealt with should go a long way towards resolving at least a couple of the major problems facing the country. And the more Brett looked into the law, the more he had to acknowledge he was entering another minefield. He was grateful for the down to earth support of Tom and Sam, a man who seemed constantly willing to go where politicians feared to tread. Brett was also aware that the other two shared more banter with their female colleagues than he did, and he was somewhat envious. He supposed it was just another downside of his schooling.

Looking ahead, Brett could see the changes they were making could lead to other societal shifts, without too much extra effort. For instance, the pitfalls of alcoholism and drug addiction, so prevalent amongst all echelons, tended to originate in some deep-rooted and unaddressed emotional problem. Whether down to genetic dysfunction, mental health issues or any form of abuse, the blanket result was to remove the future addict's self-esteem, whilst later destroying their family and relationships, as everyone struggled to maintain outward appearances. A dismal situation for many. When he thought about it, Brett saw that many of society's ills could be eased by improving individual self-worth, as Sky had suggested, and his enthusiasm for providing employment for everyone who wanted to work was renewed. For those who had habitually avoided getting a job, or been deemed unsuitable by employers, it was important to get to the bottom of the reason why. It was easy, but damaging, to class someone as simply lazy, dysfunctional or an addict and Brett had always sought to understand rather than condemn. Another worthy trait he had inherited from his parents.

The True Treat

Brett digressed to the way in which people learn to regard certain things as a treat, and found himself at Sal's office door. With her knowledge of health issues she would be a good person with whom to discuss the subject and, as he had been telling himself for quite a while, it was about time he practised speaking to more women.

'Good to see you, Brett. To what do I owe this pleasure?'

'Good morning, Sal. Have you got a little time for me to bend your ear on a few things I've been mulling over?'

'Of course, I've always got time for you,' she replied, with a smile. Brett could feel that feint knot twitching in his forehead and hoped it was not visible to Sal. She was not flirting with him, was she? He had not given her the wrong impression, had he? Surely she was at least ten years older than him, wasn't she?

Sal appeared the slightest little bit irritated by Brett's hesitation. Courtesy came naturally to her but, realistically, she was pretty snowed under. Nevertheless, she carried on smiling, centred herself and asked what she could do to help him.

'It would be very useful to have your input on some consideration I've been giving to the development of personality, rewards and incentives.'

Sal looked at him, blankly. 'Do you mean treats?'

'Yes, that's right. That is what I mean. Treats.'

Sal opened the door a little wider, unintentionally enabling Brett to see how busy she actually was, from all the stacks of paperwork around the room. 'Oh, of course, I'm sorry, I can see it's not the best time.' Brett moved to leave but Sal patted his arm and pointed him towards a chair.

'We're all busy but we're also here to help each other and to "get the show on the road". So - treats - one of my "areas of expertise"....'

Sal smiled, to herself as much as anyone, as she had a sudden flashback to that chubby little kid with the blonde pigtails, stuffing down chocolate bars in front of the telly. Boy had she worked hard to lose all that weight. Well, most of it.

Brett relaxed a little and positioned himself neatly on the proffered chair. Sal poured two glasses of water, swept a pile of papers from the table and placed the glasses between them. 'I seem to be finding some unexpected links between different projects and I'm not sure if it makes sense,' he began. Realising he had her full attention, he continued. 'I've been dealing mainly with employment, as you know, and that has led me to consider why so many people have been unhappy with their jobs and their prospects, or unwilling to work in the first place. I'm sure I'm preaching to the converted but I'm guessing one's upbringing can have a bigger effect than I've ever really considered.' Sal nodded for him to continue, wondering when the subject of treats was going to come up. 'I got to thinking about how one's family problems can lead to drinking or taking drugs and I wondered if that might be linked to the rewards one received as a child?'

'Or the treats,' Sal responded. She seemed very keen on that particular word. Amongst many other things, Brett was learning the importance of phraseology and semantics and how different these could be amongst any group of individuals. Sal giggled a little, at herself. 'I'm sorry, I must seem a little obsessed but, between you and me, I was a bit of a compulsive eater when I was a kid. My parents didn't have a lot of time to invest in me, so they gave me chocolate instead of affection. But I believe it's time that shows love, not food or gifts. Time is the true treat. I find it very strange when couples profess their love for each other, or parents for their children, when they never seem to want to spend five minutes in the same room, let alone go on a day trip together. And it doesn't help that we have expressions like "The way to a man's heart is through his stomach", or that men are taught they can behave however they wish on a date if they turn up with chocolates. Or flowers, I suppose.' Sal shook her head to bring herself back to the point. 'No wonder so many women joke about being addicted to chocolate. It's encouraged from such an early age.'

'But it is a joke, isn't it? It's not a real addiction.' Brett was briefly unaware of the can of worms he had opened. Less appealing than a box of chocolates and seemingly a lot more contentious.

Sal sighed a little and adopted the air of someone who again has to inform the unenlightened about something which should be common knowledge. 'Everyone has their weaknesses and I believe sensitivities to certain substances, of any type, may result from our experiences in childhood. It's quite possible a lot of these addictions have continued through generations and it would be very interesting to study the families of publicans or pharmacists, for instance. I've heard evidence to suggest that some of those with the easiest access to drugs and alcohol may have chosen their career, or carried on the family business, for the very reason that it offered that access.'

'Do you think the results are always negative?'

'Well, I suppose if you were brought up by a family who were obsessive about fruit and vegetables and rewarded good behaviour with a carrot, then you might grow up with a healthy attitude towards grub. Or you might rebel by turning to fast food and cigarettes. Who knows? Humans are weird creatures.'

'Indeed they are. I mean, we are.'

'And it's not all about things you consume in one way or another - perhaps the worst addictions are to certain types of behaviour or a particular way of relating. Have a think about people you know and how many of them have made exactly the same choices, or mistakes, as their parents, or find a partner who turns out to have the same issues. It can be particularly damaging if the ancestral way of relating has been through a negative trait, such as anger. And even if your family weren't drinkers, it's harder to be a non-drinker than a drinker, in our culture, because every celebration is a reason to bring out the booze. As are Friday and Saturday nights, working lunches and pretty much any other occasion you might suggest. It takes a strong character to make different choices from those around them and most of us aren't born to stand out like that. If your friends get into heroin, the chances are you will too.'

It sounded pretty heavy to Brett but he could see Sal's point. The earlier you got off the right track, the harder it was to get back on it later. If you started on the wrong track from birth, could you ever recover from that? He asked Sal what she thought.

'I reckon it would be pretty bloody hard, to be honest. That's why we're all feeling the pressure of opportunity now. There are so many ways in which we can attempt to change things for the better, but such a fine line between creating a lot of happiness and messing things up completely.'

'I totally understand. I thought it was only me who felt that way.'

'Perhaps none of us are so different after all. Now we just need to get another seventy million or so people on board and we'll be sorted.'

At which they clinked their glasses together and had a bit of a laugh. Still one of the best forms of medicine.

Country Break

Spending a few days at a quaint little pub in the country had sounded like the sort of break Tom had been looking for. He had almost invited Jess and the kids along, but managed to find an excuse that satisfied his sense of fairness. Now the reality of the situation had hit him and he sensed a little divine retribution in the air. That would teach him.

As he surveyed the burgeoning crowd gathered on the village green, Tom wondered if this could be the only place in the country where there was such vocal competition for jobs. And not even paid ones. These were all voluntary positions, which did not sound that exciting to Tom, and he gave credit for the turnout to Brett and Andrina, as the more public faces of the Pubsidy campaign, so far. Tom had received some positive comments regarding the short community information films he had featured in but he was not yet comfortable in taking his share of the public approval. He had only been himself and spoken about what he believed in. Apparently people liked that. Now he had the task of sorting out this baying mob.

'Come on, mate. I was a carpenter for twenty years before I got made redundant. I just need to get back in the swing of things.'

'I've never had a job but I'll work harder than anyone here if it gets me a good reference.'

'We've got our own caravan over there, look. We can work during the day and be caretakers at night too.'

'I don't suppose you need a lot of cooking done yet but I can feed all the workers and keep the kettle on the boil.'

'When I was in the city, I organised elite corporate events. My husband and I purchased the local manor house last year so I am sure you would like to avail yourself of MY expertise,' came a rather haughty voice from the back of the throng. Tom was tempted to tell her where to go but checked his secret leaning towards inverted snobbery and made an unplanned announcement on the spot, holding his hands aloft for silence.

'Ok, ok, as my colleagues have promised, we'll do everything we can to provide a suitable and rewarding job for everyone who shows the effort, enthusiasm and initiative to look for one. As you all clearly have, so you're all hired.'

Instead of the cheers Tom had expected, there was barely a murmur. Confused faces looked at each other and at him.

'What?' said someone.

'Is that it?' asked another voice.

'Don't we have to fill out forms and supply references and CRB checks and things?' asked another.

'I suppose some of that might be helpful later but, for now, you're all hired. You've all been kind enough and keen enough to venture out here and, on behalf of my colleagues, not least Her Majesty the Queen, we truly appreciate your commitment to acting as trailblazers in this new venture. We sincerely hope this will be the first of many, many such venues to be brought back to life, to become the hub of a thriving community.'

Speaking 'off the cuff', as ever, Tom had used a little 'artistic licence' in his impromptu speech. This would not, strictly speaking, be the first of the Pubsidy premises, as many that had needed very little refurbishment were already taking their first tentative steps towards success, with new staff and activities. Each new venue was to go through a test period, during which they would ascertain the needs of their particular area and plan accordingly for the future. Now he was fully involved, in such a hands-on way, his enthusiasm was tangible and his excitement was only slightly diminished as he looked over to the shell of a building which he was now in charge of making good.

Tom noticed the couple from the caravan were already in deep conversation with the cook and he went over to join them. After a few minutes chat, the three of them already had plans under way to provide sustenance to those who would be involved in the initial stages of the renovation. Pam and Jim had offered Sarah the use of their caravan's cooking facilities and now they suggested that workers might also use their toilet. 'Thanks, but I think that might be above and beyond the call of duty. There are going to be a lot of people on site and I doubt your water tank could handle the volume, for one thing.' Endearingly, they looked a little crestfallen, so Tom was quick to assure the couple that he would appreciate their kind offer as a temporary measure, until the portable toilets turned up. Even the delivery of those most mundane necessities, to so many locations, had already provided a good few more temporary jobs throughout the UK.

As he wandered around the green, Tom smiled quietly to himself about an unlikely conversation he had recently enjoyed with the Queen, during which she had expressed her views on toilet twinning. 'It's really quite wonderful,' she had enthused, 'three of the lavatories in the east wing have been twinned with ones in Rwandan villages and those in the stable block have been matched with some conveniences in the Himalayas. It's really rather sweet, sometimes they send us postcards - the locals, that is, not the toilets. I'm not quite barmy yet, despite what some of the press have been insinuating.' He was pleased to have been able to add to the Queen's cheery mood by opening up further discussion about how the reduction of pollution during the lockdown had affected the environment. Apparently, villagers a hundred and twenty five miles away from the Himalayas had been able to see them for the first time in thirty years, and there were numerous similar reports from around the world. It made him happy to see an old lady smile.

It took some time for Tom to circulate, to ascertain the mixture of skills and experience amongst the group and the hours they would be available to work. He was surprised and pleased to discover how much expertise was on offer, but what he had not managed to find was any cheap, local accommodation for himself. The New Ministers had willingly agreed not to take advantage of the expense accounts enjoyed by their predecessors, hence Tom found himself left in the lurch. Again he thought, that would teach him. He had not banked on the attention of Pam and Jim, who had been observing him from their window as the darkness closed in. It turned out the caravan was larger than it appeared and Tom was fairly comfortable in the kiddy bed, so long as he did not try to straighten his legs.

Next morning, having tossed and turned uneasily during the night, so far as he was able, Tom overslept. He awoke to the smell of eggs frying on the stove, a couple of feet from his tousled head. They certainly are keen around here, he thought to himself, as he noticed it was Sarah doing the cooking. Tom thought her return had been a bit premature until he opened the door to discover that most of the prospective workers from the previous night had already turned up and were awaiting his instructions. He was relieved to see his recently acquired assistant, Gary, pulling into the pub car park in the work van, replete with building plans and materials. Once the scaffolding arrived and the essential health and safety procedures were completed, they would be able to get things started.

Quiet Night In

The Queen and her perennial prince were having 'a little Sandy time', as they liked to call it. A short break up in Norf Norfolk ('so good they named it twice') had always reinvigorated them for another round of tedious state functions back in town.

Like any other long-married couple, they liked to put their feet up in front of the telly, give the footman the night off and settle down with a little snack. 'Are you sure this pheasant isn't a bit orf?' asked Philip, lifting the lid of his sandwich and sniffing at it suspiciously. 'And what's this bloody rubbish? Not another "reality show"? Reality my arse!'

'But you like this one, dear. You know, Celebrity Wine Club. Last week you guessed the exact time the first celebrity would slip into a drunken stupor.'

Philip chortled, 'Oh jolly good, yes, that one. What was her name again? Dolores Dungpuddle or something?'

The Queen drew a very slight breath, 'I believe it's not an English name, dear. They said she won the first of those big talent shows.'

'And why is it that all our footballers and cricketers and athletes are all Johnny Foreigners these days?'

'Because we do like to win some sporting contests occasionally, dear.'

Philip snorted and expressed regret that his regal status took him out of the running for the new series of Grumpy Old Men's Club, in which former celebrities played practical jokes on the unsuspecting public, sometimes on a notably disruptive scale. The latest episode had consisted almost entirely of wrinklies who nobody recognised anymore, simultaneously pretending to break down at busy junctions at rush hour, ostensibly to make a point about how everyone else was in too much of a hurry, but seemingly to allow them the chance to shout, 'What's the matter, can't you take a joke?' at anyone who looked the slightest bit frustrated by their hilarious antics. At least no-one was goaded into eating badgers goolies on the show, but it may only be a matter of time, the way things were heading.

The Queen attempted to lighten the conversation a little. 'Did you see that article in the newspaper, about celebrities and their children's strange names?'

'I don't know, Cabbage, what did it say?'

'I'm not sure of its validity but their "investigative journalist" wrote that he's uncovered evidence which suggests all those names of fruits and things are actually a smokescreen to protect their privacy. He claims, for instance, that he has copies of the real birth certificates for Mr. Geldorf's children: Sharon, Tracey and Diane.'

'Well, I think there's far too much obsession with these people anyway. The sooner your little regime gets things back to how they were the better.'

'Regime is not quite the term I'd use, it seems a little severe,' the Queen said, gently biting her lip. 'And we're doing our best to move things forward, rather than back. I can't wait to see our little country lead the way in bringing the human approach to people's lives, to see everyone healthier and happier....'

'You always were such an idealist, my love,' Philip kissed the top of her head and turned towards his sleeping quarters. As he opened the door, he could not help himself stopping to pass on a final thought, 'and if it all turns into another right royal cock-up, at least we won't be around to endure it for too long'. He shut the door behind him, which was a good thing.

As was her custom following such interactions with her husband, the Queen gently hummed the tune 'Unforgettable' under her breath. Only she knew that, in her mind, she had changed the lyric to 'unforgivable'.

Going It Alone

Sam and Brett could not help but notice the Queen had a particularly resolute air about her as she ushered them into her private drawing room the next morning. Even Alison was nowhere to be seen and the usual tray of tea and biscuits was noticeable by it's absence. She clearly meant business.

'Firstly, gentlemen, I would like to thank you once again for all your commendable work so far.' It was par for the course for Sam to sense the vibration of an impending sacking, but the feeling was new to Brett. However, it turned out they had no need to worry, at least not about that. 'Secondly, it has become apparent to me that certain persons may not be taking our joint commitment as seriously as they might. I feel this is something we need to address with the utmost urgency.'

Brett and Sam glanced imperceptibly at each other's impressive show of calm and confidence, whilst simultaneously striving to control the feeling that their insides had been taken over by a washing machine that was about to break down.

'As I am sure you are aware, the timing of my long-delayed decision to step forward, as I have now done, to bring yourselves and the other New Ministers on board with my, perhaps rather ambitious, plans for our nation, has a great deal to do with the fact that we have reached a unique period in our history. In this previously uncharted territory, in which we in the United Kingdom had chosen to "go it alone", before even more monumental, enforced changes landed in our laps, it seems wise that we all learn as much as possible about self-sufficiency, whilst doing our utmost to build strong and supportive communities on which everyone can rely. This applies to our personal circumstances, through to our international relationships. There is great strength in numbers but it also pays for individuals to know how to meet their own needs, where possible. An effective community can certainly thrive on the inner strength of one individual but that can also lead to an unrealistic and unfair displacement of power and/or responsibility. Right now, we need to concentrate on taking forward the initiatives which will best convey our intentions for the future and set us firmly on the right path. Have we reached the stage where we can hold the Tax Ballot, for example?'

Brett heard a confident, faraway voice assuring Her Majesty that the ballot could be prepared within the week and held by the end of the month. Nothing seemed real anymore; the way official changes were taking place so quickly and, particularly, the fact that the faraway voice turned out to be his own.

Sam was similarly put on the spot about the rewording of major laws and statutes. He had never been so grateful, as he was now, for the highly astute and well-informed team who had spent the last weeks trawling through the finer points of every rough document he had prepared. Since the Queen had thrown her support behind the Plain English Campaign, with well-publicised vigour, it had suddenly achieved the dizzying heights of allegiance that the founders had been seeking for years. In simply decreeing that all official documents must, henceforth, be adapted to make them easy to understand for anyone with the most basic literacy and language skills, the Queen had taken a major step in levelling the playing field of British society. Additionally, the new rules were not to be restricted solely to written language.

Gone, with the stroke of Her Majesty's pen, were the days when a courtroom being used for a highly emotive lawsuit could be reduced to an arena in which to resurrect a couple of old Etonians' playground rivalry. What fun the barristers had enjoyed, smugly trading quips and witticisms, safe in the knowledge that any of the injured parties (or plebs for short) who dared to vocalise their indignance at the trivialisation of tragic deaths or major incidents, would be promptly ushered out for contempt of court. Whilst ordinary families quietly lost their loved ones, their life savings and their minds to the seemingly misnamed justice system, the legal teams had raked in the rewards like corrupt croupiers. From now on, with the immediate banning of legalese, anyone who was able to present their own case would not be penalised in any way for making that decision, whether appearing in court or completing forms which had hitherto been the restricted domain of solicitors or other professionals.

The Queen had to be satisfied that she was doing everything in her power to leave a positive legacy. It was too late now to worry about ruffling feathers or upsetting the order of things. That time had passed and she had no choice but to finish what she had started. She was prepared to suffer the consequences, so long as it improved the lives of others. Her life had been extraordinary, though not necessarily the one she might have chosen, and she was well aware there was no-one else in the country with this opportunity available to them. She had slavishly adhered to protocol, she reflected, for over ninety years. Now, while she still had the time, she would continue with this new tack for as long as she was able. The United Kingdom was broke and she would fix it, if it was at all possible for her to do so. With a little help from her friends.

Group Sects

Whilst the serious meetings continued daily, Sky and Sal welcomed a little levity into their lives by monitoring the popularity of the Free Friends and Family website (rapidly growing by the million) and by occasionally attending the inaugural events of the rapidly proliferating new community groups. Every so often it was necessary for one of them to step in and have a word with someone whose helpfulness knew no bounds. Sometimes it was for the sake of that person and sometimes for the benefit of others. Although both of them were inclined towards being 'too helpful' themselves, it was interesting for Sky and Sal to witness the gamut of characters included amongst those who would classify themselves as good people. They found men and women (and everyone in between) of every conceivable religion, political persuasion and adherence to organisations bordering on (or right over the line of) being a cult or a sect. They found outwardly kind and spiritual folk who barely recognised the strength of their own egos and their quest for power over vulnerable souls. And sometimes they found genuinely honest, fair and thoughtful individuals who, like them, truly just wanted to make the world a better place.

As those with experience of setting up groups had been discovering for years, 'there was always one'. One who was negative or grumpy or commanded all the attention for themselves and their ideas, or did not follow through on their promises, was a bit of a bully, set up rivalries, stomped off in a huff, or did not turn up when they said they would. The list was endless, as it is with personalities. Sal longed to bring others together in harmony but had to admit that her deep rooted sensitivity made it nigh impossible for her, personally, to feel truly at ease in a group. Picking up the feelings of everyone around her may be an unusual gift but it was one she could certainly have done without.

Despite all the possible pitfalls and thanks to the growing feeling of positivity pervading the country, almost all the new centres found their feet quickly, as the efficiency of Andrina's New Media ensured that the public were aware of all the groups available to join and the venues which were about to open. Many friendships were being formed, even at the little opening ceremonies of the pubs, clubs, hubs and havens. With a new way of thinking filtering down from their small group of ministers, Sky and Sal continued to have high hopes for the collective future.

There was no end to the inventiveness of those who formed imaginatively titled groups and there were to be no official leaders but, realistically, there were always going to be a few individuals who were willing to take on more than their fair share of the organisation. So long as everyone treated each other with fairness and respect, there were no rules to govern the running of the groups.

Most of the venues arranged local walks and regular swap shops (not just for clothes but anything the owner no longer wanted - with the exception of 'live goods' such as lazy partners or noisy children). In areas with predominantly young couples, there were Parents for Parents groups (for mutual support rather than dating), Non Parents groups (for those who were fed up with hearing about their friends' kids) and Family Fixers (for those who were good at sorting out other people's kids, or parents). There were Trauma Buddies and Loners Together and some areas were already putting together teams of Welfare Wardens, to ensure that support was always available in the community, away from the centres, for those a little less mobile or a little more agoraphobic.

A few Prime Time groups were set up, where the locals had agreed that late afternoon could be the most solitary part of the day; after regular cafes had closed, most pubs were still empty and those with families or partners had returned home to them. As these groups of single people became closer, they bonded over how many ads, speeches and well-intentioned initiatives had upset them during the health crisis, as endless video clips demonstrated how hard it was to only speak to your family via computer or smartphone and how great it would be to meet up with all your old friends again. Nothing could have been more isolating for those who did not have those future options to look forward to. Being repeatedly told 'we're all in this together' had felt like a real kick in the teeth to those sitting at home, totally alone and unable or unwilling to use social media, for all sorts of reasons that had left them feeling they were safer by themselves. With confidence coming from their new camaraderie, they cheered themselves up by promoting the idea that all eating and drinking establishments should start providing a 'meet a new mate' table. And, for good measure, that 'Super Singles' deals would be as common as '2 for 1', allowing those who were eating alone to take the second meal home in a 'doggy bag', return for a 'free' meal on another occasion or pay a little extra for a starter and a dessert to accompany their original meal. The Prime Timers also discussed the possibility of approaching the New Ministers with an appeal to make disolation (discrimination against solos) a crime, or to petition the various purveyors of meals for being singlist, should they not take to the Super Singles suggestions with the desired enthusiasm.

For the even less sociable there was the Share-a-Shed scheme, where those involved might avail themselves of another's workbench for a while, in exchange for assisting with the assembly of a flatpack or a similarly tedious task. If the initial swearing did not form a natural bond, there was always hope that a few words or a beer might be exchanged over a future project.

Of course, some less welcome members of society suggested rather inappropriate ideas for improving their lives through attending groups. Amongst these, the 'dirty old men' contingent could prove quite a challenge. Promoting, as they did, the idea that frequent (unwelcome) hugging, and having 'nice young ladies in short skirts' serving refreshments, would keep them very happy indeed. Whilst some nouvelle ladettes saw the groups as just another alternative to swiping left or right - maybe worth a look on the way to a night's clubbing, with a half bottle of gin tucked away somewhere. If these two (unofficial) groups happened to coincide, they could be quite a match for each other.

With all the different activities on offer, it was quite common to find someone dressed for Morris dancing sitting down to a sedate game of chess, having turned up on a Tuesday instead of a Thursday. So long as they kept their little bells quiet, it could be the start of an unexpected friendship. Serendipity can be a beautiful thing.

As amateur comedy nights and fund raisers gave way to skittles and open mics, mediumship demonstrations and support groups, Tom's team travelled the country, supervising the completion of new premises, cutting the odd ribbon and even cracking a bottle of champagne against the occasional bow. For 'where there's a will' and all that; in isolated communities with no old pub to resurrect, if there was a tumbledown shed at the bottom of somebody's garden or a disused barge on a silted up river, then why not put it to good use? Sometimes the unusual surroundings induced further creativity in the locals and some very interesting new groups sprang up.

Who Do I Think I Am?

Andrina hated to be torn away from her more serious tasks but she could not help being excited about the subjects Maggie had recruited for the first series of Who Do I Think I Am? Having made quite an effort to loosen her attachment to her self-professed 'close knit family', Andrina found it hard to comprehend that quite a number of her countryfolk seemed to spend all their spare time (and sometimes a good deal of their not-so-spare money) trying to uncover facts about obscure relatives who died centuries ago. If anyone had asked, she would have been quite willing to hand over a few of her live ones. Particularly Uncle Anay.

Meanwhile, others suffered sleepless nights trying to piece together snippets of information and half-memories lost to the tides of time, desperate to connect with a living soul who shared just a little of their blood. It seemed there were a great many who were estranged from their living family and some folk who really had no relations and no-one to relate to.

As Andrina had predicted, her IT specialist, Laura, had proved her worth, especially in forging a connection between those working on WDITIA and the Free Friends and Family team.

Taking an interest in all the new projects going on around her had got Alison thinking. In fact it led to her devising a rather cunning plan, to put the Queen's mind to rest over someone she had been unable to forget, since she first read a certain letter. The one which had elevated her level of interest in her correspondents to the stage which had given rise to current events. Having read the message and borne witness to the effect which it had on the Queen, Alison believed the country owed quite a debt to that one specific letter writer. The problem was, the person who had tugged so strongly on the Queen's heartstrings had given no clue as to who they were or where they might be found. It had the makings of a real Cinderella story, in Alison's rather romantic imagination. Coming from a nice, suburban, middle-class family, she had little knowledge of how life on the streets really worked. But she now had access to the sort of minds who could find ways of contacting someone completely anonymous to the world at large.

Have Faith

Following many debates and much metaphorical hand-wringing about how not to offend any individual adherent to any one of the world's four thousand, two hundred or so religions, and with the full backing of the Queen, Andrina released the following public announcement:

'In the interest of promoting harmony and cohesion amongst all citizens of the United Kingdom, we ask you to hear and accept the following with open hearts and open minds. After extensive consultation with the most senior representatives of our major religions, it has been mutually agreed that all faiths will now share responsibility not only for the spiritual wellbeing of anyone who wishes to request guidance or support but also for addressing some of the more practical difficulties which we face as a nation.

Whilst anyone in the land lacks the basic necessities of a decent home, sufficient food, adequate health care and protection from any form of abuse, discrimination or violence, it cannot be acceptable for any religious organisation to seek donations merely for repairs to places of worship, nor for purposes that do not serve a tangible purpose for those members of our society who are in the greatest need. With the agreement of the religious leaders who represent the vast majority of those in the United Kingdom who follow a faith, lists are being compiled of all sacred buildings which are in need of repairs, for which funding is not readily available, with the intention of adapting these for use as accommodation for those currently homeless or occupying inadequate housing. With this change of purpose, funds for the necessary refurbishment will be made available from taxes and other sources. Where the building is deemed to be past repair, a suitable replacement will be built and used to serve those most in need.

Furthermore, it has been agreed that faiths will share their operational places of worship where necessary. Radical as this may initially seem; with the variation in holy days, practices and times of worship, it is believed this will not only be feasible but will serve as a major step towards truly uniting our kingdom for the future, by introducing adherents to the practices and beliefs of other religions. Worshippers will be free to use their time, their prayers and their money, in ways which most truly reflect the positive tenets of their respective faiths. It is also to be emphasised that the inclusivity and respect which is to be afforded to all those of a religious persuasion is equally to be shown to the majority of the population who are not. Mutual acceptance is paramount.

As most of you will be aware, the success of the new community hubs is growing by the day and everyone is invited to attend the events at their local, or indeed at any location of their choosing. Multi-faith services will often be available at these venues, as befits a true public meeting place.'

Not everyone was going to be happy with such monumental changes to the constitution but they were by no means sudden, in the Queen's eyes. Indeed, the seeds had been sown a good ninety years ago. Even as a child she had been a deep thinker, long before she had known what life had in store for her. Recently, and reluctantly, she had decided it was too soon to take the step of renouncing her role as Head of the Church of England, despite the inherent divisiveness of the title, but trusted she would be making the announcement before too long. The challenge would be in explaining that this move would serve not to reflect a new lack of respect for the positive elements of Christianity, but to enable her to openly offer the same level of respect for the admirable aspects of all beliefs.

The less helpful elements of the media, having grown bored with making unsubtle little digs about changes which were clearly going to happen despite them, now returned to form. One broadcaster/ columnist, who could have won awards for the speed with which he changed his allegiance, resolutely failed to see that the initiatives around religion were planned to bring people together. His diatribe concerning the new measures quickly descended into a rather facile suggestion for a game show, in which the different religions would compete to prove theirs the best. He envisaged the Archbishop of Canterbury poised uncertainly on a greasy floating platform, struggling to recover his balance as he attempted to catch the rubber bricks thrown at/to him by a multi-denominational group of vigilante ministers.

When the Queen heard his inevitable jibe about Edward, she saw red. 'That Dirty Little Tabloid man has been at it again,' she exclaimed to Philip.

'Oh yes, the DLT man. What are you going to do about him? Shall I call the Tower?'

'Oh no, I have a better way of dealing with people like him.' Which, being the gentlewoman she was, would be to ignore the columnist and take some positive action instead. She had been thinking, if you can't beat 'em (which she would really rather have liked to), join 'em. Or at least beat Mr. DLT at his own game.

Poor Edward had never been allowed to live down 'It's a Royal Cock-Up', as his attempt to recreate a popular, slapstick 1980s tv show had been euphemistically tagged, and the Queen immediately saw a way of killing at least two birds with one stone (which would make a change from shooting them anyway).

It was not long before an excited Edward announced his plans to produce a new panel show, Church Challenge, in which members of the congregation, ministers and employees of various churches, mosques, synagogues and temples would attempt to answer questions on their own religions, in round one, and the other panels religions, in round two. To make things more interesting, round three would consist of short films intended to demonstrate the respective efforts each group was making to address the most pressing issues facing their community. The studio audience and viewers at home would be scoring this round, using their own judgement to evaluate the success of the different faiths in supporting their brethren, introducing community initiatives such as litter picks, and on more crucial matters. If one group scored low on handing child abusers over to the police, it could ruin their whole game.

Life Diary

The Queen still loved to stroll in the palace grounds and she invited Sky along to discuss their latest thoughts on transforming the education system. 'May I tell you a secret?' asked the Queen conspiratorially. Obviously it was a rhetorical question, as if anyone would not feel privileged to share a confidence with her. 'I've never been a great fan of "systems". They seem to be the offspring of individuals and organisations who complicate their practises so much as to bring things to a standstill for all those except the exclusive few who understand the rules of the game.'

With the bravado of her new role and the Queen's acceptance, Sky felt confident enough to respond with a direct question, 'Are you saying it's time to change the rules or the game?'

'Everything, Sky, it's time to change everything.' She paused. 'How did you get on at school? Did you enjoy it?' As soon as she had asked, the Queen regretted her thoughtlessness. Sky had cast her eyes down and was clearly struggling for a diplomatic answer. 'As I thought, my dear. Might I ask if you are aware of how little education I, myself, had?' Rhetorical, again, clearly. Sky looked at her with surprise and the Queen smiled back, 'Exactly. It does not seem to have done either of us too much harm does it?' She went on to explain how she liked to follow the careers of those who had been brought to attention for their lack of qualifications, but succeeded in their chosen fields nonetheless. It was clear the Queen believed their time had come. 'I fully agree with you with regard to how many children's lives are mapped out for them and I believe that is an area of serious concern. Ours is considered to be a free society but it cannot continue to be viewed in that way whilst many citizens' choices effectively continue to be removed before birth. It has been shown time and again that the early years of life play a most important role in one's future prospects and it's time to put individuals in charge of their own destiny, right from the start.' The Queen headed to her favourite bench, under the old oak tree, and patted the seat beside her to indicate that Sky join her. 'To ensure that every child is given the most fair start in life, we are going to introduce a new initiative. Firstly, every natural or adoptive parent or carer will receive a Life Diary for their new baby, or older child, in which they will be encouraged to record essential details, plus milestones, significant events and notable changes that occur at different stages; contact details for important people in the baby's life, their likes and dislikes, details of any problems, illnesses, injuries and all the remedies investigated, whether helpful or not, allergies and intolerances and anything else which may be of use or interest to them in the future. As soon as the child is able to write, read and understand the purpose of the book, they will be encouraged to complete the entries themselves, or participate as far as their abilities allow at each stage.'

Sky furrowed her brow a little as she responded, 'It's a great idea but might some people think it's a little bureaucratic? Or even autocratic?' she ventured.

The Queen appeared rather crestfallen. 'As I understand it, merely from a health point of view, diagnoses and treatments will be much easier to clarify if the patient themselves has a full medical history readily available to them. And so many acquaintances of mine, old and young, complain about their poor memories, I felt many frustrating hours could be saved if one's most important records were always to hand.'

'And I'm guessing that subject preferences, hobbies, exam results and awards would be added when they go to school?'

The Queen perked up, 'Indeed they would. Philip wanted to add a few pages for foxes accounted for and that sort of thing....' Sky frowned a little more and the Queen continued quickly, 'but I had to explain that sort of thing is not quite as popular with everyone these days. I realise many people think my family are constantly waving shotguns around but actually Philip never hits anything. He has not for years. His PA has a lad pop over to Fortnum and Mason for a brace of pheasants a day or so in advance of a shoot, and the beater pretends to find them where they fall. It's lucky Philip never asks why the beater carries such a large bag, although I understand there was a close call a couple of years back, when the bird he presented hadn't quite defrosted.'

Sometimes it was not easy for Sky to assess the correct reaction to the Queen's remarks, so it was fortunate she returned to the subject at hand, without further delay. 'My plan is that every child will have an independent and comprehensive annual assessment, to ensure the best plans are put in place for their future, starting from their first birthday'. She noticed there was another question on Sky's lips and raised her eyebrows for the response Sky was so clearly eager to voice.

'I'm just wondering whether a child would be that keen to spend their birthdays at a sort of official meeting....' She could not help adding a tongue in cheek suggestion, 'unless you're thinking of having lots of cake and a bouncy castle and inviting all the children with the same birthday to attend.' Sky was smirking gently but the Queen's reaction came as a bit of a shock. She clapped her hands together and exclaimed loudly,

'What a splendid, excellent idea! Why on earth did I not think of that?'

A bit perturbed, Sky clarified, 'Actually I was joking....'

'Oh yes, my dear, I know you were, of course you were. But it's still a wonderful idea! Do excuse me now, won't you?'

Sky watched, slightly open-mouthed, as the Queen fairly scurried off towards the palace.

Goodbye Guys

Sal was currently engaged in matters concerning the other end of life. Or death, for the less coy. Her own circumstances had led her to display what some fair-weather friends had termed an unhealthy obsession with the subject, fortunate as they were not to have faced it too early, in particularly tragic circumstances or, perhaps, at all. It certainly drew a line between folk and Sal had an instinct for those who had been through that particular mill. She could almost feel their grief. But she was not maudlin about it. In fact, at the moment, she was having quite a lot of fun with it.

As a little break from her seemingly endless plans for resurrecting the health service, Sal had turned her mind to the ultimate outcome of good, bad or a total lack of, healthcare. She had soon realised that people's opinions on dying were just as divided as those on the best ways to treat the living. She was not too involved in her colleagues' plans for changing the face of religion but she did find it odd that the differing views of the faiths somehow seemed to add up to keeping lots of people alive when they did not want to be. Sal had never spoken to anyone who stated a preference for slowly losing their marbles in a nursing home, while their family suffered the despair of witnessing their deterioration and some faceless corporation raked in the pennies they had saved so hard for their retirement, to bequeath to their nearest and dearest or their favourite charity. When Sal recalled the high profile court cases which some individuals had been subjected to, when attempting to end their lives with dignity and prevent their loved ones being arrested for assisting with their suicide, she considered the lawyers' actions criminal.

The fun part of death, so far, was in promoting the idea of Live Happy, Die Peacefully, as coined by a small, forward thinking team of East End funeral directors (or 'The Goodbye Guys', as they preferred to be called). With a gift for marketing, Big Gerry promoted his new venture with flair and flamboyance, reminiscent of his days as a drag queen. His only problem was in convincing his customers he would not be conducting the dispatch of their dear departed in full make up and evening dress. Unless, of course, that was requested.

Like the boss, the premises could hardly be ignored, with a lurid neon sign flashing FAF every couple of seconds, in metre high letters. Some disappointed party animals were upset to find a nightclub that was closed at night but the locals soon came to know the true nature of the business, with the arrival of the thoughtful 'ten per cent off for true cockneys' flyers which were delivered door to door in the neighbourhood. 'Fun Accessible Funerals with no faffing' read the front page, in large block letters. 'We'll bury anyone'* stated the reverse. In six point type at the bottom, just below the contact details, an asterisk noted 'providing they're no longer alive'. With the history of the area, you had to be a little bit careful about clarifying things like that.

Despite outward appearances, Gerry was a thoughtful and sensitive man who was a keen supporter of voluntary euthanasia. He remembered the speed with which his dear old mum's beloved poodle had been put down when she could not afford the treatment for his bad foot, and Gerry had noted the irony as he watched his mum herself fade away in agony over twenty years. How many times her eyes had begged him to do something which she could not ask of him.

After his mum had finally passed on to the better place in which he liked to imagine her, Gerry had vowed to help people have 'a pleasant passing', whenever he could. There had only been one tricky occasion, when a couple of notorious local brothers offered him their support and took some convincing that his intentions were directed only towards those who wanted to choose the best way out for themselves. Whilst campaigning for changes to the law, Gerry decided the most practical way to cheer those who had no choice in the matter was to help them plan the biggest, brightest or most outrageous funeral they could. Many decided to literally 'go out with a bang' and FAF was soon destined for a place in the record books, as the company who sent the most customers off in a rocket.

Gerry was not just a pretty (and sometimes beautifully made-up) face, secretly having been quite the science whizz at school. His questionable obsession with pyrotechnics aside, he had also been pursuing a far more serious goal. For Gerry was heading up a most ambitious and explosive project, with his own elite team, at a state of the art lab deep in the Sussex countryside.

Men Wanted

Tom was quite busy enough with building projects and environmental campaigns but had somehow found himself drafted in to recruit more men for the Free Friends and Family website. It might save him a bit of earache from some of Jess's mates anyway. Tom could not count the evenings he had listened to them sitting around the kitchen table bemoaning the fact that everywhere they went they outnumbered the men by at least ten, if not twenty, to one. Apparently even the mousiest little chap could have his pick of the bunch from a whole load of attractive, fun and intelligent women 'of a certain age', just for being the only male to turn up at an event. It sounded like quite a sad state of affairs for the women and Tom did not have any regrets that he was not single himself. Except it seemed he would be considered a great catch these days, if he were. He tried not to remember that when the kids were creating mayhem and Jess was shouting at him for one thing or another.

With Sam being a bit scary sometimes and Brett being a bit Brett, it had been decided by the female ministers that Tom was the man for the job, again. The average 'man on the sofa who never goes out, but stays home to drink beer and watch football' would be most able to identify with Tom, they reasoned. His point about how Sam and Brett actually were single themselves and, therefore, more suited to the task, went unheard. It seemed he was the one these women wanted.

As lethargy and lack of motivation probably played a large part in the growth of the couch potato, the direct approach was deemed to be best. Although Andrina had to refuse the suggestion which one of her younger female assistants had come up with. 'Get the ****off the sofa and get a life' was felt to be just a tad too direct.

Being good sports, Sam and Brett agreed to be shown in the ads, along with their living rooms, but not their faces. Tom was to do a voiceover, along the lines of, 'Come on mate, don't sit home alone. Haven't you heard that pretty much every social group in the country needs more men to join. Get out there now and make new mates! What's stopping you?' At which point, Sam and Brett would be shown to leap up from their respective, lonely sofas and rush for their jackets.

It was hoped that all the things which might really be stopping men from leaving their homes would be sorted out through the various initiatives dealing with drugs, alcohol, abuse, physical impairment, mental health, relationship problems and the many other issues which tied people in knots and left them home alone. Tom had assumed that the single buddies who had gradually faded from his life were still out and about having a great time. If that was not the case, he hoped they soon would be. He knew the groups were not really aimed at dating but reality dictated that most couples found family life kept them quite busy enough.

A Flippant Remark About Cake

It was not long before the Queen summoned Sky to another meeting. This time, to reflect the importance of what she was to announce, there could be no other venue but the bench under the old tree, planted so long ago by one of the Queen's noble ancestors. He may turn in his tomb in the Abbey, once she let this one out.

'How lovely to see you. What a beautiful day.' Sky was taken aback, she had become used to the lack of formalities but what was going on now? Was the Queen actually showing excitement, again? 'You really had to be the first to know, as it was you who gave me the idea.' Sky looked none the wiser so the Queen continued, quite breathlessly, 'Your suggestion about the birthday parties - I looked into it immediately and plans are under way as we speak.' The Queen was wearing a satisfied smile and looking for appreciation.

'Okay,' replied Sky with trepidation. 'So you are going to make every child spend every birthday filling out forms, then give them all a party in a big office?' Oh dear, she knew she had not put that well but she really did not like the idea at all. If she had been put in that position she would have had to run away a few more times.

The Queen's face suddenly changed and she actually started to laugh. 'My goodness, no! I can imagine that idea might have appealed to some of our past politicians but I am committed to a more gentle approach. I thought you realised that,' she said, with a little disappointment.

'I'm sorry, I'm still a bit confused though. What are these plans that are under way?'

The Queen moved a little closer and resumed her conspiratorial stance, 'I think birthday parties for everyone in the land is a lovely idea. It should also put an end to all the complaints we receive about how our stately homes should be put to better use and free for the public to visit, once we start holding the parties in them. We are also in consultation with the larger charities and organisations which are responsible for similar buildings. In fact, I have expanded on your suggestion somewhat and plans are now underway to offer numerous free events on all those days which are intended to be special but are, I have now learned, the loneliest times for many - religious holidays, public holidays, national celebrations and so forth. Our initial enquiries suggest that many of the companies which are now looking at curtailing their current endeavours will be only too willing to adapt to providing whatever comestibles and party items we require. So, with carefully planned sponsorship and grants, this initiative of yours will generate a huge amount of jobs, redistribute wealth and, above all, make a lot of people very happy.' The Queen sat back and smiled, content.

'Much as I would love to take credit for all your great plans, they are your plans. I'm afraid I misunderstood you and hadn't thought any further than a flippant remark about cake.'

'Ah, but one flippant remark is sometimes all that is needed to set in motion a great chain of events. I have been looking at staging birthday parties every day of the year, at venues around the United Kingdom, for anyone who was born on that particular day and wishes to attend. From what I hear, there are a good many in our society whose birth may never be celebrated otherwise and I believe, aside from the social aspect of these parties in allowing people to meet many strangers with whom they have at least one thing in common, it will serve as a lesson in valuing oneself, for all who attend. It should not be hard for individuals to prove their birthdate, with the new initiatives in place to recognise the rights of the homeless and other marginalised people. In fact, and I digress, I feel you will be rather pleased with another idea which came to me in conjunction with this. I trust I will not have trodden on any of the ministers' toes too much but I have been made aware that an insurmountable stumbling block for certain people has been their inability to provide a home address, when they are not fortunate enough to have a stable home. I have learned that this sad state of affairs may then render them unable to claim the benefits they need to buy the most basic necessities. As we will now be opening up some of our most impressive residences to the public, on a scale never seen before, I suggest we also offer these buildings as official mailing addresses. With Tom's initiative to ban all "letterbox junk", including that delivered by the Royal Mail, we should not find it creates too much of a problem. And, at some point in the future, it may even be that a number of these stately homes will offer residential accommodation.'

Sky was gobsmacked or flabbergasted or something like that. The Queen had obviously done her homework. 'Can I say, "Well done, Your Majesty"?'

'You certainly may, providing you remember not to address me in that way ever again.'

The Queen then explained what a keen interest she had taken in the advances made by all the New Ministers and their teams. She saw her own role as co-ordinator of the numerous and diverse initiatives and, indeed, as the one with whom the buck would stop, should any disasters happen. 'I have no doubt that you and your colleagues feel rather more than a modicum of apprehension about the many important schemes which you now find yourselves instigating and overseeing. I can, however, assure you wholeheartedly that none of you will be required to take responsibility for anything with which you are not comfortable, nor without any support you may require. I wish to ensure that you and the other New Ministers are clear that my door is always open to you, should there be any concerns. Please feel free to pass that on,' she finished, in the manner of a clear instruction.

Aspirations

When Sky relayed the Queen's message to Brett it came at a good time, and he realised the pains in his chest were more likely due to nervous dyspepsia than an impending heart attack. He had been lectured by Sal about how they happened to fit young men as well as 'overweight slobs on a high cholesterol diet' and he had every intention of finding a way to relax soon. When he was not so busy. The past week had been particularly hectic and, now the preparations for the Tax Ballot were fully under way, it was time to put on his 'Jobs' hat again. The thought provoked vague memories of a bus conductor's cap, passed down from some obscure relation. Brett remembered it being summarily removed from his eager grasp and, no doubt, replaced with an item of a more aspirational nature. Alas, his proclivity for daydreaming every so often had probably impeded his climb to the even dizzier heights his parents had predicted.

Since last weekend, however, following an unusual display of affection from his distinguished father, Brett and his siblings could be in no doubt that their parents were proud of them all. They were proud of Brett for his valiant efforts to right the wrongs of British society and they were proud of Nathan and Jolie for retiring. It had been a struggle to maintain the dignity appropriate to the senior Pearces' position whilst the tabloids had constantly featured photos of their younger children falling out of taxis, throwing up in various inauspicious places, and over undesirable acquaintances. Thank goodness they had not been using the family name during these exploits.

Brett had been surprised to learn of the changes planned for the education system but felt a quiet delight in the dismantling of the 'jobs for the boys' hierarchy. Although he could hardly claim to have come from a deprived background, the veiled racist remarks in the dormitory showers had not gone unnoticed. He would truly love to see a time when all available jobs served a real purpose and posts were always awarded purely according to merit, rather than to whom one was related or the schools one had attended. Brett had been made only too aware that a cursory letter of commendation from the head of an elite public school was worth 100 GCSEs from a regular place of education. What he most hoped to see the end of was the system of 'Them and Us'. He had never been quite sure which category he fell into and he had an inkling that many felt the same way. 'Roll on Equality' Brett thought to himself, as he signed the paperwork which would turn Eton into a comprehensive.

It could not be denied that education and employment had always been inextricably linked and would, without a great deal of change, continue to be so. Which was how the New Ministers found the lines between their roles blurring, as had always been the Queen's intention. If those currently in command of the country's most senior posts were able to demonstrate their ability to share responsibility, effectively collaborate on tasks whenever necessary and delegate praise as appropriate, then it should only be a matter of time until others automatically acquired the same skills. It would be ideal if true equality could be cultivated but, at least for the moment, it had to be accepted that there was still a top level from which it could be assumed behaviour would filter down.

Brett had been amused to hear stories of multi-millionaires facing compulsory retirement with glee and embracing the chance to get down and do the dirty work on their building sites and fruit farms. Their new-found enthusiasm, for sharing the real graft that was the root of their amassed fortunes, was already rubbing off on their new recruits, as they learnt from the best how to do the job and why it was ok to aspire to bigger things.

The standard priority, which all businesses and organisations were now obliged to adhere to, was 'People Above Profit'. It had not been accepted by everyone, by any means, so it was drawing an interesting line between a revised 'Us and Them'. Any companies who continued to flout the rules of fair and decent behaviour faced penalties of a previously unknown level, with the introduction of new laws fast-tracked under the umbrella heading of Organisational Abuse, which had previously applied only to institutions such as care homes and hospitals. In recent times, not only had the importance of many other lines of work become crystal clear, but also the scope for mistreatment of employees in every type of job, at all levels. The instance of victimisation and bullying appeared to be rife across many industries, with employees practically lined up and forced to sign Settlement Agreements. At least the new name was more honest than the previous one - 'compromise' had not featured strongly when workers were paid off with a small sum, which would prevent them from receiving benefits until the money had been used up. Careers could be destroyed as employers casually broke the terms of the agreements, whilst the unemployable ex-workers lived in fear of breathing the wrong word to anyone. Rendering them unable to discuss their experience with ex-colleagues who had suffered the same treatment; thus preventing recovery, increasing unemployment and ensuring the companies in question need have no concern about being brought to justice.

The Queen and her new colleagues found it particularly unpalatable that certain people had sought to profit from the crisis by selling inadequate safety equipment or fraudulently parting others from their cash through various scams. Even using everyone's desperate need for connection to spuriously insist that individuals hand over more details than necessary, to receive online services or use their computers and appliances efficiently. No longer was it acceptable for internet service providers, websites, the tech giants or anyone else to freely collect or disseminate personal information. And there would be no room to hide behind reams of jargon, because this was automatically outlawed under the re-enforcement of the Plain English campaign and the unwritten rules which were obvious to those seeking to inhabit a fair society.

It was a challenging time for many of the less ethically minded, but a cause for celebration amongst those who could now value their privacy and freedom again, without being viewed with suspicion purely for choosing not to share their every movement online. Others were sickened as they realised the insidious way in which they had become indoctrinated into viewing true friends as the enemy, when it turned out they were the ones who had read and understood the small print. There were numerous types of Organisational Abuse to be investigated, which again would create a great number of interesting and worthy new jobs for decent people.

At last, decent was a fashionable word again, along with innocent compliments such as nice and kind, which were now dusted off and retrieved from the 'bland' bin, following a short speech the Queen had made to further explain some of the sweeping changes happening across the country. She had concluded thus, 'Wealth, power and status are as nothing if one does not enable others to feel good about themselves. I have met many, many important people in my lifetime - those considered the most intelligent, most gifted, most enlightened; the most wise, rich and powerful in the world. And I would like to share with you the attributes which I consider to be the most important in any individual. They are simply to be nice and kind and generous of spirit.'

Brett admired the Queen for her refusal to be drawn into the media frenzy, which fell just short of demanding her incarceration by this stage. He had wondered if there might even be a revolution, but he and Sam had come to the conclusion that the Queen was actually leading the revolution herself. In the obsolete corridors of power the Old Guard wandered around muttering to each other; referring to the Queen as a commie, an anarchist or a treehugger, apparently depending on the day of the week. They were interesting times and some began to ask themselves the sort of questions that normally occur only to 'third-world' citizens of openly unstable countries. Questions such as 'If there's a civil war, will the army be on the Queen's side or that of the government she effectively fired?'

The answer seemed fairly obvious, when one considered that all the moves the Queen was making were to improve the lives and the safety of the ordinary folk who populated the Kingdom (or Queendom, as it might have been since the 1950s). Ordinary folk such as rank and file soldiers, for instance. No doubt their superiors would remind them they were duty-bound to follow orders but, were the Queen giving the orders, there would be no contest. The Queen fervently hoped that such a situation would never arise. Having instigated all the changes for the good of the people, she could not bear to be the one who caused them any further harm. She could only imagine the looks on her generals' faces if she admitted she had always harboured pacifist leanings. With the increasing mass destruction of lives and countries in recent centuries, how could she not?

Drug Deal

Life today was a walk in the park for Sal and Sky. The sun was shining and it was a relief to get out in the air to discuss the latest developments, surrounded by as much nature as it was possible to find in the inner city.

'Shall we start by running through some of your new health initiatives?' Sky fidgeted with the notebook in her pocket. She did not understand how some of her colleagues seemed to remember everything without assistance.

'Good idea,' agreed Sal, opening her bag and sifting through the contents. As she produced her own notebook, Sky waved hers in the air with fellow feeling and a look of relief. 'I'm glad it's not just me,' smiled Sal, 'I thought the kids in the office had some sort of special memory powers, but then I realised they're all so quick at typing they're probably making notes on their phones.'

'Or recording every conversation on some app or other.'

'I'd probably feel quite intimidated and useless if I wasn't helping run the country.'

'Yeah, me too.'

With a shared smirk, they got on with the business of doing just that.

'I'm fairly pleased with how things are going but you know I'm desperate to address the lack of immediate health care available to everyone, particularly regarding the dire situation around mental health support. Anyway, lots of volunteers have come forward for Help to Heal, so I live in hope.'

'How exactly is that going to work?' asked Sky.

'It's bound to create a bit of a stink but I reckon there are enough folk out there who share our opinion on qualifications to realise there are many instances when they needn't be the primary concern.' Sky perked up, this being one of her favourite subjects, and Sal continued, 'If someone is suffering, in any way, what they really need first is immediate support, so that's what we're going to give them.'

'That sounds great but we can't exactly have an eager mechanic ripping out someone's tonsils as if they were spark plugs.'

'You really do have a way with words sometimes,' Sal adopted the stance of a tired mother dealing with an unruly toddler. 'Of course the professionals will have to deal with operations and things, but there's plenty of evidence to show the majority of patients are looking for fairly basic advice, or a sympathetic ear, when they seek a medical appointment. What exacerbates many problems is the hassle involved in making an appointment in the first place, the waiting time involved and the stress that results from that, particularly while many are afraid that hospitals and surgeries are no longer safe to enter. Now we all know that stress is likely to be a major factor in any illness, so we have to find the best way to avert that.'

'And that way is to let untrained people, like me, treat the general public?' Sky hated the term 'devil's advocate' but somehow seemed to find herself playing one quite regularly, given her penchant for ensuring that she gave equal regard to all sides of an issue.

'In a word, yes. Think about it - when you were a kid and you fell over, or were bullied at school, what was the first thing you wanted?'

Sky glanced off to the left, to her thoughtful place. 'I wanted to be looked after. I wanted someone to really listen to my problem and to care about me.'

'Exactly. And that's what every child, or adult, really wants when they're ill or damaged or troubled. It's so simple! We can't immediately fix the waiting times necessary to consult a GP or a therapist but we can offer people support, which might even make them realise they don't need an appointment after all. It turns out there are loads of kind, caring, and sometimes highly qualified, individuals out there, who would love to have this sort of purpose in their lives and are happy to provide their time on a voluntary basis.'

'How are we going to escape the "health and safety police"?'

'The same way as dating sites have been doing for years, by advising everyone to meet in public and not deal with anyone who makes them feel uneasy. If I'm feeling terrible, I'm alone and scared and a friendly person comes to sit with me and offer words of comfort, I'm not going to ask to see their medical papers. I'm just going to feel bloody grateful!'

'And I don't care how obscure a treatment might sound - if it makes me feel better, I'll be happy to stand in a bowl of custard for an hour,' Sky enthused. They were still on the same page.

Sal smiled, 'I'm so pleased the new groups dealing with pain management, healthy eating and trauma support have taken off well. Then there's Final Straw.'

'Which one's that again?'

'It's for those who feel like killing themselves, or who've had a loved one commit suicide, after dealing with endless bureaucracy, the benefits system, lawyers and so on. It looks like it's going to be a pretty big group. And you know I'm really keen to prioritise the Drug Deal.'

Sky, whose attention sometimes tended to fail her unwittingly, perked up, thinking Sal was testing her. 'I am listening, honestly, these subjects are really close to my heart. And I know you're not going to mess up your new job by becoming a dealer.'

'Actually I am, in a way - I'm going to be arranging new drug deals. We can't keep sitting back and watching international pharmaceutical companies put their own - ridiculous - prices on saving lives. And we can't keep reading reports of families selling their house to seek treatment abroad for their dying child. Especially now it's so much harder to go abroad for anything. I've been able to confirm there are lab directors in the UK who are only too keen to work on replicating drugs which have proved successful, and releasing them through the NHS at their standard rates. It's a fitting way out for some of those who, in the past, have profited from their unethical greed. And there are others who have never aimed for such profits but haven't received sufficient funding, largely due to their positive ethics - particularly refusing to test on animals. If only the public would support the smaller medical charities who realise why it doesn't make sense - either we're so different from other animals that the results will be useless, or we're so similar to them that it's even more morally questionable to perform the tests. Especially when animals such as dogs are so valuable in detecting various illnesses in humans, and so much more helpful when used in that way, rather than being pointlessly tortured in a laboratory. So many useful drugs have been held back because of these practices, when those who are dying or suffering badly are only too keen to personally test whatever is being developed.'

'Well that doesn't make sense.'

'Exactly. Like a lot of things. We need to start making it possible for everyone to "write their own prescription", perhaps to choose homeopathy or acupuncture instead of a medication which may not be suitable for their particular body or mind. As you know, more and more people are having reactions to foodstuffs, vaccinations and all sorts. Personally I believe it might have a lot to do with pollution - there are so many unnatural things floating about in the air and the water these days, I'm not surprised that many sensitive systems find any additional invasion too much to cope with.'

'On a different note - Maj has been quite excited by the response she's had from her various distant relations. Some of them sound really pleased to have the opportunity to pension off a wing of their stately homes for use as a "retirement co-op".'

'What?'

'You know the scheme. The state pays towards the upkeep of the building, the residents recruit and pay their own nurses and cleaners and so on. Lots more people get jobs and lots of others get better care for less money.'

'No, I mean, who are you calling Madge these days?'

Sky squirmed a little, then broke into a smile. 'Oops, yeah. I was finding it hard to avoid calling her anything, then I accidentally came out with the name some of us used to refer to her in the old days. Turned out she quite likes it.'

Sal was the tiniest bit envious of the apparent bond her new friend had with their most illustrious colleague, but she admired them both and was happy to continue building bonds herself.

Sky had returned to considering another issue. How to break it to the Queen that the UK is heading for around 190,000 birthdays per day. So, if her intended parties turned out to be really popular, it would be like holding Glastonbury every day of the year. Just training up enough staff to handle the logistics would be a nightmare (and perhaps there actually was a limit to the amount of new jobs that needed to be created). Maybe the tickets could just go to Nifties or something. There was always a lot more for Sky to think about.

Tom's Run Off

Unlike some previous ministers, the 'new guard' were happier to be out and about improving things for the public in tangible ways, than patting themselves on the back about the intellectual merit of the latest laboriously produced, yet unhelpful, confusing and unseen, policies and reports which they chose to hide behind. The

New Ministers had agreed amongst themselves that some of the best brains in the world are not designed to sit behind a desk. Also, that any of them ever heard using the phrase 'I'm following the science' would be expected to tender their resignation immediately.

Tom certainly did not relish spending time in an office but was willing to make an exception when it concerned his efforts to do what he could for the environment. He also welcomed the chance to work with Andrina, having found there was a little way to go in turning some of his new assistants into the 'new men' he had hoped to be mixing with. It seemed it was going to take more than a generation to wean the average labourer off topless calendars and racist jokes, no matter how much legislation was in place.

Andrina's office was busy as ever, with numerous assistants moving around the place quickly, quietly and with great purpose. One of them approached her, regarding a certain senior tv executive, 'Sorry Andrina, but I've had Bill Smith on the line again. He said, "My newsreader has a great set of pins and it would be a shame not to let the viewers appreciate them".'

Andrina raised her eyes and let out a small breath of annoyance, 'I happen to know she also has a serious back problem and will be happier presenting the news whilst seated behind a desk, wearing flat shoes, as was always the norm. You can tell Mr. Smith that our concern for health and welfare applies equally to everyone, so it's high time we change the fashion for going out of our way to make people uncomfortable, in any circumstances.' The assistant nodded and Andrina turned sharply back towards Tom, making him a little uncomfortable. 'Now, we need to come up with a snappy title for your "green innovation" show, or it could come across as a little dry.'

'We will. There've been a few good suggestions but I'm waiting for something that sums up what it's all about. We don't want to appeal only to inventors but to anyone who has a great "planet and money saving idea" or who is "disinventing" by bringing back old methods, skills and tools. It's not a contest or a game show but there'll be awards and prizes involved, to attract more interest. We'll also be introducing suggestions for changes on a bigger scale, to gauge public reactions before we bring in new laws....'

'Such as?' Andrina enquired, concerned that the light-hearted programme they had planned was about to turn political.

'Well, for instance, many people hate automatic tills and dealing with robotic call centres, so on the first programme we'll start with a phone-in to find out what people really think....'

'But how will their views be recorded?'

'By real people who've been given real jobs to find out what really matters to the viewers.' Tom hoped he had got the emphasis right on that one.

Andrina was quite unaware of the effect her directness could have, but she was pleased Tom was not afraid of her. She could not understand why a lot of men appeared to be, but her mum always said they must be intimidated by her beautiful eyes and flowing black hair.

Tom was talking about environmentally friendly portable toilets now, enthusing particularly about a new Scottish company that had cunningly come up with the name Wee Care. Tom's own water recycling system had also been well-received but had given rise to some confusing jokes, when everyone started using the 'working title' of Tom's Run-Off. Personally, he took the issue very seriously and was proud that all new builds would now automatically recycle the clean water wasted while attaining the right temperature for the bath, shower or washing up. And he was currently perfecting the system whereby the water already used for those purposes would be saved for secondary use in the garden, for washing the family car or flushing the loo. He hoped that older buildings would all, eventually, be converted to the system. The amount of water saved, nationally, every year, really would be something to feel smug about. Perhaps he would win some sort of award himself. Maybe not an OBE or anything, he knew the Queen was far too upstanding to play favourites.

'I'm also looking forward to hearing how you are going to make our viewers fall around laughing when you bring up the subjects of sustainable building materials and ethical pest control,' Andrina said, with a bit of a smirk.

About to reply 'That might take a little more thought' Tom was interrupted by his phone suddenly coming to life, blaring out a favourite punk tune from his youth. Making an apologetic face, whilst thinking the clichéd 'saved by the bell', he heard Jess's usual tone of slight annoyance,

'Yes, what do you want? I thought you didn't like interruptions during work time?'

'But you called me. What do YOU want?'

'No, you've called me three times in the last fifteen minutes. I'm busy too, you know.'

Only confused for a moment, Tom realised a small downside to Andrina's dedication to duty. She never seemed to sit down, or invite anyone else to, so during their discussion Tom had been trying to make himself comfortable by leaning awkwardly against one of the long tables on which Andrina's many projects were spread out. Consequently, he had inadvertently 'bumdialled' Jess, as Billy would say. Three times, apparently.

By the time he had explained the situation to Jess, Andrina had moved on to something more important and all he had to worry about was whether Jess was back on the coffee. She had seemed calmer for a while - sometimes he could be home for five minutes before he got a bollocking.

Lentils

Brett liked to keep himself smart, fashionable and well-groomed, so he decided tearing his hair out might spoil his image a little. His hair was also too smart, fashionable and well-groomed to get a good grip on. It amazed him how effectively he was able to appear cool as a cucumber when he was shaking like a jelly inside, much of the time. Funny how he always seemed to think about food on his way to see Sal. All the practical tasks necessary to the Tax Ballot were nearing completion, so Brett was able to give time to other issues whilst metaphorically wetting himself about the potential results of the ballot.

Brett and Sal were passionate about Ethigreen, the new supermarket chain which was being set up to sell only goods which were healthy, cruelty-free, from sustainable sources, produced by companies who complied fully with equal opportunities, sustainability and fair trade guidelines. When the press caught a whiff of the plans, they had a lot of fun printing cartoons showing stores selling only lentils spilling out of paper bags. And as the journalists tumbled around in the pub after work they mimicked blind Ethigreen assistants attempting to serve customers without spilling the lentils, and disabled assistants trying to reach up to the top shelves without spilling the lentils. Of course, on paper they were not going to let go of political correctness so easily but their views did not seem to matter too much anyway; the general population were clearly on the side of the New Ministers, again. Job applications had flooded in to Ethigreen from around the country, as soon as the first cartoon appeared.

The only possible threat to the success of Ethigreen was Sensibuy, the new 'green arm' of one of the major chains. As with everyone else, they had needed to think quickly to keep afloat in this latest sea-change.

By the time the Ethicaffs were causing whispers, the jokes about menus only offering lentil dishes fell on deaf (hearing impaired) ears. All the supermarkets and fast food chains were starting to get very nervous indeed. Their money had always been of great use to the media but things could change overnight if the retailers had less money coming in to pay for advertising, or if the media took the view that the tide was changing and they would serve their own interests better by supporting the drastic move towards good health and true ethics. Many journalists had no qualms about changing their views at the drop of a hat, so there would be no problem convincing everybody that the way to a loved one's heart was no longer through a steak, a bottle of wine or a box of chocolates, but via ethically sourced muesli. Or possibly lentils, of course.

'Do you remember my idea for new hospital gowns?' asked Sal, changing the subject and bringing to Brett's mind a rather disquieting couple of Sal's own, cartoonish, drawings. 'It really is unacceptable that we're still forcing some poor old thing, who's been admitted for a complicated tooth extraction or something, to wear a gown that a sprightly contortionist would be unable to tie up behind their back. I'm surprised the NHS didn't go bust years ago, because of lawsuits brought by people who were traumatised at the sight of a lot of saggy bottoms, well before the "powers-that-be" destroyed it.'

'Quite.'

'So, what's your plan?'

'You'll be pleased to hear that I am negotiating with several factories in the poorer African nations, former colonies where they have experience of producing simple clothing from natural materials. It was not hard to find a more sensible design, considering they are already in use in most countries, and even in some parts of ours. And as I had already placed some extremely large orders for protective clothing for all our medical staff, to avoid any future mishaps, I don't see any problem with also obtaining the appropriate items for our patients.'

Sal beamed. She loved to hear that indigent people would be benefitting from her idea. She also loved it that she was being heard, at last. And that someone like Brett appreciated her ideas enough to take them on board and act on them. Sal hoped he might even go with the name she had suggested for the gowns; she thought 'Moddies' had a nice ring to it and brought a little fun into the serious issue of preserving one's modesty. Sometimes she felt she became more old-fashioned, the more society progressed. But the fact she was not happy with a lot of those 'progressions' had brought her to her current situation. And she was pretty chuffed about that.

Legally Bolshie

Since the day they were all first introduced by the Queen, Sky and Sam had not had so many opportunities to work together as they had with some of the other New Ministers. They were pleased to be changing that now, having sensed there was an element of the kindred spirit between them. Sky hoped Sam would not bring out her inner bolshiness and Sam hoped she would not twig that he was actually as sensitive as she was. There was a lot to discuss and it was clear they shared similar thoughts on most subjects, which made things a lot easier. As did the comfy surroundings of the small sitting room which Sky had recently discovered, hidden away from the main offices, with a good view across the gardens.

Working closely with Brett had given Sam a better understanding of the current job market and tax plans, whilst he and Sky probably had the closest connection to those whose lives had been lived at the lower end of the scale.

'I'm so pleased you're tackling the benefits system head on,' she said, with feeling. 'I'm afraid people might think it's scaremongering if I talk about some of the things I've seen. I'm sure there's been some sort of cover up and lots of claimants have actually killed themselves because of the way they've been treated. Has Sal told you how many members have joined Final Straw?' Sam was not used to being taken aback by someone else's outspokenness, but he was now. He had known they would get on.

'I'm with you there and I'll bet it's in the thousands. But we're still going to have to tread carefully. There are too many people who "just can't handle the truth", he said, feeling obliged to adopt an American accent to befit the movie he was quoting. 'Personally I'd love to see certain members of the outgoing government, or former governments, dragged through the courts to answer to some of their decisions, but (he almost went into the accent again) "that ain't never gonna happen". And we're still in a pretty uncertain position here, to say the least.'

'As precarious as walking a tightrope, perhaps.'

For a passing moment each of them almost fell into the well-hidden pit of despair that resided somewhere deep within. Sky was the first to shake herself free and resume her role as the one who cheered others up.

'So, what we do now is the best we can, as far as we can.'

'Agreed.'

'Have you talked to Brett about the release date for the free legal packs?'

'What, in all the spare time I've had?' He had not meant to sound that defensive or angry or whatever it was Sam feared everyone thought of him. He was actually trying to make a joke, while he thought of a better answer.

'It's ok, I know you've been busy making it easier for everyone to handle official matters for themselves and I'm looking forward to seeing the information guides and all the necessary forms available for free. You're going to be helping a lot of people by easing the stress of getting divorced, wording a lease, writing or executing a will and all the other things which solicitors have intimidated people out of doing until now. The whole system seems to have been set up to cause unnecessary anxiety to everyone and it was all tied up in the old legal jargon for so long that it wasn't obvious most of these things are easy enough for anyone to do, if they're reasonably intelligent and can understand English ok.' Sky was feeling bolshier all the time and Sam was liking her all the more for it. It cheered him to realise someone else got as fired up as he did about all these issues.

'Absolutely, that's just how I feel; that's why I want to make it easy for anyone to represent themselves in court, with any back-up they might need. And, obviously, to provide the extra support necessary to those whose English isn't so good and anyone who has additional needs of any sort. We're all keen to see the end of the unjustifiably high salaries paid to lawyers, particularly when it's a dodgy one who's reaping the rewards. Brett actually believes it may be possible to treat their salaries as "proceeds of crime" in some cases.'

'Brilliant, I can't wait. It's about time victims got the payout for their suffering, instead of the lawyers.'

Sam could not help noticing how Sky's expression changed; fleetingly replacing her initial enthusiasm with the shadow of a memory, and he felt the need to bring back her usual smile. 'We're also planning to make all government and big business spending truly public. It should help everyone appreciate the changes we're making, once they can see what the last lot were really up to. Talking about forms again, I should mention we'll be "backtracking bureaucracy" by replacing the current ridiculous requirements for medical staff and emergency workers to complete reams of paperwork whilst they're attempting to save lives. And we don't want to hear of any more surgeons running around the hospital trying to find a bed for the patient before they can start an emergency operation, so we're looking at a major overhaul of the whole system.'

Picnic

The Queen was delighted when she woke up to a sunny morning. Everyone had been working so hard she had decided a little break from all their tasks would be good for morale. A picnic on the grass in the gardens was always so much more fun, without having to drag all the marquees out. Not that she often had to help with that.

Chef had barely managed to contain his inner brat when the Queen had unexpectedly asked for a vegan spread, for the first time ever. After she had been subjected to one of Sal's earnest, well-meaning (and 'accidental') lectures on the animal welfare side of healthy eating, the Queen had come to realise this currently popular diet may not be just a fad after all. Indeed Sal had made a point of stating that veganism was a principle, not a preference, that it was the best option for the health of people and the planet, as well as the animals, and even that a British court had ruled ethical veganism a philosophical belief. Sal had expressed her sincere wish to replace the (often surprisingly unhealthy) menus in all hospitals, schools and other community buildings with plant-based fare, as soon as possible. So the picnic was intended not only to be a relaxed social gathering but also a chance for the Queen to gauge how the rest of her ministers, their now numerous assistants and the Inner Circle reacted to the vegan food, before she conclusively determined to back Sal's plans.

The Queen could not help noticing that Chef had made a small stand by sneaking in a few platters of Scotch eggs and sausage rolls. At least that would keep Philip happy. Surprisingly, to the Queen, there was little mention of the food. It seemed to be going down well and everyone was too caught up in finding out the latest on each other's projects to be interested in sandwich fillings, or the other delicacies on offer. What seemed to be on everyone's lips was how drastically the results of the Tax Ballot might affect the finance available to pursue all the issues which were becoming increasingly important to each of them.

'How are you feeling about everything?' Sam ventured to Brett, knowing it had not been an easy task for him to be prised away from his desk, to stand awkwardly away from the main throng in the garden. Having been party to the game of politics for some time, Brett was more keenly aware than the others just how unpredictable the public could be, let alone the effect which the Old Guard and former government may still be able to exact via their chums in the media. And if a major celebrity split 'happened' to occur in the few days around the ballot, it would not be the first time that the most important issue of the day had been hidden away inside the papers, whilst a popular soap star and her aggrieved boyfriend each vied to tell their side of the story on the front page. Brett's delay in answering encouraged Sam to voice his own opinion, leaning closer and taking on a more conspiratorial air, 'You know we're all with you mate.' He noticed the concern in Brett's eyes. 'We're all bricking it,' Sam clarified, knocking back his sugar-free elderflower cordial in the most rugged manner he could summon in the circumstances.

A few picnic rugs away, some of the ministers' younger assistants were having a mildly heated debate about the terminology used on dating apps, websites and tv shows. One man, who looked barely old enough to be dating, let alone entrusted with a role at the palace, was attempting to uncover a definitive explanation as to what 'friends' meant these days. 'So, if you tell me you just want to be friends with me, does that really mean you don't want me to ever speak to you again?' he directed towards a particular brunette.

'No, it means I just want to be friends with you.'

'No it doesn't,' interjected another new female colleague, 'it means I'm keeping my options open and I haven't decided if I fancy you or not.'

This prompted a spotty young man to suggest, 'No mate, it means she doesn't fancy you enough to go out with you but you might be alright for an odd night's "friendship".'

In the end they arranged to go to a Speedy Friends night at a new local Pubsidy; to survey everyone else's opinion or chat people up or make new friends or get laid or whatever it turned out 'friends' meant to the others who attended. Sky and Sal, who could not help overhearing, were quietly amused by the predicament. 'Was it that complicated back in our day?' Sal mused aloud. 'Anyway, I'm just off to get rid of some toxins,' she added, as she turned towards the loos.

'Surely not from Chef's vegan specialities?' Sky smiled, guessing they were not his preferred speciality.

Much as the Queen admired the splendid work her gardening team did in keeping the formal lawn manicured to within a few millimetres of its life, and the flowers dead-headed almost before they had fully bloomed, she reserved a particular fondness for the wilder parts of the garden. Philip teased her by referring to the area as Ballysandy, knowing how she loved to escape to her country homes whenever the opportunity arose. But duty decreed the Queen could not always do as she wished, and neither could those who worked with her. She knew she had put pressure on Brett to push the Tax Ballot through sooner than he had suggested he would be able, but much of the effort being made by the New Ministers and their teams would be to no avail should the tide of public opinion flow in an unexpected direction. It was imperative they ascertained the mood of the nation as soon as possible. As usual, those around her believed the Queen to be the only one totally unruffled by the unfolding events. If only they knew.

An important point which she was keen to acknowledge to the assembled throng was how many groups and individuals had made contact to politely inform her that, perhaps for some years, they had been dedicating themselves to initiatives similar to those currently being credited to the New Ministers as ground-breaking. It saddened the Queen to learn how unaware she had been of the extent to which efforts had already been made to support underprivileged people, animals and any number of causes she had never even heard of. It had become clear that one's financial position or standing in life were often the governing factors in whether one's enterprises were successful in reaching a wide audience; thereby receiving additional income, respect and appreciation. This situation appeared to be the direct opposite of the vicious circle so often referred to by those less fortunate subjects who contacted her. Without treading on further toes, she vowed to work with the current organisers of award shows for ordinary citizens, publications listing charitable and community organisations, plus individuals fighting to support a particular cause, to ensure that no-one went unappreciated for their attempts to improve the world. She also hoped to bring like-minded souls together, to avoid situations where funds and resources were being spread thin, purely because those with similar goals were unaware of their potential collaborators existence.

With her increasing age, and tendency to see herself as ultimately responsible for everything going on around her, the Queen was grateful to have younger associates available to deal with social media, new technology and the sheer volume of information entailed in all the tasks at hand. Just the size of the current world population was overwhelming, even without the effects of the virus and other ongoing disasters.

Old hands at dealing with the sovereign, Alison and James observed her fondly. He nodded towards where the Queen stood, apparently engrossed in what one of Brett's assistants was telling her. 'She's not listening, is she?'

'Of course not,' Alison agreed. 'She's worrying her socks off about the Tax Ballot. And everything else, like the rest of us.'

Brett Has a Dream

It was the first time a ballot had been put to the nation in such a way, so the procedure was being undertaken with the solemnity it deserved. Ultimately, Brett and his crew held their collective breath, crossed their fingers and unleashed the form to the internet at the appointed time. Only a minority had requested paper forms, thanks to the boost given to libraries and other public buildings to be able to offer more free technical support, and it was expected that the results would be fairly clear within two days.

Tension was high, with everyone's plans in limbo until the forms had been fully analysed. Most of the responses could be compiled automatically but there was no room for mistakes, so Brett had insisted on security checks being completed by humans as well as robots. He trusted his own team but, unfamiliar with handling this amount of data on a national scale, it suddenly hit him how hard it really was to ensure that no tampering, or simple mistakes, could take place. If he could fully trust the IT specialists, could he trust the computer systems and the method of checking that each National Insurance number was used only once? Would the system be capable of analysing narrative answers accurately? He knew he was living in a society that had made everybody paranoid to some extent, with good reason. If he kept his fingers crossed for long enough perhaps it would all work out and this ballot, HIS ballot, would be the key to the big change everyone was hoping for....

Brett suddenly became aware of voices around him, which meant - Oh God, he'd fallen asleep at his desk. Had someone said the system had crashed, or was that a dream? Why were his hands aching?

Sympathetic to the pressure he was under, and not being in the dorm at his old school, no-one had taken the opportunity to write obscenities on Brett's face with permanent marker, tie his shoelaces together or pull his trousers down around his ankles. And the strange sensation in his hands was easily explained - he really did still have his fingers crossed.

Sky came through the open doorway and approached him, with a coffee and a smile. 'I thought you could do with this,' she said, studiously ignoring his attempts to bring his fingers back to life. She placed the mug on his desk and sat down next to it. 'I'm no good at the techie stuff but moral support is my speciality, if you could do with a bit of that. Some of the others have gone for a break, figuring we can't do much until we know what we're dealing with. But I knew you wouldn't be able to relax until it's all done and dusted.'

'Thanks, you're right there.' Brett managed a slight smile and accepted the drink gratefully.

'Well, seeing as it's not an election and the tv stations can't analyse the results endlessly as they come in, shall we be positive and make some provisional plans, assuming we do get the results we're hoping for?'

Brett relaxed a little and his smiled warmed, 'Actually that sounds like just what we should do. Good idea.'

'Great, let's start with education. I'm guessing that'll get quite a lot of "votes". And it'll be good for children to get tested, very gently, when they're really young - so the right plans can be put in place for their future.'

Brett's brow furrowed slightly and Sky picked up on it immediately. She gave a brief laugh, 'Oh, don't worry, I'd be the last person to suggest labelling a kid with IQ tests or anything like that. I've been speaking to the Queen a lot about this and we need to find a really insightful method which will give a clear indication of personality, sensitivities, suitable schooling and learning style.

You still don't hear too much about all that but I think it's really important. Speaking as someone who hated school from the word go.'

Brett noticed how Sky kept smiling when she was not really happy about what she was saying. No wonder he was still so confused by women. He would have liked to agree, he had also hated his school. But his background decreed 'what happens in the dorm, stays in the dorm'. Besides which, his parents were so proud of the education they had provided for him that he had never found it the right time to tell them he wished they had sent him to the same school as Nathan and Jolie. Still, he supposed their school would probably just have messed him up in a different way.

Brett explained how eager he was to reduce the pressure which had been brought about by the seemingly never-ending demand for Ofsted reports and turning schools into not-for-profit companies. He was sure that some were profiting from the changes but felt it unlikely it was the pupils or teaching staff. Explaining all this to Sky elicited an enthusiastic response.

'Good on you, Brett. After the way education's been disrupted we must do all we can to improve things for the future. Now everyone's used to learning from home, how about we make all the course material available to students online - or on paper to take away - so they can work at their own time and pace, at school or elsewhere?'

'Why not? None of us could have predicted the situation the world is in now, but one of the few good things to have come out of it is that new ideas aren't immediately laughed out of existence, as they may well have been in previous years. And, with the current level of unemployment, any methods we can introduce to increase someone's chance of getting work is going to be well received. Now that practical careers are more truly valued, a lot of academic courses will be replaced by on the job training anyway. I'm expecting apprenticeships to make a big comeback.'

'Don't bite my head off for saying this but, in a way, our jobs don't need to be as hard as they might seem....' Sky paused, tempting fate. Brett did not bite her head off, so she continued, '....because the public are in control of the decisions now. We just have to put them into action. And keep coming up with suggestions for their approval - like different types of schooling to suit the whole gamut of kids' characters, and letting them come up with their own subjects so they'll actually enjoy their education and set themselves on the path they really want to follow.'

'When you put it like that it does make me feel better, thank you.' A little relief spread across Brett's face. It would be really enjoyable to keep coming up with ground-breaking ideas, have the public agree and 'rubber-stamp' them, then go home early for a relaxing evening. If only it were going to be that simple.

Result

Following the brief respite of the New Ministers' picnic, the hectic pace had continued for all at the palace. Despite a tacit agreement that the former government and the Old Guard were to be ignored as far as possible, whilst the real work of undoing the unholy mess into which they had plunged the country was accomplished, they had their way of sneaking their views into the public arena. In fact, in the last few days all hell had broken loose, as every columnist in the country seemed to have been fed a whole smorgasbord of carefully contrived propaganda, to be presented as their own personal opinion, in an audacious attempt to sway the answers to the ballot.

In the streets, pubs, cafes, boardrooms and living rooms, everyone was speculating about the likely outcome. The privileged minority firmly believed the plebs would know their place and refuse to cross the line when it came down to it, realising it was of paramount importance to maintain the arms industry (aka the defence of the country), the pharmaceutical/health industry (formerly the NHS in the UK) and all the systems which had been in place for hundreds of years. Who on earth would dare to oversee the re-writing of history?

Well, it seemed the Queen was about to be that very person.

As the results of the ballot started to roll in, it was hard for the New Ministers to fully appreciate what was happening. There was a stunned silence in their meeting room for much of the time, as everyone sat glued to screens, large and small. Breath was bated, food left uneaten and words unspoken, lest chickens were counted too soon. Hardly anyone went home, not wanting to miss the momentous experience they sensed was about to happen.

After two days of tension and tenterhooks, the implication of the results received so far could be denied no longer. An old Aussie expression 'stunned mullet' came to mind as Sky observed Brett's unshaven face and bewildered demeanour. He seemed to be finally plucking up the courage to speak, when the door opened and, unceremoniously, the Queen stepped into the room. For the briefest moment she looked serious, then suddenly she moved around the room: shaking hands, smiling widely and congratulating everyone excitedly. It was time to admit that the change had been made. The New Guard were in charge at last.

In the most simple format, the preferences of the people had been made clear. Health and happiness really were the priorities for the population at large. Safety, support and inclusion were primary concerns and preserving the environment was seen as essential.

Drinking and Smoking

Pleased to be back to earth, literally, after the events of the last few days, Tom instructed his latest batch of volunteers on the plans and layout for the latest hubs community garden.

As usual Pam and Jim had turned up with their trusty caravan, always ready to provide a cup of tea, a friendly ear and a place to rest. Having travelled the world together throughout their lives, they had now settled into a routine of turning up at the fledgling hub sites whenever possible. Tom was always happy to see them and found they provided the essential familiarity to support the new teams.

Pam rubbed her hands together with glee and her good humour was infectious, 'I'm so pleased to see all this enthusiasm for starting up outdoor spaces as well as the hubs, pubs and whatsits. It's so much better to get outside when we can. Far be it from me to applaud global warming but it looks like we'll be having more sunny days in the future, so we may as well make the most of it.'

Jim looked at her lovingly, as ever. 'Top up the endorphins and all that,' he agreed with a smile.

What a great couple of old hippies they are, thought Tom affectionately. He hoped he and Jess would last as long and prayed she might soon find her inner Zen. Before he lost his.

'It shouldn't be long before we can organise the retractable canopies, so there'll always be options for staying outside, if you're feeling hardy. I want to make sure there are welcoming places for people to get together everywhere. And there are endless ways to harness heat and light from the sun and wind, to provide energy indoors and out, so that will all come in good time.' Tom had a clear picture of his task list and saw the projects stretching out into his retirement.

'What about the smokers?' asked Jim, a little hesitantly.

Tom looked at him uncertainly. He didn't have Jim down as a smoker and would be a little disappointed if he was. He could not think of anyone amongst the New Ministers and their crowd who smoked (or would admit to it, at least).

'I mean, Pam has her asthma, and that's one of the reasons we always travelled with our own accommodation - so we didn't have to do too much passive smoking. Sometimes we've been in a beautiful beer garden, watching the sunset cast that lovely golden glow through our glasses, and we've had to leave our drinks when the place was taken over by smokers.'

'And I hate it when that happens on the soaps. Have you seen how often a character orders a pint, then immediately gets up and goes off somewhere else? They must be made of money.' Pam always found a new link to her other half's conversation.

'They probably are - soap stars, made of money. But don't worry about the smoking - it's far less popular these days and smokers really did have a good run for their money. Smoking isn't going to be permitted in any public places any more, indoors or out. It's our turn now.'

Seeing the happy couple smile back at him reignited Tom's enthusiasm for a pet project he planned to introduce through the innovation show. His idea for refurbishing vehicles destined for the scrap heap, written off by insurance companies or anyone who could not afford the repairs needed, really appealed to his frustrated, free-spirited side and he would love to escape in a little Carvan of his own sometime. Offering a unique opportunity to trainee coachbuilders, it would fit Tom's remit nicely if a car could be saved from destruction and simply converted into a 'mini camper', thus providing a temporary home, a means of travelling for work, or both. They would be great fun too. He envisaged the simplest models merely having seats which would fold completely flat, to enable comfortable sleeping, whilst his imagination sometimes ran riot with plans for incorporating every home comfort into a regular sedan. At the very least, the 'over-steering-wheel tray' would be useful for eating meals in relative comfort, or perhaps for consuming food cooked in the mini oven, if it were a luxury model. Some had already found creative ways to reuse old buses and he saw endless scope in that too. As well as supporting the move to bring back rural bus routes and open up old train lines. Exciting times.

One Hell of a Mess

Back in London everything had gone into overdrive; the ministers were gathered together and, unexpectedly, Brett had started to sympathise with their predecessors and how they must have suffered the same feeling of being snowed under. But Sam had no time for them. 'They're the ones who got us into this mess. If it wasn't for them we wouldn't be having all these hassles now. How are we meant to turn around a system that's so completely bloody screwed, before the public turn on us?' he asked, with a brief lapse of the bravado everyone counted on. It was unnerving for the others and glances were exchanged.

'I get you, I really do,' sympathised Sky, quickly. 'We've inherited one hell of a mess. But we're not like the previous governments and that's why we're here. We can't afford to get edgy or overwhelmed now. What we can do is be honest; with ourselves, with each other and with the public. I wish all the necessary changes could be put in place right now, this minute, but they can't. Let's just keep supporting each other, prioritising what's most important and doing everything we can to provide what the public want and need.' Sky's rallying cry seemed to do the trick and the atmosphere perked up a bit, but it still took her some time to convince Brett that he would not be singled out as wholly responsible for the changes he was about to oversee. 'No, that's the whole point, you - we - are putting in place what the people have asked for. We knew that a minority wouldn't agree that it's a good idea to reduce the armed forces to a peacekeeping organisation, nor to cease our involvement in the arms race. Or the 'space race', or any of those things that have cost a fortune but don't benefit anyone except the tiniest percentage, who already own pretty much everything and don't seem to care how much anyone else is suffering. But the great majority of the public don't want us to waste any more of their money on supporting conflicts that make no sense but kill huge numbers of innocent civilians. They don't want us to keep spending ridiculous amounts on shooting off to mess up other planets when we should be fixing the problems we've got on this one. They've made sensible choices; they know what's most important to them and they realise that none of their concerns can be resolved without considering the impact on the environment.'

'It's about time the adults woke up and realised what those hundreds of thousands of kids, all round the world, were protesting about. And it seems they have, here at least,' added Sal. 'There's not much point in pouring additional funding into supposedly combating terrorism, or even throwing virtual billions around in an attempt to fix the economy, when global warming is going to finish everyone off anyway, if we don't act now.'

Gradually the atmosphere calmed and plans were made, instructions were given and assistants organised themselves into groups to address specific tasks. The most pressing task being to let the public know what they, themselves, had decided.

Brett could have kissed Andrina when she told him she had been planning an appropriate press statement for weeks and had merely needed to drop in the salient facts, as the results had come in. He blushed at the thought, of kissing her, but quickly decided he had matters of state to attend to and could not afford to be distracted by passing fancies. And that was another reason why he was more suited to a government role than many of his predecessors.

Random Homeless Guy

Andrina's assistant Laura had been pleased to take a break from endlessly exhausting her IT skills. When Alison had approached her with a more personal task, Laura had felt very flattered. Not that she had been provided with too many details about the task she was to undertake but, nevertheless, she was determined to prove her worth to Alison. Also, it sounded quite fascinating.

Laura did not know why Alison needed to find 'as much information as possible' on this random homeless guy, but intended to do the job to the best of her ability. She had always quite fancied being a detective and found it a bit of a thrill to turn up 'incognito' at the shelter where he was currently staying.

The worker on duty had been given as few details as were necessary to convince him that Laura was on legitimate business and represented an organisation that may be able to offer long term support to the man. As he shuffled into the meeting room unsteadily, she was taken aback by his age and could not help commenting.

'Truth be told, I'm surprised to still be here meself,' he said, with a rather incomplete grin but an endearing smile playing in his eyes.

Laura followed the instructions she had been given, enquiring whether the man would be open to receiving assistance from an anonymous benefactor. The answer being a resounding affirmative, she asked him to tell her as much or as little about his life story as he wished to. And, two hours later, she realised what a story it was. In fact it was hard to gently encourage him to stop telling it. She did not know if she would be seeing him again but, for now, she had just one more task to complete, 'Would you please write down just a brief outline of what you've told me? For me to pass on.' Laura smiled at him. He seemed like a decent guy, he deserved a break.

After ten minutes of writing, Laura gently suggested that he save the rest of the details for another time, and he reluctantly pushed the pen and paper over to her. As per instructions, she placed the paper in an envelope, sealed it and placed it safely in her pocket. Getting up to leave, Laura held out her hand and the man shook it firmly.

He had not often had the chance to shake someone's hand and she did not know how he appreciated that, her smile and her time. He hoped he would see her again. No-one had ever really listened to his story before.

Telling Tales

Feeling they may as well throw themselves in at the deep end, Sam and Brett had been making plans for turning around the criminal justice system. It was not particularly high on the list of ways in which people wanted to spend their taxes and Sam had some ideas on how to cut corners.

'I appreciate where you're coming from but I don't think we're going to be able to get away with stringing child abusers up in that manner,' responded Brett carefully. 'What I will be suggesting is that we introduce a system whereby sentences are far longer and passports are permanently withdrawn from anyone who has been convicted of an adult crime.' Sam looked a little uncertain and Brett continued, 'It's an idea I've been mulling over for some time and I think you're going to like it. Also, from some of the comments we've received, it seems to fit with public opinion. Many believe that someone who commits violent or sex crimes should be tried and convicted as an adult, whatever their age. If a "child" is responsible for a savage assault or a rape, for instance, then it's believed they should automatically waive their right to leniency.'

Sam's eyes lit up as he spoke, 'If you can't do the time, don't do the crime.'

'Exactly. Particularly in these sorts of cases, there will be no funding available to provide new identities, nor rehabilitation, for those who are independently deemed to be incapable of remorse, or unwilling to show any to their victims. They will be subject to a permanent ban on use of the internet and the money which has previously been used for providing support or home comforts to such criminals will go directly to their victims or to organisations which offer whatever help victims may need. We will ensure that it's no longer acceptable for anyone to play "blame the victim", nor to engage in covering up the truth of a case by hiding behind loopholes in the law. Pejorative terms are to be wiped out, so "whistleblowers" and others who rightly report crimes or injustices will never be seen as the ones who are at fault. We'll bring the right people into our police force by revising the current legislation to ensure that decent citizens and decent officers will be afforded more protection than someone who has committed a serious offence. The supposed rights of a dangerous criminal cannot be permitted to take priority over a minor infraction in the interviewing process, nor the safety of the public. Though, of course, strict measures will be put in place to ensure that absolutely no-one is above the law, in any situation. As society moves swiftly towards favouring those who do no harm to others, it will naturally follow that the police force will become more diverse, as those from ethnic minorities, women and the LGBT+ community are able to trust they will be safe and accepted if they choose a career in law enforcement.'

It was clear Sam was impressed and he nodded emphatically. 'You know we didn't come from the same background, but we're coming from the same place now. I never got it when the other kids thought the worst thing you could do was "grass" or "tell tales" or "dob someone in". And I didn't see why I should be "loyal" to some scumbag who was picking on another kid, just because the bully lived on my street.'

'Absolutely. If anyone sees or hears of a harmful act being committed, it should be their moral duty and obligation to report it. As was once the case. Fortunately the public seem to agree with us on that one too.'

'So long as we don't breed a culture of people harassing the neighbour they've taken a dislike to or reporting their annoying brother-in-law for crimes against fashion or things like that.'

'Certainly not. Wasting police time will still be a criminal offence, where it has actually occurred. And anyone who abuses a position of trust, such as a police officer, minister of religion, doctor, teacher or sports coach, will have cause to be particularly concerned about the full weight of the law which will descend upon them.'

Sam smirked a little at all this, beginning to realise Brett may not be as green as he was cabbage looking.

Ethical Minefield

Sal had not been home for several days. In fact, she had being making full use of a little bathroom near her office and had been virtually sleeping on her desk. She had found her mission in life and was determined to fulfil it to the best of her ability. She was not open to any interruptions but could no longer ignore the phone ringing.

'Yes, hello?' she said, a little more snappily than intended.

Big Gerry paused briefly and did not sound his usual ebullient self once he started speaking. As he did, Sal had the strangest vision of his hair singeing gently, for some reason.

'You remember my secret plans?' Gerry asked, in a muted tone.

'Well no, not really, you refused to tell me anything about them. You said you were going to save the announcement for a special occasion or something....'

'Oh, ok.' The usual flair had definitely gone. 'Well, at the moment it's not going to be quite the surprise I wanted to give you....'

Sal wanted him to cut to the chase, so she could carry on with the seventeen tasks she had been in the middle of, but could not be mean when Gerry sounded so deflated. Biting her lip, Sal closed her eyes to avoid looking at all the piles of papers, as there was not a part of the room they had not spilled into.

'It's my special project,' Gerry wailed. 'You know, the Sussex project!'

'This doesn't have anything to do with Harry and Meghan does it?' Sal asked nervously. If Gerry had accidentally harmed a couple of prominent ex-Royals, that would really throw the cat among the pigeons. One or two of the others, ok, but these two were still pretty popular, given their unique situation.

'No, no, of course not.' That was a relief. 'But there's been a bit of a mishap with our efforts to harness the power of....' He stopped, then continued in a stage whisper, 'you know....'

No, I bloody well don't - for NDD's sake spit it out, was what Sal wanted to say. No need, as he was now continuing in a barely audible, real whisper.

'..... spontaneous combustion.'

Sal assumed she must have slipped into some sort of alternate reality, thanks to her recent habit of not eating, drinking, sleeping (or practising what she preached about healthy living). 'What the....'

Silence.

'I said "what the f...."'

'I know what you were about to say,' came the huffy response. 'I thought you said I could count on your support at all times.'

Sal frowned. Had she really said that? Probably. Too bloody helpful, as usual. 'Sorry Gerry, ok.... what exactly are you talking about?'

His usual form returned a little as Gerry excitedly outlined the rather vague details of the project he still hoped to return to at a later time 'once the building stops smoking'. Following an intense conversation which Gerry and Sal had previously enjoyed, on the subject of how it might be possible to make cremations as 'green' as burials, it turned out that Gerry had thrown himself wholeheartedly into making their wishes a reality. Reasoning that spontaneous combustion was a natural phenomenon, he had been pursuing the development of it enthusiastically ever since. Hence the explosion, the fire, and yes, the singeing.

Gerry having agreed to 'put the trials on hold for a while' (or 'the foreseeable future' in Sal's mind) at least meant that was one thing Sal did not need to give more thought to for the moment. Gerry was happy to delve deeper into his ethical embalming project instead. He was no fan of the regular post death procedures that few were aware of: including embalming, which he considered unpleasant, unnecessary and terrible for the environment. However, he thought some may like the idea (instead of having their body filled with toxic chemicals) of getting properly 'tanked up' one last time with their favourite spirit, in celebration of setting their own spirit free.

On a future occasion he would speak further to Sal about their plans for Sensexec - a low-cost, trustworthy, co-operative service for those who had no reliable friend or family member to act as their executor. No-one could experience so much angst regarding their own death, nor feel so lonely and unloved, as those who expected to die with only a solicitor to make the last decisions on how to execute their estate, and how much he or she could get away with skimming off for their own expenses. To act as a personal and sensitive executor for a stranger, in good faith that someone else would be doing the same job for you when the time came, would be the ultimate way of Paying it Forward.

The Big Issues ('not the magazine')

Andrina continued to impress her colleagues with her ability to remain cool, calm and collected, despite some of the remarks aimed at her due to her high profile role in publicising the results of the Tax Ballot.

Whereas Maggie could be relied on to overheat quickly and give her opinion with little encouragement. 'It's just not on. How do these "journalists" still get away with all this racist, sexist crap? You're doing a brilliant job. I'd like to see any of those misogynistic little twats manage half your projects.'

Andrina cringed visibly, just a little. 'Thanks again for your valiant support, Maggie.' She felt obliged to add, 'You might just want to change that terminology a little,' with her sweetest smile. Maggie looked confused and one of the younger men in the office appeared to take some amusement from enlightening her.

'You all know by now that I'm made of tougher stuff than some of the other media sources give me credit for. Please don't worry that you might accidentally refer to my race or my skin colour or the fact that I'm a woman. I see them all as legitimate, identifying factors. When I took my - white - boyfriend to visit my extended family in

India he stood out like a sore thumb, but he didn't expect them to pussyfoot around his ethnicity by describing him as "the one in the red shirt" or "the tall one with the fair hair". Can we all just start being people, first and foremost? That's the message we're trying to spread to the rest of the country after all. I have always believed that the most hurtful insults are those aimed at an individual, not someone who merely represents a group which encompasses millions, or even billions, of people.'

Astute enough to realise that certain hacks would have been just as keen to attack anyone in her position, whether they were pink, green or purple, Andrina felt happy to have made her point. Now she could get back to what she did best - work, work and more work. Ironically, she was keen to address the issues of 'reverse' racism and sexism, but quickly decided this was not the right time. She was already feeling pretty het up, having spent most of the previous night reading up on the extent of hidden slavery, sex trafficking and child abuse rings in the UK. Now they were the sort of issues that really made her blood boil. The same applied to all decent people, of course, including her fellow New Ministers and the rest of her colleagues. However, finding individuals who could maintain their own sanity and strength whilst dealing with the worst depths of depravity was another matter. The resolve shown by Andrina, Sam, Brett, and the others who were attempting to address these most confronting matters, was simply due to their mutual commitment not to let anyone walk free from these crimes in the future, whoever they may be and whatever their status in society. It was time to reinvestigate some famous reports and statements which had mysteriously disappeared. And to look into the inappropriately long sentences handed down to those who continued to assert their innocence whilst imprisoned, following their accusations against powerful players. Basically, time to bring a lot of evil scum to justice.

Sam had guessed what Andrina was dwelling on and decided she needed a break. The pub Sam had visited with Sal and Sky, after their first introduction, had become the local for the ministers, on the rare occasions that any of them stopped for a breather. It was mid-afternoon, a quiet time of day, and Sam had been pleased to find a free booth for a private chat.

'How did we get from talking about horrendous sex crimes to my boyfriend?' Andrina laughed, glad to find something funny again. 'Anyway, he's not now - my boyfriend. He's very "ex". Why do you ask?'

'No reason,' replied Sam, smiling into his glass.

Second Childhood

Sky and Sal were taking a wander through the palace grounds, dodging the corgis and pigeons and catching up on all the latest community initiatives. It had been hard to drag Sal from her office, so Sky had employed a little unusually sneaky persuasion along the lines of 'it's not going to reflect well on us if the minister for health has big bags under her eyes and a generally pasty look about her.' Not that the general public would be seeing them, in that part of the garden, but it did the trick and Sal started to remember just how much better she felt from a little fresh air and sunlight.

'And, later on, I really want to initiate Health Food Banks, maybe at the community pubs or attached to shopping centres and supermarkets. Have you seen the sort of junk that gets donated to food banks? And that's what gets donated because that's what they ask for.'

'What, the people going there for food?'

'No, the ones who run some of the food banks.'

'I suppose it's like the papers telling us they only print gossip because it's what "we" want.'

'And manufacturers filling stuff with sugar "because the public wouldn't like their food without it". We need to start treating our fellow citizens like grown ups and actually give them the chance to make sensible choices about everything, instead of telling them what to do but not making the right things available.'

'Are you up to speed on all the latest groups?' Sky enquired, before Sal could expand further on her favourite subject. 'Quite a few SAD retreats are being planned, particularly in the north, in readiness for the gloomier months.'

'We must try to come up with a better acronym though. People with Seasonal Affective Disorder are already sad enough, without having the word rammed down their throats.'

'How about Foul Weather Friends then? I think it sounds quite catchy and alludes to the idea that the members will really stick together and support each other all the time. But I don't think "happiness" can be over-used, so we could call them the Happy SAD Groups. We really want all the groups to be happy, don't we?' Sky pondered, in conjunction with her Inner Child. 'Anyway, they should have the desired effect if we provide light boxes, comedy films and books, art and craft materials and....'

'the right drinks and snacks.'

'Stop it,' said Sky, giving her friend a playful slap on the arm, and a grin. 'Seriously though, let's also get the Real Retreats up and running, as soon as we can. And, to make them more relaxing, let's aim to keep them all tech-free. I've felt pretty desperate in the past and spent ages looking for a basic retreat for a cheap break, where I could find other people who were after some peace and quiet and a bit of mutual support. Maybe others who had been through some difficult stuff and also had no-one to talk to. All I could find were upmarket places offering spa-type weekends for extortionate prices, or courses which were tailored to a very specific group, had prohibitive regulations and long waiting lists. I just know there are so many folk out there who desperately need a break, for any number of reasons. We need to do something to help them.'

'Say no more!' Sal triumphantly recovered a large piece of paper from her bag and waved it in the air. 'Here's my list of small hotel and guest house owners who would love to supplement their income by offering just what you suggested. So many businesses have completely gone under that the remaining ones are very approachable now. We may even give some the incentive to start up again.'

Sky looked surprised, 'You followed that up?'

'Of course I did, I always listen to you Sky. You have the best ideas.'

Sky blushed a little and moved on quickly. 'Thanks Sal, it's good to hear that business owners are more open-minded about new ideas now.'

That brought a bit of a laugh, with Sal responding, 'Although some thought WE were being a bit TOO "broad-minded" when I raised the subject of adult playgroups....' Sky started to smirk '....and when I mentioned ball pits it only made things worse. One guest-house owner, with the most tightly curled blue rinse I'd ever seen, virtually grabbed my collar to march me to the door.'

Sky could not resist saying, 'He sounds lovely,' and they both collapsed in giggles. Perhaps Second Childhood Days would be a better name for a group where grown-ups could unwind by innocently playing with toddlers' toys.

'Anyway,' Sal resumed a more solemn expression as they reached the outer wall farthest from the palace, 'I'm planning to introduce an emergency 24 hour helpline as an alternative to the current health service based line, which generally advises callers to contact their doctor about whatever issue they've got. With the changes that have taken place recently I'm pretty sure there will be specialists from all sorts of fields available, and keen to volunteer their expertise. So callers can be transferred straight through to a trauma consultant or a naturopath or whoever they believe can assist them most effectively.'

'That's great - fantastic. The country certainly needs all the support it can get at the moment. A lot of lip service has been paid to the subject of mental health over the last few years but help doesn't seem to have reached people at grass roots level very effectively, and there are so many more with issues now. We must ensure that support groups remain a top priority at the new hubs and havens and all the community centres. I know there are some influential characters out there who think we're a bunch of namby-pamby liberals who are too invested in how everyone's feeling and that the way to fix the UK is to throw everything into their personal money-spinning projects. We just have to prove them wrong and keep the country on the right track.'

Antique Sale

It was rare for Tom to attend the palace these days, with most of his work taking him around the country for days or weeks at a time. He was intrigued to be shown into one of the state drawing rooms and he admired the luxurious furnishings. Not really to his taste but he could appreciate the quality.

The Queen seemed to read his mind, 'You know, it's not really to my taste but I did not have much choice in the matter. Can you imagine the outcry if we had a lot of skips delivered to the forecourt and dumped all these priceless antiques in them?'

Tom had a sneaking suspicion that she was toying with him, testing out her sense of humour and waiting for the right reaction. He smiled one of his winning smiles. 'I'd be happy to take some of them off your hands, if you wish, Your Majesty.' Touché.

Returning his smile, the Queen indicated that he should sit down, on a gold couch which was probably worth about what he would be willing to sell one of his children for. Good job he had changed from his usual work clothes for the occasion.

'I have rather an important matter to discuss with you today. You are of course aware of the considerable amount of refurbishment which is currently in progress at the palace, and probably aware that our other residences will require similar levels of input in the near future....'

Following the result of the Tax Ballot, it crossed Tom's mind that maybe the Queen really was going to ask him to unload antiques for her. Did she see him as some sort of Del Boy character? The notorious chandelier scene flashed through his mind. If Tom was not so good at turning his hand to anything, his parents might not have pushed him into building in the first place.

He realised the Queen had stopped talking and was waiting for him to renew his attention. He felt like a naughty kid, more than he ever did as a naughty kid. '....As I was saying, Philip and I feel this offers the ideal opportunity to introduce more apprenticeships at the palace. Under your tutelage.'

Great, Tom thought, another job for the list. A moment later, he realised what an honour it was. And he said so.

'Of course, we realise how very many tasks you already have "on the go". However, it will be an opportunity for you to share a project with Brett, in putting together a new team, offering further job opportunities to young people and....,' she hesitated, 'hopefully, keeping our costs down to placate the rest of the nation.' She too had obviously noted the inauspicious position the Royal Family occupied on the Tax Ballot.

Merchant Bankers

Brett was on form as he continued to enact the results of the Tax Ballot, in accordance with the wishes of the population. He had been relieved to find that the objective of being fair to all had shone through, as he and his colleagues had so fervently hoped it would. Unsurprisingly, the general public were not keen to spend too much tax on things (or people) they considered irrelevant or damaging to them. Brett could see politicians were going to be in for a rough ride, not being one of the occupations which could be said to have cheered everyone up or kept the country going in its hour of need. The first principle had to be 'the more unethical or harmful the product or service provided, the higher the tax to be paid on it.' Violent computer games, hard core pornography and the like would be priced out of the market by books about puppies and shapes in the clouds.

While designs for greener transport were improved, further taxes would be introduced to reflect the vehicles currently in use. An old car with a small engine would still be affordable but, should you own a collection of huge, new, gas-guzzling monsters, you had better hope you also owned a bank. Which perhaps you did. As banking was going to be one of the professions hardest hit, you would be in trouble either way. The tide was about to turn, with the monetary system gradually being ousted in favour of non-profit credit unions and bartering systems - the big launch of the Kindness Exchange would soon be taking place in all the hubs and public buildings, in print and online; changing the currency from cash to kindness and offering a progressive take on previous schemes which, sadly, had not taken off as widely as they might have done. Now the time seemed ripe for just such a method of obtaining goods and services without any money (and more acceptable than stealing them).

The airlines had, in the past, been phenomenally successful in disguising the dangers of sending land-based mammals into the sky for their annual two weeks in the sun, but that had all changed now. Disregarding the vast amount of individuals who had been disabled by, or died of, deep vein thrombosis and other illnesses related to such transport, there could be no denying that one hundred thousand or more commercial flights each day had not done a lot to help the ozone layer. Now that so many airlines had been killed off, the ones still struggling to survive were in no position to flout new environmental laws and, in choosing how to spend their own tax money, the general public were clearly more enthusiastic about holidaying locally and having the basic essentials to live a good life than they were about propping up big businesses. Any permitted flights would no longer be cleared to leave British soil with less than ninety-five per cent occupancy, nor would it be commercially viable for them to do so. With regard to protecting the natural environment there had been a long way to go with air travel. But perhaps not now, Brett reflected.

Technology had, surprisingly, turned out not to be as popular as the industry would have us believe. Apparently, since everyone started struggling to make sense of 'the new normal', most people were happy to use any method of communication available and could live without the latest gadget. Brett was going to offer them further encouragement to do so, by introducing hefty taxes for frequent upgrades and constant usage. It may even get people to have real conversations and make real friends again. Any company that encouraged use of technology above personal interaction would find their tax bills increased substantially, pro rata, creating a lot of headaches for many industry bosses and a major source of funds with which to build a better, and more environmentally friendly, Britain.

Manufacturers of plastics would be some of those to suffer most, tax wise, as a token payback for all the turtles, dolphins and polar bears who did not get to vote. There would be no more smoke-screening about recycling and no company would have the option to refuse to recycle any of the goods they supplied. Indeed, all retailers would be obliged to create what, for the larger outlets, would amount to a second place of employment, as they could no longer pass the buck of the waste they had created to local councils or solo greenies. Making individuals and businesses responsible for their own mess was guaranteed to pay dividends, once the initial protests had died down. It was going to be a challenging test of everybody's goodwill but Brett was not as fearful as he might have been. On an individual basis, he sensed that many may be breathing a sigh of relief at the changes. What a welcome release it would be not to have to keep up with the latest fads, or to stress out over where one could actually recycle all one's plastic wrappers. He could already picture keen eco-warriors unwrapping all their shopping at the tills and dumping it on the bemused shop assistant, who was about to start earning more than her boss for the service she was providing. Clearly, the higher up the ladder you were in an unethical organisation, the less the rewards would be. The message was pretty straightforward - get green or get out of business. For those looking for alternative methods of waste disposal, the signs would be equally blunt - 'Dumping? Fine'.

It would still be possible, and acceptable, to be (relatively) rich, famous and successful, if that was your thing. So long as your success was in helping, not harming. People, animals, the country or the planet - all would welcome a little extra support. Climate change was finally to be pushed to the top of the priority list, which would save a lot of mild-mannered accountants and schoolteachers from feeling compelled to expose themselves in (any future) parliament or chain themselves to tube trains during rush hour.

Brett could see that, even with the large amount of funding which would now be available for health and social care, a sliding scale of some sort would need to be created. Was it really right to give someone a new heart when they had relentlessly abused their old one with cigarettes, drugs or alcohol? Or should a healthy young person with children be prioritised? Was it time to start rewarding those who had always led a caring and unselfish life, rather than attempting to rehabilitate individuals whose lifestyles had brought pain or distress to others? Quieter types who found their thrills in knitting would not be expected to fund operations for those who continuously engaged in dangerous sports; the odd skydive or bungee jump, maybe, but not when every weekend was just an accident waiting to happen.

The ministers would soon need to revise and finalise the opt-out scheme for organ donation, to increase the level at which these were actually carried out. Also to ensure nobody was forced to stay alive against their will, if they had been debilitated to an extent they had already decreed would be unacceptable to them. Brett had personally heard accounts of bereaved families ringing around desperately and unsuccessfully trying to find anywhere that would make use of a loved one's body parts, in accordance with their final wishes. The impression was often inferred that only a perfect body was useful for anything; which led him, fortunately, to changing his line of thought - to the issue of unnecessary cosmetic surgery. Unfortunately he had not been able to forget the nickname for the new breast enhancement tax, which had immediately suggested itself to some of his more brazen young assistants, once the tattoo removal tax had been dubbed the Tat Tax.

As part of encouraging everyone to appreciate natural beauty, in their environment and themselves, it had seemed like a good idea to offer a financial incentive to discourage the fashion for artificial enhancement. Whatever the reason for deciding to alter the shape of one's features, or cover them with piercings and ink, taxing the procedures would, hopefully, give pause for thought. Those with distressing abnormalities would still be able to apply for assistance from the health service but others, desperate to modify their perfectly normal body, or their image, due to peer pressure or low self-esteem, would now have the excuse they could not afford to make the changes. Whereas the emotional or psychological support they might really need would now be readily available for free. Working at the palace did not involve a lot of running around naked, so exactly what any of the ministers might be hiding under their clothes was not widely known. But several of them had agreed they would not like to hang the same pictures on the wall for their whole lives, so they certainly would not want permanent artwork on their bodies. Especially the sort of images they might have chosen in their teens or early twenties.

The energy companies which offered no green alternatives would quickly disappear unless they made major changes, as would producers of any vehicles, machines or goods which were harmful to the environment. There was no time for further discussion on these matters, so Brett gave quiet thanks that the majority of the good people of the UK had made it clear their thinking was in line with the New Ministers, the Queen and most others. He looked forward to an imminent future where more countries would accept that the only war worth having was the one against environmental destruction.

Having decided early on that he would not wish to bring his own children into a world which was in such a state, Brett found it impossible to comprehend the blinkered approach some parents seemed to take in making decisions which would affect their offspring so significantly, the first one being whether it was really a good time to conceive a baby. Fortunately there was a larger group, often singletons like himself, who felt the same way and had taken tax decisions into their own hands, on behalf of the less well-informed and less well-meaning. At least he would soon be benefitting from generous tax relief on not having children. As would all those who only had as many kids, cars or homes as they really needed. He wanted to encourage everyone to ask themselves how much their own consumerism was costing the earth.

Touchpaper

Alison had been so pleased when she opened the envelope, she did a little dance around her office. The handwriting analyst's report confirmed what her untrained eye, and intuition, had already told her. The man in the shelter really was the letter-writer whose words had touched the Queen so deeply, and lit the touchpaper on such a historic chain of events. Alison did not know quite how James had managed it, but he had found the man and she was so grateful. Until now it had been impossible for her to repay the kindness shown to her by the Queen. What does one give the woman who truly has everything?

James took one look at Alison's face, as she ushered him in a few minutes later, and guessed exactly why she had called him. She merely beamed and nodded and, without thinking, he suddenly gave her a hug, before they quickly leapt apart. Protocol seemed to be catching. 'That's marvellous,' he enthused, allowing his usual demeanour to slip for a moment longer, 'so, what happens next?'

Neither of them had thought past confirming the man's identity and now they both wondered how they might broker a meeting between the Queen and her unsuspecting muse. They looked at each other. 'How about a cup of tea?' suggested Alison.

Laura knocked on the door, happily anticipating what task Alison might have for her this time. She was surprised to see James there as well, having only passed him occasionally along the corridors of the palace.

'Do sit down. Cup of tea?'

'Thanks.' Laura could not work out quite what else was brewing.

'As you know, that little mission I sent you on last week was of a most private nature. In fact you, James and I are the only ones who know about the meeting you had with the gentleman in question.'

Laura put her head to one side and listened more intently.

'James has suggested to me that the gentleman may be highly suited to being a subject for the genealogy show which you are working on. I believe one of the intended participants has had to pull out?'

Laura was a little disappointed, feeling a further adventure slipping from her grasp. 'That's right, they did. I'd love to be involved but you know the programme is really Maggie's baby....'

'Absolutely. And none of us would wish to tread on Maggie's toes....' Alison said sincerely, assuming Laura would be as nervous around Maggie as she was, 'but this is a delicate situation and it's not the right time to involve anyone else. We would like to keep things that way, for the moment, if we can rely on your discretion?'

'Absolutely.'

'And your further assistance?'

'Definitely.'

James was quietly amused by the two women, both apparently eager to make a mystery out of circumstances that were par for the course in his line of work.

Collective Conscience

Andrina was sorry she did not have time to devote to the more light-hearted matter of the television productions, but she had bigger issues to deal with. Currently she was in negotiations with the major players in IT and social media, pitting them against each other as she attempted to exhume their better natures and thus secure agreements which would benefit the world at large. Particularly those who were most vulnerable in it. She was gradually gaining mileage in convincing some of the planet's most highly paid executives to put their hearts where their profits were and finally start putting people first. Their moral duty, she argued, was not to protect the privacy of the lowest level scum who they permitted to operate through their systems, but the decent customers whose privacy had meant nothing as they were bullied, groomed, abused and driven to suicide. And the innocents who were too young to operate a computer but had become victims of those who made use of the system in the most disgusting ways imaginable. When Andrina wanted to make a point, she did not cut any corners.

With English being the universal language, and it still being quite a powerful little country despite all the odds, Andrina felt empowered to appeal to the collective conscience of the world. If she ever faltered, she just needed to remember the faces of the children in those videos she had forced herself to watch. She could not bear to remember what she had seen of their poor little bodies, or she might actually go mad. It all had to be stopped. Simple as that.

Complaints from the Old Guard had gradually diminished over the weeks and months. They seemed to have given up believing the New Ministers could be stopped. Particularly since they refused to 'play the game' with the old media. In turn, realising where their future bread and butter would be coming from, most journalists appeared to have taken some secret pledge of allegiance to the New Guard overnight, becoming the cohesive support any government could only dream of. Which could well be due to the fact that the People's Media, introduced by Andrina's team, was now the source of news and entertainment preferred by the great majority. Especially as it was free, environmentally friendly and offered a fair mix of independent views.

As they had with their denigration of the Queen, the Old Guard's views on the New Ministers swung violently between labelling them dictators or commies. A lot of dummy spitting went on in the gentlemen's clubs of Westminster, as it always had. But the enthusiasm seemed to have gone out of it now.

The New Ministers were finally able to relax into their roles, knowing they had the public backing to move forward with more long-term plans. Everyone was clear on what they needed to prioritise and free to ask for whatever assistance they needed. Some of them even gave thought to holidays, sometime in the future. Perhaps camping, walking, volunteering at a local animal sanctuary, or something similarly altruistic, which would not infringe on their ever-increasing principles.

Film Star

James set up the camera in a cosy little room at the shelter. Normally used for counselling sessions, it was a bit snug for the three of them, but it was do-able if he flattened his back completely against the wall while he looked through the viewfinder. James guessed his subject might be wary of men he did not know, who may be seen as a threat after all his years on the streets, so he was content, as ever, to assume a quiet but reassuring role in the background.

Laura knew the session was not about her either. It was all about getting the most important points of the story on film, in a natural way. She was to provide encouragement and moral support, due to the fact that, having spoken to the man once, for less than three hours, she had somehow assumed the role of his closest confidante. She was genuinely honoured.

George had given a lot of thought to his big break. He was not sure what this was really all about but he planned to make the most of it. Naturally shy, he had been tempted to sneak out for a bottle of something last night, but he could not afford to risk his place at the hostel, nor whatever it was that this girl's boss might be offering him. Maybe he was getting sensible in his old age. He was a little disappointed that Laura had not appeared to notice his efforts at smartening himself up, but he had to admit his standards may not be quite the same as most people's. Still, they would hardly be keen to offer him help if he had suddenly turned up in a three piece suit and a cravat. He had tried to have a bit of a shave but he seemed to have lost the hang of it after all this time.

'Don't worry about the camera, just look at me and talk to me as you did last time,' Laura smiled and nodded. George stared at her blankly, for quite a while.

'Whenever you're ready,' James was glad it was not an 'old school' camera; they would have got through film pretty quickly at this rate. But he did not really mind, something about the old boy made James feel sympathetic towards him. He must be softening in his old age. James did not even like to admit to himself that he had actually been pretty soft all along. But a background like his, and the demeanour of an action hero, had somewhat miscast him in life.

In his own good time, George started to tell his story again, in rather a spellbinding way. It was as if he had rehearsed it all night. Which, in fact, he had. He could not have these people thinking he was as dim as his eyesight. Once upon a time, when he had occasionally attended school, he could have been top in English, had his circumstances been different.

It was easy for James and Laura to take a back seat. George needed no further encouragement and the filming went like a dream. All that was left was for Laura to obtain his written permission for her to enter his details on the DNA website, so they could set about trying to turn up some family members for him. George's attitude changed abruptly at that point. Laura was sure she had already explained things clearly, on the phone, but it appeared not. When she mentioned she would also need to take a little saliva, he stormed out and slammed the door.

A few minutes later, Mike, the duty worker, appeared, with an accusing look on his face. He was fiercely protective of the clients and not too clear himself who these visitors were, though he knew his boss had cleared it for them to speak to George.

The misunderstanding was sorted out once James reassured Mike about the purpose of the saliva sample. Apparently George thought they did not trust him and it was some sort of drug test. He had not always been the most honest or upstanding person but he was proud enough to resent anyone else suggesting that might be the case.

Aura of Calm

Sam felt as though he had not seen daylight for weeks, having been submerged in the sort of legal paperwork that gave him nightmares. He hated dealing with it but he cared so much that he made a better job of it than most solicitors would, sorting out the much simpler rules and regulations which would govern the running of the country in future. Obviously a team of trained lawyers would be checking everything over but, with legalese abolished, they would find little to correct. The country had not yet foreseen the aura of calm which would arise from all citizens accepting they now had the right and the freedom to personally handle any issues which interested or concerned them. They still found it hard to believe there would always be someone sufficiently well-informed to help with a problem, address with a query or advise on how best to put forward suggestions and speak out for themselves. Having those options firmly in place would ease minds to the extent that fewer people would find it necessary to avail themselves of the assistance on offer. Once everyone felt their autonomy was respected and their voices heard, the country could heal. Peace of mind is a wonderful thing (and it's been a long time coming), smiled Sam to himself.

As the population had risen over the years, the governments and the ordinary people had become overwhelmed, with everything. It was time to acknowledge that instead of making things easier, the many official departments, charities and NGOs that had sprung up with the goal of addressing various issues, had merely served to complicate lives further. Many had become bewildered by the plethora of contradictory information on offer and the workers in call centres often seemed as bemused in their roles as those who approached them for advice.

'Simplify, Simplify, Simplify' had become Sam's motto. For that was the only way he could see the country really moving forward. As with individuals, organisations of all sorts needed to be brought together to work for the common good. Rather than one desperate soul spending weeks or months calling around in an attempt to find the help they needed for, perhaps, a specific mental health issue, there needed to be a central agency which would hold comprehensive and up-to-date information on the most appropriate places to contact, and have the ability to transfer the individual straight through to the right person.

Sam's profile was one of the lesser known of the New Ministers, but that did not stop a substantial amount of messages filtering through to him from the public. One account after another related how the efforts necessary to obtain a benefit, represent oneself in court or find a particular therapy, ended up causing more distress than the original problem. His respect and admiration for Sal had grown as he engaged with her over her plans to support the population to look after themselves, and each other, at least until the health service could be rebuilt. They would certainly be spending a lot of time putting their heads together over mental health, and he decided to pay a visit to Brett on the way to his meeting with Sal.

Brett's door was slightly ajar and Sam could hear voices, or Brett's voice at least. Sam stood quietly for a moment, not wanting to interrupt an important meeting.

'We can no longer afford to fill our prisons with those who have committed crimes of a merely commercial nature and are of no physical danger to society. The judicial system does not exist to mete out punishment for the wounded pride of large companies in embezzlement cases, when the minds that devised such scams can be usefully turned to work for the good of the country. We believe that, with the right guidance, a scheming mind might well be the sort of logical and logistical mind which may be suited to, for instance, devising a system whereby the re-nationalised train service will actually run on time and its replacement buses will return to operating on forgotten country routes.'

Silence. Sam thought that was a pretty good little speech but the silence continued and he felt sorry for Brett, who must be squirming at the lack of response. With one finger, Sam quietly pushed the door open a little further, to see Brett gazing out of the window. There was no one else in the room. Sam tapped on the door gently and Brett jumped a little. As Sam walked in he could not help himself, 'It's the first sign you know.'

'Hi Sam. What? Oh, yes, I see what you mean. Were you listening?'

'Just for a minute. It seems pretty good. Who's it for?'

'Well, you'll do for a start,' Brett smiled. 'Is it just me, or are you and the others feeling we've all slipped into some sort of parallel universe? A few months ago we were living our lives; getting on with our mundane, everyday duties, and now we're charged with changing the whole country.'

'Not sure I like the word "charged" in there. Especially after your speech on prisons. Sometimes I wonder if we might all end up in the Tower or something. Things have been moving fast and I'm sure a lot of the major players must be plotting ways to get rid of us.'

Brett grinned. 'We're not living in a gangster film, Sam. The public are pleased with the changes we're making and, besides, look what they've let all the past governments get away with. We'd have to do something really dreadful to upset them now.'

'I'm not so sure about that. The tide was definitely turning before we "took over", as it were. A rebellion is only a short step from a revolution and I've been expecting one of those for a long time. The country's changed and we need to keep changing it for the better, quickly and drastically, or the revolution could still happen. I know I sometimes sound as if I'd be right into that but actually I wouldn't. Underneath this gruff exterior I'm really a peace-loving old hippy who just wants everyone to be happy.' Both Brett and Sam were surprised he had put all that into words.

'Don't worry, Sam. The only one who could put us in the Tower is the Queen. And we're working for her.'

'It's what the Old Guard and their cronies might be planning that worries me. More than a few people who've rocked the boat have met with some pretty curious accidents over the years. And the Queen's not going to live forever, is she?'

'You know, the way things are going, I think she just might.' Slick politician that he could be, Brett knew when to end a difficult conversation on a positive note.

But, as Sam headed for the door, he turned back to offer a bit of friendly advice, 'And you know what? It's ok to talk to yourself. We all need someone to talk to and I reckon there's nothing wrong with having a bit of a chat to the telly or the radio, or a passing cat or whatever, if you're spending a lot of time on your own. But if Boris tells you he's been talking to me, don't believe him.' Sam left the room and left Brett confused again.

A Special Person

Sky stuck her head round the door, in response to the knock. The New Ministers' doors were always open to each other so she guessed it must be Brett, unable to overcome the rules of his upbringing. She was far more of an equalist than a feminist and she could not help being a little charmed by the occasional display of old-school courtesy. 'Hi Brett. I've made the list you asked for, but I think you probably had it all in hand anyway.'

'I hope so - it was hard to forget your sentiments on education. The remark about "pickled bunnies" conjured up quite a troubling picture.' He shook his head slightly, as if to erase the image, and Sky looked confused for a moment.

'What? Oh, yes - that was the reason I only ever went to one biology lesson. Because of the "pickled bunnies" in jars around the walls - that sort of thing is pure torture for a sensitive kid. I've never forgotten it.'

'You don't say,' responded Brett, sarcasm unintended.

'So, you really are going to go ahead with letting children decide their own subjects, right from the start? I'd have had no idea what alternatives there were to choose from but I guess you'll be making it easy for today's kids to find out about everything that's available.'

'Absolutely. It has been most valuable to get feedback from so many people, with experiences of all types of education. It made me realise I was quite entrenched in believing the system I was a part of was the way it should be. That's not to say I really enjoyed it, or felt that I benefitted from school as much as I might have, just that it seemed to be one of those things that couldn't be questioned.'

'Like the political system, the health system and the general hierarchy?' Sky's sentence, along with a teasing eyebrow, raised slightly at the end.

'Exactly like all that,' Brett relaxed suddenly and sank into a comfy chair. Sky's little corner of the palace always felt welcoming. He knew she was not a mum but he could not help thinking he may have had an easier time with a mum like her. Her ambition for her kids would, he was sure, just be for them to be happy. Brett often felt the pressure of his legacy, to prove his right to a place in this country, and this world. He felt truly gratified to be a part of the generation which would turn the focus on bringing everyone together.

Sky produced her list. She was pleased she was finally getting the hang of 'cutting to the chase' and 'getting to the point'. It was so much easier to do that when people were actually listening, and acting fast on ideas which were likely to change things for the better, no matter who they came from.

Brett gave the list a once-over and frowned a little. He looked up at Sky. 'Do you really think children know what they want by the time they start preschool?'

'Well I did.'

'I'm sure you did, but you're quite a special person....' He hurried to add, 'in a good way, of course.'

'Thanks Brett, I'll take that as I'm sure it was intended,' she replied with a smile. 'I suppose we're all inclined to believe everyone sees things the way we do, and I've always needed the freedom to do things my own way - boy did most of my teachers and bosses get pissed off by that....'

Brett still had to hide his shock at women swearing, particularly when he was daydreaming about Sky being the sort of surrogate mother who would have been more likely to ask about his latest girlfriend than his school report. He thought he would probably have had more of the former if he had not been under so much pressure to think about the latter.

'....but I realise now, some kids actually like to have rules,' Sky shuddered, finding it hard to believe her own remark. 'You know the Annual Check is going to be the real key to changing everything, don't you? When everyone feels heard, from the youngest possible age, it'll be far less likely that so many'll turn to drink, drugs or crime, or develop issues with their mental health. And if there's the slightest suggestion of any ill-treatment or abuse, that'll immediately be investigated, sensitively - for the good of the potential victim, not in a "tick the boxes, cover our arses" kind of way.'

Brett actually quite enjoyed a little gratuitous swearing, it made him feel part of the gang. He had never been in a gang before and he never expected to join one at the palace. He wondered if the Queen knew she had a gang. He wondered if he should stop daydreaming and pay attention to Sky. But she was on a roll and probably had not noticed his mind wandering off.

'And while I'm on the subject, we need to prioritise the monitoring of anyone who is suspected of using their role to cause harm of any sort. Whether it's a school caretaker or a member of the elite who is targeting a child or an adult. There's been an epidemic of covert abuse going on for many, many years and it often starts with the victim's self-esteem being destroyed in ways that no-one else notices. Families might call children spoilt, selfish, whiny or difficult, accuse them of throwing tantrums or being fussy eaters. These sort of putdowns give the child a clear message that they aren't important, understood or cared about, their legitimate concerns aren't taken seriously and they aren't going to be listened to. The child learns that, basically, they have no value, and that's the best way to turn someone in on themselves. It can set them up for a lifetime of being targeted by bullies, narcissists and abusers. Later on they may be silenced by the labels hypochondriac or victim, by being accused of self-pity or feeling sorry for themselves if they attempt to seek support. Health professionals are in the best position to do the worst harm and they often do. I can't believe some of them still use the term "cry for help" in an accusatory way, instead of apologising to a patient who has got into a desperate state due to the failings of the system. There's many a therapist or support group that's causing further harm, rather than providing assistance.'

Sky became aware that Brett was attempting not to look slightly startled by the passion in her words, and decided she had better lighten up a little. 'So that's why Sal and I are doing our best to keep an eye on anyone who starts taking control in the community groups. And you're the one making all the headway regarding further education. I was so pleased to hear you say that aptitude is going to be more important than exams and that our priority is to fix our current problems, rather than funding students to discuss outdated ideas, undertake unethical research and - what was it? - "indulge in pointless intellectualising". Brilliant! I remember when I first heard what philosophy is - I couldn't believe it could be seen as a course or a career - it seems to me it's what we all engage in all the time. Who's to say that someone who lived two hundred or two thousand years ago had ideas more relevant to modern life than you or I?'

Flattered by Sky's words, and enthused by her fellow feeling, Brett took his leave and hurried off to discuss ecobricks with Tom. There were suddenly going to be a hell of a lot of them available for new projects, now that all plastic (as well as pretty much everything else) was subject to compulsory recycling. It was going to be a fairly simple task to adapt the cutting equipment in newly-redundant factories into plastic-shredding machines. Also to make portable versions available to individuals at all the community hubs. That would save quite a few cases of RSI amongst the really keen environmentalists who, particularly during lockdown, had become quite obsessive about spending their evenings chopping up plastic wrappers in front of the telly. Brett had heard it could be quite fun to stuff all the little pieces into plastic bottles, to make the 'bricks', but somehow it had not caught on, until now. Green finally was the new black, and he thought it was ok to say that these days. Perhaps until the Martians landed.

Timing

As always, James arrived in good time. This morning it was for a meeting in the city. Sometimes he mused that he would have an easier life as a taxi driver, with his knowledge of shortcuts and secret parking spots. Not that he parked in cab ranks or regular car parks. There were a lot of facets to his position which he was not at liberty to reveal.

The office block was pretty standard - 99% windows, none of which opened to let in the 'fresh' air. There were plenty of little annoyances involved in his role but James was thankful not to be stuck in a place like this all the time. However, on this particular day, he was curious to discover the reason for his invitation.

James was shown into a large corner office with a priceless view down the Thames, as befitted its occupant. The mature, smartly dressed woman rose to greet him, with a polite smile and an outstretched hand. Following the standard pleasantries, she proceeded to heighten his curiosity.

'This is a somewhat sensitive matter, involving information which may be a tad surprising, so if I were speaking to someone else I would be strongly advising them to sit down. However, knowing your role in Her Majesty's household, and your somewhat personal involvement in this situation, I would merely like to offer you a seat. Cup of tea, perhaps?'

James waved his hand, refusing the tea and eager to hear what this was all about. He was normally the one creating the subterfuge, rather than subject to it. Although he had not previously met Athena, he was now aware of her standing in the field of genealogy research, and wondered what her interest might be in him.

Athena's assistant silently crossed the room and closed the door behind her. It was suddenly very quiet, save for the almost imperceptible hum of the air conditioning.

Laura swore to herself, under her breath. She still thanked her lucky stars that she had landed this job and she was as careful as she could be never to put a foot wrong. So she was fuming to be stuck on a bus, crawling along, with the minutes ticking away until her appointment. There was less than a mile to go but she knew bus drivers were not currently permitted to employ their common sense and allow passengers to jump off and run to their destination in an emergency, when it would be quicker. Which, Laura had learnt, seemed to be pretty often. She did not know why James had been unable to give her a lift but she secretly enjoyed all the little mysteries involved in her new world.

Meanwhile, James had arrived at the hostel early and had been a little concerned about whether George would be happy to make polite conversation with him, while they waited for Laura. Therefore, James was surprised when, of his own volition, George launched into some very interesting tales, barely pausing for breath. It seemed the floodgates had well and truly opened.

'...and there was this particular time,' George paused briefly to wipe his nose on his sleeve, thought better of it and produced a surprisingly pristine cotton handkerchief from his pocket, used it quite proudly, replaced it neatly and continued, 'when there was a lot of them posh scumbags around. You know the type - the slimy ones in their suits, who come looking for the young girls. Bastards!' he spat out, suddenly, heightening James's attention. 'And there was this skinny little thing - she'd been on our patch a few days, kept herself to herself. Right timid, you know?' He looked up at James, who noted the pools of remembrance in his eyes. Not tears. Those probably dried up years ago. There's only so much one person can cry, passed through James's mind, a half-thought sentiment that maybe he had heard, or felt, long ago.

'Then, one night, there was this rumpus, suddenly, and there was this smart arse trying to drag the girl off, and no-one was stopping him. They were all too bloody pissed, as usual! And she started screaming, except it wasn't really a scream. It was more of a whimper. Like she knew she couldn't fight it, like she knew it didn't matter what happened to her. Like nobody would care anyway.' George momentarily looked even sadder, but sensed James's unspoken plea to continue. 'And I couldn't take any more of it. How dare he, how dare they, steal our lives and our self-respect and take these poor girls off to who-knows-where? And I thought, "If it's the last thing I do, I'm gonna fucking kill 'im"....'

There was a longer pause and James was desperate to hear the ending. Even though he was pretty sure he already knew it. With little encouragement, George continued, 'So I was holding this bottle and then I'm swinging it at 'im and I don't know if I've hit 'im and I don't really know what's going on anymore but some of me mates are shouting at me and bashing me and I'm trying to look after meself, but I want to save the girl and then I see she's gone and then there was this other, older woman in the corner and....' with a dramatic gasp, George stopped talking, dropped his head to his knees and started sobbing, harder than he had done for as long as he could remember. Hard enough to bring Mike in, his face glowing with a 'what the hell have you done to upset him this time?' look. James's anguish was almost as clear as George's and a quick glance led Mike to think better of intruding. Somehow he knew it would not be doing anyone any favours. He retreated quietly and left them to whatever the hell was going on.

Eventually George's tears dried up and he slumped further, almost whispering, '....and she was gone too. She'd only arrived that day and I couldn't save her either and I don't even know who took her. If only I hadn't been such a fucking waste of space I could have helped them, I could have helped my family, I could have helped lots of people. Why didn't I see where she went? Why?'

George looked at James with such pleading that James felt compelled to do something he had never done before. 'I think I can help you with that,' he said quietly.

First World Problems

After a tip-off from Sam, Tom had succeeded in dragging Andrina away from her office. Sam was concerned that the darker side of the job had been getting to her and he guessed Tom's tv show might offer an opportunity for them to work on something a little more fun.

The first Stuff Up challenge was being recorded and there had been a huge response from schools eager to take part. Children were lined up with their empty bottles, big tubs of newly shredded plastic and a variety of sticks with which to pack the plastic tightly into the bottles. It proved an effective way of showing the public how to make ecobricks, whilst turning it into a competitive sport and providing some laughs. Later in the day Tom would be recording a more serious clip, on further inventive ways to effectively re-use the plastic which might otherwise end up in a variety of creatures, of all shapes and sizes. For now, he was happy to see Andrina smiling again.

Tom had not been on camera for a while, due to his compulsion to oversee the building projects for which he ultimately felt responsible, all over the UK. More issues became obvious all the time - number one (and number two); the need to reopen more public toilets. And there were a lot of other things which would make life a bit more comfortable for everyone, without too much difficulty. Much as he had an eye for innovation, Tom could also appreciate certain circumstances in which it would be more helpful to turn the clock back. He could not really pinpoint the year when someone should have called time on certain advancements which had gone on to do more harm than good, but he could remember when it was much easier and cheaper to have a wee. How had everything become so complicated and so commercialised?

In recent years the inclination, in some quarters, towards viewing all those who owned commercial or residential property as greedy, uncaring and unscrupulous, seemed to have increased to the point where anyone who owned a modest house or a small shop might be seen as the enemy by those who did not. Indeed Tom had been involved in an interesting discussion with Sam, who had been fiercely aware of the injustices which face those who struggle with pensions, food banks and finding decent accommodation but had been less understanding of the ones a little further up the scale. However, being a fair man, he quickly came to understand the problems of Tom's friends, who had found themselves victims of an unacknowledged type of discrimination. Once Sam learned how it might be landlords left clearing up the mess, feeling the stress, losing time and money to tenants (who may have wrecked their properties), and not always vice versa, deposit protection was added to his list of rules to rewrite. He realised the identity of the underdog was not always apparent and that true impartiality was essential in making all decisions.

Another of the first world problems which Tom and Sam had agreed to address, involved situations that many would find themselves in at some point in their lives. Sam had been talking about the first flat he had shared and the drama that ensued when he could not turn a tap off. Of course the situation had occurred late at night, when he and his flatmates had been drinking. None of them could find the stopcock for the water anywhere, so they had to maintain an all-night vigil to stop the bath overflowing, until they could contact the estate agent in the morning. Tom had responded with his own tales of the times he had gone to a house to repair the damage after a DIY enthusiast had put a nail through a pipe or blown the electric when trying to hang a picture.

They quickly made plans to bring into force an idea that had been on Tom's mind for a while. A very simple new regulation which would save a lot of time, hassle, accidents and, ultimately, lives. It was to become law that every new property: owned or rented, large or small; would come with a full architectural plan, which would have to be updated whenever alterations were made. So there would be no more attempting to knock down supporting walls or guessing where hidden wiring and pipes were most likely to be. No fallouts with helpful friends or lawsuits brought against inept handymen.

There almost seemed to have been some sort of conspiracy to make work that could easily have been avoided. Now more jobs would be created as workers were trained and recruited to detect exactly where the pipes, wires and other important features were situated in each older building, enabling retrospective plans to be produced for every property.

Cream Cakes

The Queen had gradually been stepping back from her many duties, even with regard to her involvement with all the initiatives undertaken by the New Ministers. Thrilled as she was by the apparent success of her grand plan, she was keenly aware that it would be counter-productive for her to continue to play a major role in mapping out the future. It was bittersweet to admit the time was coming when she would have no choice but to let go of the great responsibility which she had quietly resented, yet embraced, for so many years. Even she was not immortal and she was determined to do her damnedest to ensure the right people would be holding the reins once she was no longer around to do so.

Alison placed the Queen's favourite cake stand on the small table between them and the Queen helped herself to a chocolate eclair, poking gently at it with a pastry fork and giving Alison a questioning look.

'They are real cream, for now,' Alison smiled. 'I presume you've heard about Sal's plans?'

'I believe one of her assistants discovered a vegan patisserie, where "one can't tell the difference"?'

'That's right. Sal believes vegan cream cakes could be the key to changing the nation's eating habits. If all the 'naughty but nice' foods can be replicated in a more healthy and ethical way, it could be a big step towards changing diets and the environment and leading the way for other countries to do the same. At least, that's what Sal said.'

The Queen smiled with satisfaction and took a large bite of the eclair. She was Sal's greatest fan (and, obviously, the greatest fan of all her New Ministers) but she was of a generation that could only take so many changes in one lifetime. And vegan cream cakes could be one step too far for her. But Sal had been trying her best to radicalise the palace staff, in her own gentle way, and Alison did not think the Queen would see it as a sacking offence, after so many years loyal service, if she were to sneak a dairy-free selection on to the cake stand next time. After all, the Queen had not noticed the sugar bowl had been filled with xylitol for weeks now.

'On a slightly more serious note, I really must turn my attention to my final meetings with the Prime Minister, by which title he still appears to be referring to himself. The man really cannot seem to take a hint. And it's time to escape this good government/bad government system we seem to have acquired. Where some poor soul is, apparently, refused money by one department, offered solace by another and then forced to attend a tribunal, if they can maintain the strength to do so, all to obtain what they were entitled to in the first place.'

Alison's jaw dropped a little, 'Oh, you've heard about that?'

'I do keep my ear to the ground, you know.' Alison's eyebrow twitched, unwittingly, and the Queen continued, 'Well, yes, I have people keep an ear to the ground for me. And I am truly horrified at some of the things which I - you or they - hear. One of the proudest moments of my lifetime was observing the founding of the Welfare State and my dearest wish is to see it return to, and indeed surpass, its original aims. Even in our current climate there seems to be a prevailing attitude of "every man for himself". Particularly, I am sorry to say, amongst certain world leaders.

We must, of course, continue working with other nations towards equally sharing the burden of welcoming refugees who have no safe home to return to. However, there is little choice now but to prioritise looking after our current citizens and to aim for independence as far as possible, particularly from past allies whose values do not tally with those towards which we are striving....'

Noticing Alison's silence, the Queen centred herself a little and re-focussed from her unintended speech, '....sorry, was I doing it again?'

'Just a little, Your Maj.... just a little.' To avoid putting her foot in her mouth any further, Alison stuffed an eclair in quickly.

The Kindness Board

Sal sometimes felt overwhelmed by how much she had on her plate. If she was not explaining the moral issues around factory farming she was discussing her proposal to introduce the term 'hidden crimes', for the types of behaviour that can cause serious emotional distress which often goes unrecognised. She was very keen to see justice meted out, not only to those who committed the most obviously serious crimes, but the far more common types of everyday intimidation, harassment and worse, such as those described simply as domestic abuse, neighbour disputes, playground or workplace bullying. All of which have been known to end in suicide or murder. Sal was well aware the police had their wrists firmly cuffed by the current laws, being unable to act on their instincts 'until a crime has been committed', no matter how obviously distressing to the victim, if the issue is deemed to be a civil matter. She also knew the relevant laws would be changed as soon as Sam, Brett and their teams had everything in place to do so. They would be increasing the powers of organisations which sought to protect the vulnerable of any species, to ensure that suspected acts of cruelty or aggression would always be followed up. Sky had been enthusiastic about Sal's plans and they were well on their way to introducing the Kindness Board, which would initially support the victims of hidden crimes.

'Are you sure it doesn't sound too soft, for an undertaking like this?'

Sal, who had given too much thought to it already, put some of those thoughts into words, 'I've been wrestling with that but then, as we intend to completely turn the country around and make life all about everyone treating each other well, maybe a soft name isn't such a bad idea? If our new terms sound as official and negative as the old ones, that could make it easier for everything to stay the same. I don't want to waste time getting hung up on words and we haven't come up with a viable alternative, so maybe it's best to just go with it.'

'It's probably "meant to be" then.' Sky smiled, knowing how much time and effort Sal put into everything. Hopefully not too much for her own good. 'And they are going to oversee other things too.'

'Exactly. For a start, the Kindness Board will be the branch that arranges the annual checks for children. I'm glad we decided to organise them for a month or so before their birthdays - however we set them up, they'll probably still seem intimidating to some of the kids. And there's the issue of the parties - I'd love to see them open to everyone but it could be a massive undertaking.'

'Yeah, I know - I think she got a bit carried away at some point, but the Queen really intended to prioritise those who wouldn't normally get to celebrate and that'll probably apply to more adults than children. Hopefully we'll be able to organise annual checks for adults too, once we sort out the resources. I know it's an immense task but ultimately we should be seeking out anyone who's slipped through the net and not had the help they deserve in life. There are so many obscure issues that can screw someone up for good.'

'Not that we want to encourage the mentality which insists everyone is labelled and stuck in a box forever.'

'Especially as most people fit in several different boxes - it could get pretty messy. We just need to show everyone they're accepted and appreciated as individuals, that they don't have to take on any particular label or be attached to any specific group.'

'I'd like everyone to keep in mind the phrase "First Do No Harm", for this and, in fact, most of our undertakings. It seems to have been forgotten by some in the medical community, never mind anyone else.'

'And if we have to lead the way by rubbing people's noses in it about how everyone should start being nicer to each other, and all the other animals, then what the hell? Let's go for it! And to lighten things up a bit, let's start posting ads for chuckout day.'

'Good idea. But whatever term we use, some of our friends in the Old Media will probably dub it "Crap in the Attic" or something, so shall we preempt that by using a more "aspirational" tag?'

'You're right, I guess we should. There are politics even in secondhand goods. Here we have "charity" shops - because we're such a caring lot, I suppose. In the States they have "thrift" stores, because everything's about money, and in Oz they call them "op shops", because it's an opportunity to find things you like, wouldn't see elsewhere and can easily afford.'

'I like the sound of that - how about Opportunity Day? A day for some to take the opportunity to give away things they don't want, need or have no room for....'

'....and for others to find gifts they can't afford, or household goods they desperately need!'

'Absolutely!'

Sky went to high-five Sal, who hesitated, thought better of it, then stuck her palm in the air. Sky slapped it eagerly, happy to have cheered Sal up again.

Sky had also been thinking things through. 'The public halls can ask for donations for use of their facilities, small charities can set up their stalls and accept more goods on the day, individuals can bring in their own belongings and find suitable recipients. Others can find items for free, or pay what they can afford. It's all about goodwill, not cash. If the charities don't make much money, at least they'll get to tell people about their cause. Only the big ones can afford to advertise and they may not be the ones everybody really wants to leave their life savings to.'

'I hope this'll be the way to get around the old pride issue too. It's so hard not to have money to buy Christmas and birthday presents and a lot more people are in that situation now. I'd much rather someone gave me a thoughtful gift that was home-made or cheap or free than a thoughtless expensive one. It's time to stamp out the stigma of giving secondhand items, particularly when many of them have never even been used. So we can promote that and, fingers crossed, generate enough community feeling to bring everyone together, whether they're giving away or choosing items.

Maybe we need to open the doors to those without any cash, before others come in? We don't want any nasty "bidding wars".

'Good idea - and I suppose we'll need to have a limit on the amount of items anyone can pick up, in case any traders sneak in or anything, but we can sort out the details later, with a few of the others.' Sky still found it hard to acknowledge they each had a team of assistants, but she had to admit they came in handy. 'For now, let's get the ball rolling - I'll give the info to Andrina and she can put it out on all the media sites, so the public are prepared to do their decluttering or make their wanted lists.'

'Speaking of "getting the ball rolling", where are we with the new lottery?'

'I'm glad you asked. "We" have it all in hand,' Sky smiled. 'At least, I do. You know Maj is funding the initial set up; it's another way she wants to repay the folk who have supported her for so many years. And as it was, sort of, my idea, and I'm the "People's Minister", I was keen to oversee it. The prize money has got so ridiculous in most lotteries and it's daft for one winner to receive 50 million or so, when 50 people could win a million and set themselves up for life. Or loads more people could probably manage that with a quarter of a million or a hundred thousand or whatever. This is going to be totally different to the current lotteries and, I have to say, I'm quite proud of that.'

Being proud was not a regular occurrence for Sky, who was always quick with a self-deprecating quip, so the importance of the project was not lost on Sal. 'And so you should be, it's such a great idea to have a lottery that excludes those who don't need to win one!'

Sky grimaced a little, 'I'd rather refer to it as "one ticket, one person, one pound". That's why we're planning to call it The People's Pound, as a pledge the price will never go up. We're still working out the finer points of how to ensure those with loads of money can't enter, and that nobody is able to purchase more than one ticket for each lottery, but we'll get there. Even if it's just by bringing out everyone's better nature so they won't dream of cheating.'

'Won't we be seen as discriminating against those who've worked their way up from nothing and feel they also have the right to a bit more?'

'I suppose we will. But we'll also be discriminating against them by enforcing early retirement for being successful. Maybe we can't make everyone happy, even if we want to. The thing is, I believe everyone we're working with genuinely wants to make ours a fairer society and we can't afford to get side-tracked from making that a reality, now we're all in survival mode. In the past we haven't done too badly for our official happiness ratings but, when you dig deeper, it always seems to be countries which aren't financially wealthy, where the inhabitants are really happiest. Not that we want to see everyone starving, in rags....'

'We don't want to see anybody starving or in rags. Just less people paying through the nose for tiny, pretentious meals or parading around in ridiculous designer wear, whilst others are starving and in rags,' Sal triumphantly finished Sky's sentence.

Farcical Ideas

As the United Kingdom and it's citizens gradually changed for the better, some notable exceptions clung to their domain in the private clubs of the capital.

'One for the road?' Bertie's colleague returned, with drinks in hand.

'Don't mind if I do. Have you seen their latest farcical idea?' Bertie pushed his favourite newspaper across the old oak table, bitterly aware that the news in it was no longer expressed in the way he preferred. Not much was anymore, thanks to these incorrigible upstarts who had been enabled to take over his country - by the Queen, no less. He tutted into his malt and waited for the appropriate reaction.

'They can't possibly keep it up for too much longer. The whole world is running out of money and....'

'Not my world, old boy....' Bertie had barely got the words out before laughing uproariously at his own hilarity, accompanied a little less enthusiastically by his companion. Their enjoyment waned suddenly, as Bertie's face turned puce, his eyes startled and the laughter turned to full-on choking. For the briefest moment he could have sworn his subordinate paused before calling for help.

Following a rather impressive demonstration of the Heimlich manoeuvre by the barman, Bertie was soon able to recover his composure, somewhat aided by having already consumed half a tank of whisky. His companion, who had been relieved at the thought of escaping due to the emergency, felt compelled to stay and listen to further ramblings. He actually quite enjoyed some of the ideas the incumbent government had come up with. What was it his wife had called them? A breath of fresh air? If only he got to see her more often and could afford himself the same freedom of thought.

'They're obsessed with these DNA tests now, d'ya see?' Bertie waved his arm in the rough direction of the newspaper and continued, without waiting for a response. 'I say bring 'em on. I really do. Let's repatriate all the bloody Vikings back to Denmark, the frogs back to France and all the coloured fellows to wherever it is they come from.... bloody good idea, I say.'

As Bertie leant forward clumsily for another swig of his drink, his companion made a sudden decision and took the chance to escape. He had wasted quite enough time on the obsequious banter required by his role, and not spent at home in the evenings with his lovely black bride. On his way out he passed on the tip Bertie had given him for the barman, with an embarrassed nod towards his erstwhile colleague and drinking companion.

Smiling warmly back, the barman politely kept his hand closed until the man had left the room. Glancing over at Bertie, he opened his palm and shook his head. A tenner? he thought, for saving his life?

A moment later he smiled at the thought that he could probably have got a lot more for finishing him off. He was not really meant to whistle at work but the few remaining customers were all at least three sheets to the wind and it was a special moment for him. Maybe he had a new career ahead - as a paramedic. Or a hitman.

Tea and Biscuits

James had left it a few days to speak to Laura, knowing she may have questions about their most recent session with George. He had some answers but was not sure which ones he should be giving her. As neither of them had their own office, it was important for James to find a room where their conversation would not be overheard. Although it was some time since anyone had regarded him as merely a regular member of staff, he was still entitled to use the staff tea rooms and decided it might be best to hold their meeting in a more casual atmosphere than that which prevailed upstairs. Being outside the regular staff break times, he felt confident they would not be disturbed and he showed Laura into the bright, functional sitting room.

James had even thought to collect a tray of tea and biscuits on his way, but this did nothing to set Laura's mind at rest and he could sense her anxiety. 'I expect you may have some questions about our meeting with George the other day?' he said, in an attempt to relax her. This did quite the opposite.

'I'm so sorry I was late. It's really important to me to do a good job in helping George tell his story. And I was so pleased that you and Alison trusted me to be a part of this, I really appreciate it.'

'It's fine, you haven't done anything wrong. I can see you've formed a bond with George and I can tell he's already grown fond of you. If we didn't cover what you were expecting to discuss, that was down to other matters which arose before you arrived.' Seeing Laura's remorseful look waver and then reappear, James felt he should proceed with caution. 'It turned out George and I were already - acquainted, let's say. It was a bit of a shock to him and

195

he was already feeling a little emotional, so I decided it was best to draw the session to a close. I'm sorry if you got the impression that you were at fault in any way.'

Laura immediately appeared calmer and James realised he could barely remember the days when he was a new employee at the palace. He did, however, recall how afraid he had been of putting a foot wrong and losing the opportunity of a lifetime. Generally, it had suited James's role to say little and show little, in terms of emotion. He was one of the last at the palace to realise feelings were now acceptable, perhaps even from someone who had spent a lifetime guarding the Queen and protecting her interests. He smiled. He thought he should check how much new information Laura might be ready to hear. 'Through something George mentioned, I realised we had come into contact many years ago, as part of my duties in protecting the Queen. The circumstances were rather distressing for George, so he did not wish to continue our conversation that day. Sometimes it's most important to know when to hold back, so I acknowledged his wishes.'

'I see. Thank you for telling me. I had been a bit worried that I'd done something to upset him - I'm glad that wasn't the case. Maybe it's different when you're older but I've always wanted to know the truth straightaway. Whatever it is.'

James did not know who had put those words into Laura's mouth, but they made his mind up for him. 'Do you have any interest in genealogy yourself, Laura? Apart from your involvement with the tv project, in your role here?'

Suddenly it all came out. Laura told him she had not known her birth family and had spent many years trying to find them, with hardly any clues to go on. She had tried to put it behind her, feeling there was little chance of her finding any information now. She never discussed it because she could not bear people's pity. And what was the point? It was hardly likely some stranger would come up to her at a bus stop and turn out to be her long lost cousin or something.

On the verge of tears, Laura suddenly felt foolish. She hardly knew James and she had just told him all this stuff she had been keeping to herself for ever. She hated it when that happened. It had to come out somewhere and the perils of having no family meant it could never come out to the right people.

Whilst she was speaking, James had quietly produced a sheet of paper and placed it on the table in front of him. His eyes were serious, concerned and kind when she raised hers to meet his, with a questioning look.

'Remember when you applied to work, indirectly, for the Queen - you agreed to have your own DNA results examined privately, before they were delivered to you? It's a formality for all new staff these days, in case of any sensitive issues which might possibly arise....'

Laura looked confused for a moment. She had been so eager to get the job she would have considered wrestling a bear or diving into a bucket of jelly if they had asked her to, so the quick spit into a tube and the accompanying paperwork had seemed a mere formality.

James decided to take her silence as a yes, to avoid further delay. He pushed the paper towards her, explaining that it was just a brief extract from the full DNA results, which would be made available to her shortly. In fact, apart from Laura's own details, the rest of the sections on the chart were blank except for one other person's name. It was George.

'Oh my god, he's my grandad! How can that be?'

James thought she was handling it fairly well, all things considered, until Laura suddenly burst into tears and asked him, in a barely audible voice, 'Are you my dad?'

Spreading the Love

Sam had been looking out for Andrina again. He was pleased to be back in a position where he could help strangers, colleagues, and new friends (which was how he had come to view the other ministers, some of their assistants, some of the palace staff and even, he could never admit to his old Leftie mates, a few members of the Royal Family).

It was a measure of the mutual regard felt by the ministers that they were willing to pass on some of their pet projects for input by the others. Sam had become particularly close to Sky, as he had known he would, and was not surprised when she agreed to request Andrina's help with the 'I am Loved' project. In her usual way, Sky had tried to deny the credit for her idea, stating that she had seen a similar phrase used previously, whilst simultaneously demonstrating why it would be more useful to change the wording from "You are Loved".

'It's obvious, isn't it? Say you give me a t-shirt, with "You are Loved" printed on it, then the gesture really misses the point. Phrased that way, it's more about the giver feeling they have expressed a caring sentiment than making the receiver happy every time they wear it. When I get it out of the cupboard and put it on, I'm now reading a message that is no longer meant for me....' Sky did not know if she was on a different wavelength or just a bit mad, but things which seemed clear to her sometimes seemed to take a lot of explaining to others, '....but all the people who walk past me and see the words will, like me, feel so much better if they read to themselves, "I am Loved".'

Sky was creative and artistic and all those things, but what she really loved was coming up with ideas. So it made sense to pass them on to someone who really enjoyed the nitty gritty of making things happen. Like Andrina. Having overcome the first obstacle, of the explanation above, Sky listed numerous 'I am Loved' objects and projects which she envisaged, with plenty of accompanying plans. In a way it seemed silly to her but Sky was greatly affected by her surroundings; what she heard, saw and read. She felt others must be the same, whether they were aware of it or not. And she was sure the subliminal message of being surrounded by t-shirts, mugs, banners and posters for positive events, all with the message 'I am Loved', was bound to improve the general mood of the nation. To ensure it was easy to 'spread the word' (in a totally non-religious way), everything was to be available at cost price, whilst providing work experience, plus making use of warehouses and factories that had fallen into disuse in the latest recession. Another scheme to rejuvenate and regenerate. All that was left to be done was to fine tune the details and work out the logistics. Sky could not believe how Andrina almost rubbed her hands together at the prospect, but it made them both happy. Now Sky could move on to new ideas and avoid taking too much credit, again.

A Very Good Idea

The healthy diet had been paying dividends at Tom's house. Katie and Billy, and even their mother, had finally bought into the new lifestyle. It had been quite unnerving at first, when Jess started greeting Tom with a kiss and a 'rosemary infusion' as he walked in the door. Now he was learning to love it, and her, all over again. It seemed like coming home to a new family.

Instead of the constant fighting and screaming from the kids upstairs, all Tom heard was the gentle tapping of the keyboard, as Katie researched a new project to impress him with. Or the sound of Billy beating the hell out of his drums. It was not perfect, but it was a good start.

Whenever Tom's schedule allowed, they enjoyed their family dinners together. Jess and Billy had been working on their cooking skills, while Katie clearly had ambitions to take over her dad's business empire, as she liked to call it. Being the big sister, she also did her best to include Billy. Perhaps she would let him be a junior partner someday.

'Daddeee,' ventured Katie (in that long drawn out "I'll get your attention if it kills me" kind of way kids have), 'we've got a special idea for you....' Billy's ears pricked up - he was excited to hear about their new idea, for the first time. Katie continued, 'well, Daddy, you know how you're always telling us we need to care about people who don't have nice homes, like we do....'

Tom felt a little bit guilty. Was he always telling them that? Probably. His mum had always told him to 'think of all the starving children in Africa', if he attempted to leave the tiniest bit of food. Now he was getting the tiniest little bit of pleasure out of telling her why he should not have been eating all those unhealthy foods in the first place. He turned his full attention to Katie and waited for another imaginative little plan involving unicorns and mermaids delivering food parcels, or some such fantasy.

'....so, I decided to go and see Mr.Green and I went along at break time and I knocked on his door and he said "come in" and I told him my idea and he said he liked it very much and he said, with a name like his, he really should support "eco-friendly" ideas, so he wants to meet you.'

The last part particularly grabbed Tom's attention and he exchanged a nervous look with Jess, who shrugged her shoulders. 'Ohhh Kayyy,' Tom responded (in that long drawn out way parents have when they're thinking, "What the hell have you got me into?"), 'what exactly is your idea, Sweetie?'

Katie became petulant, curled her bottom lip and adopted a condescending air, 'I've told you not to call me that anymore, Daddy. If I'm not allowed to eat sweeties, I don't want you to call me that.'

Jess's days of predicting a riot were not yet firmly behind her, so she quickly offered placation in the form of, 'maybe you can have them on special occasions....'

Like when you want to rot your teeth and end up with lots of expensive dental work, was what Tom wanted to say. Instead, he gave Jess a slight glare and tried a different approach, 'What did Mr.Green particularly like about your idea?'

'Weeeeellllllllll.... Mr.Green thinks it will be very helpful and it will be good for the pupils and the parents and the teachers and everybody in the area.'

Bloody hell, what was she proposing? Was she going to steal his building plans for that new eco-estate and employ her schoolmates as child labour? To adopt some sort of mini Robin Hood style persona and have them all stealing from the rich and giving to the poor?

Katie was looking very pleased with herself, not just because of the brilliant plan which Mr.Green was such a fan of, but also because her family clearly had no idea what she was talking about. It might be fun to drag it out a bit longer but she did not know if Mummy's temper really had gone away for good. With a sigh that clearly showed she would have to explain things very simply to the plebs, Katie relented. A nod of encouragement from Tom and she continued, 'You know how Billy cried when you told him that old man has to sleep in the shop doorway because he hasn't got a house?'

'Didn't,' said Billy, 'didn't cry.'

'It's ok,' Jess responded quickly, 'it's ok to cry if you feel sad for someone.'

'All right. Did cry. My idea.'

It was looking like a long evening and Tom was starting to wilt, 'What is your idea then, Billy?'

'What Katie's going to say....'

Katie ignored Billy's cunning hijack attempt and finally explained, 'I told Mr.Green it's not fair that people have to sleep in the dark and the cold and the rain when we have a big school that's empty at night. And it has showers and toilets and kitchens and all those things that people have in their own houses. And Mr.Green looked at me for a while, then he got up and looked out of the window for a while, then the bell went and I was going to go. But Mr.Green told me it was ok, I wouldn't be in trouble for being late back to class. Because I had come up with a VERY GOOD IDEA!!'

Katie's triumphance knew no bounds and Tom saw he would need to tread carefully. 'Mr.Green's right. It's a very good idea. Well done.' He looked at Billy's expectant face. 'Both of you. Just one small point.... why does Mr.Green want to see me?'

'Because I told him you're an expert on green things and buildings and all that. Or maybe just so you can talk to him about my VERY GOOD IDEA.'

Fortunately, in a call to the school next morning, Mr.Green, the Headteacher, confirmed his enthusiasm for Katie's idea, referring to her as a very bright and caring student. More fortunately, he did not seem to require much support from Tom at all. Mr.Green had already formulated a plan whereby he could invite the local homeless population to sleep in the school hall overnight, then shower (if they so wished) and leave, in time for the regular cleaners to come in. He did not wish to cast any aspersions but felt compelled to mention that the areas the overnight visitors would have access to were all easy to clean and disinfect.

Tom could not help feeling proud of his little 'chip off the block'. At this rate, those without homes would have quite a task choosing which offer to take up for the night. More schools and public buildings were bound to follow suit and he could devote his time to all the other pressing concerns on his agenda.

Silent Rant

When Sam was not putting in place distractions to prevent Andrina from going under, due to the strain of the issues she was dealing with, he was actually having a pretty hard time himself. In wording documents he knew were going to seriously anger some major players, he could not help reflecting on how easy it could be to make him disappear. He still felt only little Boris would really miss him, when he found himself alone in the flat with an empty water bowl.

Pushing those thoughts aside, Sam continued his efforts to protect the public from techrimination, his private name for what he saw as another insidious form of control by those who held the real power and, thus, the ability to divide the population. Some years ago there had been an outcry about the intended introduction of identity cards but there was no need for them now that virtually everyone disclosed all their most personal details, willingly, online. It was usually a case of ignorance is bliss, so keen were the public to join the latest social media platform that they did not generally attempt to wade through even the first page of a novella length document in which privacy policies or terms and conditions were cloaked in legalese. The vast majority of the population had been duped into relinquishing their privacy in exchange for the chance to view interminable videos of cats doing stupid things, humans doing stupider things and huge amounts of programmes that were ten times as rubbish as when there were only four tv channels to choose from. In those good old days the country bonded over who had shot who in last night's soap or by exchanging punchlines from their favourite comedy show.

Sam was doing it again. Silently ranting to himself, in his thoughts, instead of churning out more of the sort of paperwork he had always abhorred. Sometimes changing the world could be a real pain in the arse.

The little things were often the last straw, like being able to buy cheaper bus tickets with a smartphone and viewed with mistrust if you did not use social media. But what really annoyed Sam, apart from all the other things that really annoyed him, was when government departments did sneaky things like providing drivers' details to the dodgy parking firms, who then harassed them mercilessly. Those departments were meant to serve the people, not betray them. He had often been told he was like a dog with a bone when something annoyed him, but he knew the little things could have a real impact on lives and he was dealing with the bigger things too. Sam did not even have a car, but he cared about those who did. And everyone in general. Which made it ironic that he could be about to annoy millions of people whom he was aiming to help.

The ED card was not an ID card, but it could appear rather similar. Along with the other ministers, Sam was really torn about the issue. On the one hand, freedom and privacy were of paramount importance to all of them. On the other hand, if everyone were to carry a card containing their essential details it would, at the very least, increase the level of organ donations and enable those who lived a more itinerant lifestyle to prove their identity, right to benefits and other assistance. The current feeling was that it might be best to start by offering the cards to everyone on a non-compulsory basis, with no penalties for those who chose not to carry one. Obviously there would be extremely strict rules to govern who was permitted to access the information contained on the cards and for precisely what reasons. In time, if the system proved effective, it was hoped many more would be happy to carry the cards.

With the anticipated reduction in the use of social media and renewed preference for personal contact, changes were bound to happen. Sam would not exactly call himself a luddite but he would be quite happy to see a lot of things return to how they had been in the past.

The Big Change

Meanwhile, the Queen was forging ahead with her plans to turn the country on its head. She could not defer any longer, the time had arrived and there was the knock on the door, which she had been dreading. Alison adopted a more stiff and formal air than usual, as she ushered the Prime Minister into the room. The momentousness of the occasion was not lost on her and she retreated silently. The Prime Minister paid her little attention anyway. He would have liked to pay the Queen as little attention, had she not been dangling his future in her hands.

'Mr. Prime Minister, I do hope you will join me in a cup of tea?'

Something about her manner led the PM to believe he was already in enough hot water, but he summoned up his sweetest (not very sweet) smile and agreed.

It turned out there was little left for either of them to say. The perfunctory discussions on matters of state and the contents of the red boxes, which had held their weekly meetings together until The Big Change, were now merely another routine which had been confined to the past.

The Queen could not believe how easy it turned out to be: telling the Prime Minister that his services, and those of his colleagues, were no longer required. Although it had been merely a formality, so far as she was concerned, the Queen was pleased the Prime Minister created far less of a stink about it than she had expected. She was gratified to hear that he wished her well with her plans, appeared to have now accepted the changes and had no ill feeling towards her. Much as this humility seemed totally out of character for him, the Queen decided to ignore her instincts and take the Prime Minister at his word. How much trouble could he possibly cause, after being effectively fired by the monarch?

There were decisions to be made on whether the New Ministers might prefer to work from the Downing Street offices, assuming there would not be some sort of lock-in staged by the more truculent members of the former government. But the Queen enjoyed having the New Ministers close at hand, in the palace, and had recently amused herself by dreaming up alternative uses for No.10. Perhaps a rehab unit, a sex addiction clinic or something similarly ironic. Jobcentre was her favourite.

Another necessary duty for the Queen was to make a formal statement to the media. These days such duties were far less onerous, since she realised she had the right to dictate the terms of her own life. This, she reasoned, would again be leading by example. If, perhaps on a subconscious level, ordinary citizens previously had an inkling that even the Queen was not the one who held ultimate power over the nation, or her own life, surely that would have increased their uneasiness with regard to the way things had been heading?

It was a pleasure to leave the arrangement of her broadcast announcements to Andrina and James, though the Queen now insisted on having the final say over any words she would speak in public. Having been trained to show little emotion, whether congratulating someone on a fantastic achievement or offering sympathy to those affected by a major disaster, the Queen secretly fretted that her monotone style may come across as a little boring. Not that anyone had ever suggested that, obviously. All the same, she still intended to keep her words as brief as possible, as she took her seat in the comfy chair in her private office.

'Good evening. As you will now be aware, the former government are in the process of completing any necessary tasks prior to vacating their roles, and I would like to thank them, once again, for their service to the country.

It had been my intention to hold an election, using the generally preferred system of proportional representation, to choose their successors. However, in the spirit now prevailing, and from your communications with our New Ministers and myself, it seems you share my wish to avoid further endless campaigns, meetings, debates and enquiries, in favour of taking action and saving our valuable funds for more urgent matters. Indeed, many of you have made your feelings particularly clear on the prospect of being....' The Queen cleared her throat and tried, unsuccessfully, to stifle a slight smile, whilst quoting directly from a correspondent, "repeatedly subjected to the same breed of career politicians relentlessly evading the same questions, in slightly different ways, until all our resources have been used up by ridiculous political games".

I would like to take this opportunity to apologise for any actions taken, in your name or mine, with which you did not agree. Henceforth, the primary method by which all major decisions are to be made will be through regular voting by the electorate. It will be appreciated if you are able to submit your votes online, but other methods will always be available for those who are not able to participate in this way. As with all businesses, official organisations and bodies of all sorts, the voting system will be stringently monitored by groups of independent individuals who have consistently proved to be beyond reproach. Rest assured there will be no exceptions made for those attempting to flout any law at any level.

As we work to improve life in the United Kingdom, it will clearly be of benefit for us to secure trade agreements and mutually supportive relationships with only those countries which share our principles regarding human rights, animal rights, environmental policies and disarmament. For these are the issues which you, as a nation, have declared your priorities. Along with health, happiness, personal safety and everything which brings these about. And I am pleased to agree with you.

For far too long, as I now understand, those with less than scrupulous ideals have tended to hold the power, in many arenas. Our aim is to turn things around and to value persons with the ethics needed to run a truly successful humanitarian society. Fortuitously, because such individuals find their rewards through the satisfaction of improving life for others, not only do we envisage it to be a happier society but far more cost effective to maintain. On a final note, please remember that this is your country and every one of you is valued here. We are drawing a line under the past and the United Kingdom is now in the hands of the people, which is as it should be. We are all just people, after all....'

'Hell's bloody teeth,' choked Bertie Barrington-Smythe as he watched the end of the Queen's announcement on the television at his club. When Bertie's over-excitement again progressed in a rather worrying manner, the barman averted his eyes and went off to find some more glasses to polish. His lone customer slid gently under the table; the only sound in the empty bar, his choking fading to a whisper.

Inventions

It was almost time to record the first of Tom's ethical invention showcases and he still had not managed to come up with a title for the programme. Or, to be more precise, he had experienced several moments of great excitement, during the past couple of months, when he had thought of a perfectly witty and descriptive moniker, and held his breath as he clicked to check for its current existence online, only to find the name already being used by a Scandinavian eco-group, a small electrical goods retailer in a remote Canadian outback town and/or a happy-clappy religious group in the US. He was unsure whether checking things online was a sensible idea anyway, considering anyone might be monitoring his search, ready to whip up a blueprint of one of his breakthrough inventions and patent it instantly.

Tom was no stranger to the camera by now, having filmed various infomercials on all sorts of worthy subjects since his success with the original Just One More Thing ad. Although the shock of seeing the Queen behind the counter at a tip, handling real cash, undoubtedly commanded most of the interest, Tom was willing to accept his share of the credit. It had been his idea, after all....

The highlights of the show were to be extra-strong solar panels, built to withstand all the stresses and demands of being attached to fast-moving transport and subject to all weathers. Much energy had been devoted to publicising electric cars, which had turned out not to be the panacea envisaged, and now Tom believed it was time to look at more viable alternatives. When cars were first invented, steam was the preferred choice of power and it was looking as though there was a chance of it making a comeback in a future episode, perhaps in conjunction with the solar panels. Wind and water were likely to be following close behind. It seemed everyone had a prototype in them these days.

There were to be a couple of shorter segments, on subjects which would start by raising a smile then arousing further interest in those who were looking for just such a device, whether they had realised it previously or not. The term seemed to have transmogrified in the current millennium and Tom was keen to remind the public that not everything was about technology. Unfortunately for his plan the first gizmo was actually related to technology, being a Laptop Tent. A member of the public had sent in the rough drawing, which seemed to be functionally based on the hood of a pram, after seeing requests for inventions on the New Media channels. It had been sitting in her drawer for years, perhaps since the introduction of the first laptop, judging by the condition of the piece of paper. Appearing a little pointless and frivolous at first, viewers were likely to rethink their judgment the next time they were blinded by the reflection as the light caught their screen on a sunny afternoon. No family outing was complete these days without an attendant parent who was multi-tasking extra office work, alongside a relaxing picnic with the kids.

Bunny shoes would probably catch on just because of the name, the cute little 'black bunny' logo and their ability to be changed to a sandal, or through a myriad of colours, patterns and styles, on the same, long-lasting, thick, comfy soles. Available for men, women and children, the real beauty of the shoes was that they were designed to prevent the formation of bunions and other foot abnormalities and to prevent further decline in existing conditions. As with many medical afflictions, historically there had been a great deal of money at stake, should a real solution be found to replace all the lucrative gadgets and operations that enabled people to live with their particular deformity a little more comfortably. Now that manufacturing and healthcare were in a period of enforced change, with resources and available funds greatly reduced, items such as these shoes would be sold at subsidised prices and produced solely in ethical materials. With the new attitude that had been ushered in, by the bigger change which had hit the world like a meteor, prior to the Big Change in government, the female ministers hoped Bunnies would become the new word in fashion and high heels would be gone forever (unless you really were particularly short).

With so many people now living in isolation, enforced or otherwise, it was also time to look at the personal and societal savings to be made by addressing the needs of those living alone. Tom had learnt, from his single friends, about the mixture of embarrassed self-consciousness and guilt they suffered when opening their regular oven to cook one baked potato. How, despite flats and houses having shrunk in direct proportion to rents increasing, it was nigh impossible to find furniture and appliances small enough to squeeze into some of them. Serendipitously, he had already received designs for Cosy Corner sofas, which would actually fit through the doorway of a modern house, as well as into the corner of the living room. Only viewers who had moved into a bijou residence would understand the frustration of being subsequently unable to furnish it stylishly, what with the fashion for giant modular seating arrangements and massive tellys. Tom did not want the viewers to lose interest, so he hoped he had sufficiently rammed home his point about how everything mentioned on the show would be manufactured from guilt-free materials and available at affordable prices. Obviously with a few exceptions, such as the solar powered luxury jets which had featured earlier.

Unsurprisingly, Tom was a great proponent of the Tiny House Movement and looked forward to working with the novices who were likely to respond to his airing of the subject in a later episode. However, not wanting to appear 'size-ist', one future show would be featuring a budget 360 degree screen which could immerse a profoundly disabled, depressed or comatose individual in a positive world of light, colour, images and music, all chosen to be the most specifically beneficial to the person being treated. Another would feature a new range of computers and phones aimed specifically at technophobes, those with conditions that involved a short attention span or who just suffered from a lack of patience. These items would be simplified as much as possible and would avoid annoying features such as underlining a misspelt word before one has the chance to correct it. Also some of those (less than helpful) 'Help' suggestions, such as when you are feverishly searching for a confidential folder and 'Do you mean "share with everyone"?' pops up.

Tax benefits would be involved in producing essential ethical items, so there would be no shortage of backers ready, willing and able to make the new designs and inventions a reality, now that it had been demonstrated how fast a factory could be converted to a totally different use when necessary. Also with regard to manufacturing, Tom would be starting a push for built-in obsolescence to be outlawed in all goods. From pens that cannot be refilled to shavers you cannot buy spare blades for, right up to vehicles which have to be scrapped because parts are priced unrealistically or no longer available. He could see this was another huge market waiting to be filled, by those with the ability to make and supply the necessary replacement items. Indeed the time was ripe for people who were good at reinventing the wheel.

Film Premiere

In a largely overlooked corner of the palace, a quiet room occasionally functions as a small cinema. With the red velvet seating and gold paintwork generally admired by theatre outfitters, plus complementary drapes, handwoven carpeting and ornate light fittings, it was the ideal venue for James to hold the first trial screening of his personal contribution to Who Do I Think I Am?

A nervous air filled the room as the small and exclusive group took their seats in the semi-dark. If they had been expecting some sort of introduction they had little time to think about it, as the title came up almost as soon as bottoms hit seats. The slight rush to get sorted and settled, whilst simultaneously paying attention to the start of the programme, served well in drawing them all in, as George's face appeared on screen. In the darkness, Laura could not help smiling as she cast a surreptitious look at George. Her grandad. She had not told him yet.

James maintained his usual public persona; quiet, reliable, unreadable. Especially in the dark. Inside he was a little less relaxed. He had discovered enough about George to believe that another shock or two, in a life full of drama, would not be enough to ruffle the old chap, never mind finish him off. And, apart from a little understandable emotion at first, Laura had been happy to accept the news James had shared with her. So, no worries on either count. He relaxed and watched the screening, along with the others.

Whether heard for the first, second, or third time, it really was an amazing tale of triumph against the odds. Only George fidgeted during the screening and only George seemed impatient as the screen went dark and the lights came up. He directed a look of confusion, and slight annoyance, at James. George seemed to be expecting more. Perhaps a fully polished tv production, neatly wrapped up and ready for the public eye. 'Where's the ending?' he asked. With only a moment to take in the middle-aged man and woman sitting in seats further back, George heard James reply,

'It's right here. In this room. It's all up to you now.' His eyes were smiling and his face sincere, as James nodded to the small gathering and walked to the door. He paused and glanced back. He had wondered if he should say more but he had made his plan and he would stick to it. The others did not look at him as he left the room.

One of Them

Sal, Sam and Brett were in the middle of a somewhat heated discussion on the subject of responsibility. Fortunately, all the heat was flowing in the same direction: from them to the ex-government, as the New Ministers now liked to refer to the architects of their misfortune.

'I'm doing my best, I truly am,' lamented Brett, wearily.

'I know mate, we all are.'

'Sometimes I feel sorry for the old lot....' Sal could not always stop herself empathising with even the most undeserving cases.

Once again, Sam was quick to leap to their attack, 'Oh come on, it's their fault we're all so damn busy. I haven't had quality time to spend with Boris for days and I swear he's learnt how to work the tv control - last time I managed to get home for a few minutes I'm sure I heard the Gogglebox theme tune as I walked in.'

Brett looked confused and Sal just said, 'his dog,' which did not really help. They were all overtired, the best fuel for misunderstanding. 'All I meant was I had no idea how many different issues are involved in every aspect of running the country. And I bet most people think it's far more straightforward than it actually is.'

'Well that's the point, it could be straightforward if all the previous ministers had been doing their jobs responsibly.' Sam turned to Brett, 'Don't worry, you're doing great - you're one of us now....' Brett started to smile and Sam spoiled it by adding, 'not one of them.' Leaving all sorts of outdated questions around political correctness unanswered. He actually meant 'politicians'. Funny how none of the New Ministers saw themselves in that way.

'So how many billions are we pledging to spend on the NHS again this week?' asked Sal, with a snigger.

'We can drop a few zeros off now you keep encouraging the public to self-diagnose and self-medicate,' suggested Sam.

Sal paused, unsure whether she was meant to laugh or protest, so she took her usual route of defend first and think later, retorting, 'Well who knows your body or mind better than you do?' Silently she reflected on how long it had been since anyone had known her body, and actually she was still trying to understand her own mind. Still, her ideas and initiatives seemed to be encouraging people to take better care of themselves, plus saving money and time for frontline medical personnel, so she was doing ok. They all were.

Brett decided it was safest to reply to Sal's previous quip, by agreeing the virus seemed to have been treated as a licence to print money. He did not elaborate by telling the others he regarded it more as an insidiously creeping tide, nor voicing his real fear; that many seemed to have forgotten the thing about tides is they keep returning, relentlessly.

Happy Soap

Andrina had not loosened her grip on the most serious issues, but had listened to the concerns of her colleagues and managed to introduce a little more balance into her life. As Sam had reasoned, she would not be much use to anyone if she were locked away in a straitjacket. Andrina could not help smiling a little as she remembered how she had been quite startled by Sam's manner of speech when she had first known him, only a few months ago. Much as he would hate to hear the word used to describe him, Andrina now thought of him as actually quite sweet. He had even invited her to a special show which was being put on by a youth centre he once worked at. 'Just as friends, of course,' he had been careful to add.

For as long as she could remember, people had complained about how there was too much misery on the telly, so Andrina was delighted to have the opportunity to commission the first 'happy soap'. The breakthrough idea was to base storylines around how well people could behave, rather than writing characters to reflect the lowest common denominator. So instead of having partners cheating on each other, alternately, every month, troubled mystery relations turning up out of the blue or whodunnit murders at the corner shop, everybody would get on swimmingly. It might be boring as hell to start with but it would be great for the mood of the country, once everyone got used to watching things that made them feel better. Instead of aiming programmes at those who really had better things to do and loved ones they could be spending quality time with, it would be kinder to think primarily of those who were unable to go out, perhaps because of social anxiety, past events or current incapacity.

The weird xmas tradition of screening the biggest disasters or most upsetting breakups of popular couples was to be knocked on the head. Did tv executives really know their audience so little? Of course the viewing figures were always high for the miserable xmas episodes, because the on-screen heartbreaks meant little to those who were enjoying a happy day with their family. For those whose only family, and perhaps their only contact with the outside world, were their favourite onscreen characters; the writers, directors and producers were unwittingly compounding the depression of a particularly lonely time. So, in future, the regular plot lines might run something like this:

As little old Mrs.Nexdoor was approached by a group of surly young men on the gloomy street corner there would be no need for alarm. Obviously they were about to break into smiles and offer to carry her shopping, before walking her dog and cleaning her house.

Grim and brooding Mickey Thugboy, just released from prison, would be seen to raise his hand to his girlfriend, who momentarily appeared to cower in fear. Before looking up at him adoringly, as he bravely brushed away the wasp that had been about to sting her. They would then settle down on the sofa with tea and biscuits, to discuss how he was a new man since taking his sociology degree in the Scrubs.

Whilst all in favour of dropping the blanket tv licence, Andrina was toying with introducing what she thought of as a 'licence for violence'. Although she would be happiest with a complete ban on any programme that hinted at intentionally causing harm of any sort, to anyone or anything at anytime, she had to acknowledge that large tracts of the population were currently more in alignment with Uncle Anay's thinking than her own. Still, instead of charging decent people to watch dated comedies and gameshows on mainstream channels, she considered it would be far more reasonable to levy a steep new tax on those who liked to enjoy, for instance, grown men beating the crap out of each other. If they were prepared to pay stupid amounts to cable companies for that dubious privilege then they should be happy to pay a further amount to her colleagues, perhaps to spend on dissuading young people from taking up occupations that were likely to cause them brain damage or early death.

Sky's News

Sky and Sal had continued to meet regularly, due to the fact they worked well together, supported each other and were growing closer as friends. But still there was a relative distance between them. Today's conversation had run the usual gamut; across health, wealth, ethics, environment and improving society in general. It was when Sky became particularly vociferous about her feelings regarding victimisation and violence, that Sal was able to infer more than had, perhaps, been intended. After that the floodgates seemed to open of their own accord. Sky was speaking so fast, and so urgently, that Sal was finding it hard to follow. There was something about a man and a baby and some sort of shock and how it was all too much to take in and she was sorry but she had to go....

The door swung, then thudded shut, as Sky went.

Sky hurtled down the corridor, lost in the strange and unexpected conversations of the past couple of days. How had she managed to keep herself together? Why had not she just escaped somewhere, like she used to when things overwhelmed her? There were so many questions that needed to be answered and so much explaining to do. If he was here, at this time of day, he would probably be alone. God, he'd better be, this was not the sort of conversation where an audience would be welcome.

Sky reached the last door, hesitated, then knocked and went in. She could tell it was him; feet up on a stool, staring out of the window. Somehow he had also sensed it was her, before she appeared in front of him.

'Why didn't you tell me?' asked Alby, looking up at her. His eyes were red, his dignity gone, his tears still falling. Her heart bled for him, regressed to a wounded little boy. She sighed and dropped in a chair to face him. But she could not. She lowered her head and her mind revisited the blur of the last forty-eight hours or so. Was that really all it had been since they were in the little cinema room and Andrina's assistant had produced the piece of paper and shown it to the old man? He had looked so shocked, then so thrilled. Then Andrina's assistant had looked so happy, then they had hugged and looked at each other and, eventually, turned silently to look at Sky. And Alby.

'Why didn't you tell me?' Alby repeated. His voice sounded so pitiful that Sky wanted to jump up and explain and hug Alby and make it all better. But she wanted someone to explain it to her and hug her and make it all better for her too. And that was not going to happen either.

All of a sudden her mind whizzed into overdrive, spinning through scenes from the past. She was leaving the palace, leaving her home, boarding a plane, touching down in Australia; waitressing, fruit-picking, out in the bush, trying to fight off that drunken farmhand who would not take no for an answer. She felt her distress, recalled the dismissive farmer, hitching a lift from that passing ute, ending up somewhere on the coast. Walking, hitching, sitting in cafes, paddling for miles along those endless beaches, with all she owned in the rucksack on her back. And then she found herself back in Byron. And she slowed down and there were colourful characters and laughter and warmth. And the only man who ever made her feel safe.

And here he was again. And he was crying, because of her. But she could not work out why. 'I didn't know,' she said softly. What else could she say?

Alby suddenly looked uncharacteristically furious. 'What the fuck do you mean? She's our daughter. You gave birth to her. Nearly forty fucking years ago!' He dropped his head into his hands and they sat, still as statues, for what seemed like hours.

Eventually Sky spoke. 'I was raped,' she almost whispered.

'I know. You told me.'

Sky looked up, confused.

'I couldn't believe my luck when I found you at that backpackers. And you were the same as ever. You actually asked me if I'd come all that way to get into your knickers! And I was desperate to prove it wasn't like that and that I just wanted to travel a bit and yes, I wanted to see you. And we kept talking and talking and I wanted to be there for you and look after you and then you told me about that man....'

'and I'd told no-one else. I'd had no-one to tell, I'd been so alone. And you were so kind to me and you listened and I could see the pain in your eyes and I could see that you wanted to cry too, that you'd support me and care for me....'

'and "one thing led to another"....'

"as they say...."

Both suddenly exhausted, it was a long time before they could speak again.

Do Not Ask

James had not been himself, ever since he had spoken to Athena. He had made his living by keeping secrets, for over forty years, but there was a limit, even for him. He was glad to have avoided the DNA test himself and wondered how many felt the same, in the wider population. It was such a quick and easy procedure but, from what he had recently witnessed, it could be akin to poking a viper's nest, rather than opening a can of worms. Perhaps throwing a cat among the pigeons. Maybe something completely harmless to humans or any other life forms. With regard to his colleagues it seemed to be causing rather a lot of disruption, to say the least.

He was in a difficult position, being the one holding the most information, though not necessarily aware of how it all fitted together. When Athena had entrusted him, with the Queen's blessing, to be the one who would reveal any tricky situations to the palace and New Ministers' staff, regarding their own DNA, he felt this task really was outside his remit. Conscientious as always, James had tried to do his best but was not confident he had succeeded in this instance. All he could do was present the basic facts as gently as possible, then leave the relative individuals, appropriately speaking, to sort things out for themselves.

As he had expected, it would take more than a surprise granddaughter to shock George. When James had found out she was also a surprise daughter to a couple of his colleagues, it all became a bit much, even for him. He was not sure how the situation had come about, nor how it should be explained to the Queen, but he realised, reluctantly, that it was he who would have to be the one to try. To his surprise, the Queen seemed quite unruffled and rather delighted with the whole scenario. James supposed that, considering the exploits of her own family over the years, the intrigues of another brood might offer a little light relief.

It had taken a lot for Sky to go back into her memories, having blocked them for so long. Simultaneously, and subconsciously, having deleted the trauma of the rape and the pregnancy which must have resulted from it, there had been no place in her mind for the glimmer of comfort which had been Alby's visit. It was all part of the bathwater that was thrown out with the baby. Not that Sky would put it like that to Alby, or Laura. Her baby, Laura, thirty-eight. If only Sky had known the truth, she could have kept her. But she did not, so she did not.

No longer could she hide the truth from herself, nor anyone else. Sky was determined to be as sensitive as she could in explaining everything as well as she could, but it was going to hurt. Perhaps her more than anyone. For now, her father would have to wait, as she always had for him. Laura and Alby were her priority and Sky found a quiet summerhouse in the palace grounds, where they could talk freely.

James could not have known what a bombshell the information would be, when he called Sky and Alby together to let them know he had been made aware that they had a daughter, who was also now working for the Queen. This was just the type of delicate situation which she needed to be aware of, to protect the palace from (any further) potential scandal. James had thought they kept up convincingly blasé appearances, not knowing that he was presenting Alby, and even Sky, with the idea that an adult child could suddenly materialise out of thin air. Hence their blank expressions were down to nothing but complete shock.

This was not diminished when James immediately ushered them into the cinema room, then left them to their own devices as soon as the screening ended. By that point, Sky realised she had just watched her father's life story and she could take no more. Alby had reached that point as soon as James had mentioned Laura. As she and George had turned to face them, apparently with little interest, both Sky and Alby had hastily excused themselves, without further explanation.

Sky sat as calmly as possible, whilst Alby paced nervously up and down the summerhouse, until they heard footsteps approaching on the loose stone path. The blonde hair, green eyes and long lashes seemed so familiar now. Sky suddenly realised that Laura was, to her, the spitting image of Alby. She caught her breath and stifled a sob, as all those missing years came back like a punch in the stomach. So much for keeping calm and explaining the situation clearly.

Momentarily, Alby thought how much he would have loved to say, 'your mum and I have something we'd like to tell you.' In the event, he took matters in hand with great diplomacy and managed to convey the gist of the meeting, whilst leaving Sky to fill in the details, as only she could, once she had regained her composure. She smiled, rather tearfully, at her daughter.

'So, you know my grandad? And you've got some more information about my family?' Laura asked. Her imploring tone caused Sky to catch her breath again. Gone were the quips, the witticisms and self-deprecation with which she usually handled awkward situations.

'Sit down,' Sky beckoned. She had moved three seats close together, for the first time. They all sat silently for a moment, then Sky took a deep breath and smiled gently at Laura. And Laura's dad. Wow. What a day.

'Do you know who we are?'

Laura's brow furrowed a little, involuntarily. 'I know you're one of the ministers but, I'm sorry, I'm not sure if I've seen you before,' she said, turning to Alby. They both felt so happy to hear her addressing them directly, it hardly mattered what she was saying.

'That's right. Sky's the People's Minister and I'm Head Chauffeur to the Queen,' replied Alby, bursting with pride for all of them.

'And you've been interviewing er, George, for a tv programme.'

'That's right. And you were at the screening because you're involved too, I guess?'

Sky had been waiting for the right time and she could delay it no longer. 'George is my dad,' she said, gently but clearly, leaving time for it to sink in.

There was no way to do justice to Laura's reaction, nor words to describe it. Except perhaps as a full spectrum of lightly expressed emotions. She looked from Sky to Alby and back, several times, intrigued. They were not dissimilar. 'So, are you my uncle?' she ventured, clearly having realised her relationship to Sky and found that too much to express.

Alby suddenly burst out laughing, a confused response to everything that was whirling inside him, 'No, love. I'm your dad.' At which point Laura burst into tears, quickly followed by Sky. And Alby, for good measure.

Eventually, Laura asked why they had not said anything after the film.

'It would have been a bit too much for all of us. I'm so sorry, love, so very sorry, for everything. And to you Alby, I'm so very sorry.'

It was no easy first conversation but it had to be done. Sky told her daughter, and the man who could have been her partner, that she had no say over which memories had been blocked by her trauma response. She did not recall her night with Alby, so she had been convinced her baby was the result of the rape. Sky knew how damaging families could be and she did not believe that she, or a baby with the same sensitive genes, could possibly have a positive life, together or apart, with the knowledge of a start like that. Never mind what genes that disgusting farmhand would have passed on. Sky was hazy about the details she had given at the hospital. All she remembered was that on the third day she had fed her baby, kissed her goodbye and left a note in her cot, which read....

'....Her name's Laura and she's half English. Please take good care of her and find someone to love her as much as I do,' sobbed Laura. 'I've still got it, I thought I might need it one day. As proof of who I was, or am, or something.'

Once they all calmed down enough to speak again, Laura asked Sky and Alby when they had found out who she was. When they told her 'about five minutes before the screening started,' her jaw dropped. When Alby replied in the same way, to her question about when he had heard he had a daughter, Laura's jaw almost hit the floor.

There had been no doubt Laura would be drawn to England, from the moment she could read the note. Though she had assumed her mum must have been Australian, dumped by her English dad after a holiday romance. They had all got it so wrong. But they quickly agreed on one thing - that none of them had done anything to feel sorry about.

Educating the Elite

Sam was wrestling with his own demons. Having complained, through one government after another, that life should be easier for those who cost the authorities the least, he was at a stalemate as to how such people could prove their own low incomes. It seemed simple for billionaires to hide away most of their fortunes, whilst those further down the scale often seemed unable to get the free prescriptions and council tax exemptions they needed, because these only came as add-ons when eligibility for specific benefits had been laboriously proved. The system often left claimants with no income for weeks or months, hence the growing need for food banks. Watching Boris, Sam thought he seemed to chase his own tail as much as the dog did. He wanted to reward those who lived healthy lives and never visited a doctor, saved their money and dealt with their own emergencies or rented out their house to provide an income for themselves, and a home for someone else, instead of claiming what they were entitled to. And all the other deserving people whose efforts went unnoticed. There seemed to be a lot of loopholes in trying to reward folk for doing the right thing. And Sam was determined to close them.

He and Brett had been discussing the reality of those who 'choose' not to work, with some less enlightened members of the palace staff. Sam was learning more about the class system all the time and it saddened him to realise the impact it was still having on so many lives. Much as Brett could see the faults in his own education, others from similar backgrounds had found it hard to dispel the myth that most of those claiming benefits were, to some extent, work-shy scroungers. Not that their parents, nor the tutors at their schools, would have used such a derisory term. But it seemed the implication had always been there, somehow. Fortunately, Brett's public persona was that of an eloquent man and he had been blessed with what was almost a superpower in a politician; the ability to listen and take on board the views of others. With his diplomacy and Sam's clear explanation of the difficulties people faced due to health problems, family breakdowns, job losses or sheer bad luck, it had not been too hard to change some long-held opinions.

Filthy Tramp

The Queen had been rather chuffed to discover the lengths to which Alison and James had been prepared to go, mainly in their own time, to provide her with such a pleasant surprise. She knew it would not have been an easy task for them to think of something she did not already have amongst her vast array of possessions, so this rather unusual choice of 'gift' had been most welcome. As usual, most of the effort had actually come from James, only the initial idea having been Alison's. But only she had the knowledge to come up with the suggestion, so her input was essential to the outcome.

Being unable to contain her excitement any longer, Alison had eventually broken the news to her boss over tea one day. They had been looking through the latest post when the Queen, seemingly unwittingly, pondered aloud, 'I wonder what happened to that poor homeless person who desperately needed my help but did not tell me how I could contact them?' At first Alison did not respond, so she continued, slowly, 'It would be wonderful to let them know how they were instrumental in changing the course of our nation.' Still nothing. 'It might really help him - or her - to know that....' Finally she could see Alison's resolve weakening.

'We found him! That is, er, James did. He really is a marvel, I don't know how he did it....' The Queen felt Alison might have had

223

a soft spot for James, had she not been happily married and young enough to be his daughter. She had been looking forward to seeing Alison's face when she revealed the big news, and the Queen felt that she, herself, showed just the right amount of surprise and joy. Over the years she had become quite the actress, particularly when visiting more exotic nations - 'Deep fried tarantula, how delicious. What a terrible shame I am already quite full.'

How times had changed, during her many decades on the throne. Back in the fifties her staff would have done everything humanly possible to ensure she never had to set eyes on a 'filthy tramp', to use the parlance of the day. Now here they were presenting one to her, like a pot of gold. Fortunately, the Queen was much happier to receive news of George, having plenty of golden pots already. Alison had looked so pleased with herself, as she scurried off that day, the Queen wished the news really had been a surprise to her. However, after a little soul-searching, Athena had realised she had no choice but to contact the Queen in advance of anyone else's announcements.

Meet the Family

It was time to tie up a few loose ends and the Queen sat as calmly as possible, lightly twisting a handkerchief in her lap, until there was a knock on the door of The Gold Room, as everyone seemed to call it. Rather ostentatious for her taste, the Queen had never seen fit to change any decor which could last a little longer, but the room seemed appropriately impressive for welcoming a new member into the fold.

The Queen was a little perturbed to notice the distance Sky maintained from her father, as he strode in. Laura, walking between them, seemed oblivious to the atmosphere and glowed happily. She curtsied slightly to the Queen, who smiled back graciously. She had not officially met Laura before, so would not remonstrate with her on this occasion.

Sky had not had the time or the inclination to reach far towards George, as yet. The film had done little to heal the deep wounds of her childhood nor to solve the puzzle of so many unanswered questions. She seemed to be in shock from all the recent revelations and the Queen made a mental note to arrange as much time off for Sky as she might need. Relentless stoicism is not for everyone, she chided herself.

'A very good afternoon to you, Mr....'

'George,' he interrupted, as the Queen held out her hand to him. Laura beamed, Sky winced and George shook the proffered hand vigorously. Containing her bemusement admirably, the Queen stepped back a little further than she intended, narrowly missing a dozing Jasper. She was always amused when her podgy little dogs showed no qualms about yapping at her in annoyance. She found their attitude so refreshing, compared to most humans.

'Please, do take a seat,' the Queen indicated a large sofa with elaborately carved legs and gold upholstery, which would comfortably seat her three guests. Sky looked tempted by a separate chair but thought better of it.

'Nice place you've got here, Your Majesty,' said George, with a twinkle in his eye. She warmed to him, while Sky cooled further. She had earned her right to make those sort of little jokes to the Queen. Who did he think he was?

The Queen fairly twinkled back at George. Thank goodness for the modernisation of the monarchy. She found it so relaxing to be able to speak to everyone on the same level. 'It is a great pleasure to meet you both,' she smiled at Laura and George, 'and I have to tell you there may be more to this meeting than any of you might be expecting.' She widened her glance to include Sky and wondered if Sky was quite ready for any further revelations.

'I am most grateful to members of my loyal staff for tracing the catalyst who gave rise to so many of the changes which his daughter, granddaughter, and their colleagues are now implementing, and

I am so looking forward to further conversations with each of you.' She was pleased to notice a quiet look of satisfaction spread across all their faces. 'And what a joy it must be for you to have found each other after all this time.

Now, I am about to introduce you to someone who is solely privy to the details which she is about to share with us. Indeed, one has - that is, I have - chosen to receive this information at the same time as all of you. It seemed wrong for me to learn more of your family history before any of you and I am told it is most important, having only been added to the database yesterday.' Befitting the occasion, and with a casual nod to her dislike for modern technology, the Queen picked up a discreet little gold bell, from the small table beside her. As soon as she rang it, the door opened and Athena appeared, carrying a folder of papers and smiling politely at the assembled group.

'Good afternoon,' Athena addressed George, Laura and Sky, 'You won't recognise me but we are, in fact, linked through my position in genealogical research and I am most happy to see you here together today.'

'Your Majesty,' Athena bowed slightly as she faced the Queen, 'it is a great honour for me to introduce you to the newest members of your family....'

As the Queen regarded Athena, the others turned to look at the door, intrigued by who would be entering next. They waited. It remained closed.

Gradually, everyone turned back to Athena, with some confusion. She opened her folder and handed each of them a chart, which did not appear to make anything much clearer. Athena was beginning to lose her nerve. Normally a picture of self-assurance, this was one situation she had never envisaged being a part of her rather illustrious career.

The Queen studied the chart for a little while, before addressing Athena. 'I see one of my favourite earls is on here. He really is a very pleasant young man.' She kept her head down for a few more moments, then turned to the occupants of the sofa, 'And I see George is on the chart, just above him.'

Athena wished she could take a photo of the faces in front of her. A little levity would be very welcome right now. She believed that 'gobsmacked' would be the correct term to describe them, in other circles. 'Yes, Ma'am. In fact, being slightly to the side on the chart, it indicates that George is, in fact, uncle to the current earl.'

The Queen employed one of her famous, inscrutable looks. 'How very interesting,' she said.

Sky thought what a good time it would be to let loose a torrent of expletives, take up drinking again, or run out screaming. While she chewed over her choice array of inappropriate reactions to this latest bombshell, George decided to put his two bob's worth in, 'Do I get a castle now, Your Majesty? Or will I have to wait?'

The Queen chose to continue with the inscrutable look, whilst she decided whether she still thought George was as charmingly amusing as she did before she had learned they were cousins of some sort. First that soap star and now this. Soon she would not have to try very hard to be ordinary. The family seemed to be getting commoner every day. Without warning, she threw her head back and laughed very loud. Everyone stared at her for a moment and she regained her composure.

Laura had never seen a startled prawn but now knew what it felt like to be one. She had no idea what else to feel - shock, pride, embarrassment, shame? Though the chart had been produced with diplomacy, it was obvious George was not a legitimate member of the family and that all sorts of controversies would ensue, if this situation were ever to be made public. What a huge scoop it would be for anyone working for, say, the most prominent disseminator of news in the country. Such as Andrina. Oh shit, thought Laura. Now she understood what all those talent show entrants meant when they talked about the rollercoaster they'd been on. She'd give them rollercoasters! At least she would if she ever felt she could mention anything about this situation to anyone. Except her strange....new....

unusual....Royal Family! It suddenly struck her. It was not just George, it was her too. And her new mum. They were all royalty!

Judging by the look on Sky's face, she had just been struck by the same thought.

Judging by the look on the Queen's face, she might just be about to throw up. She rose sharply, said, 'do excuse me for a moment,' and promptly disappeared through the door, as fast as any nonagenarian can.

Seemingly taking a leaf out of James's book, Athena decided she could serve no further purpose to the group at this stage and felt it best to leave them to sort things out for themselves. She also imagined her cat would urgently need feeding, right now. Hastily, she almost threw business cards to each of them, imperceptibly crossing her fingers as she invited them to contact her if she could be of any further assistance. With a quick smile and a nod, she was gone.

George looked after her, rather smugly. 'What else can she do for us? She's just told me I'm Royalty! That'll do for now,' he chuckled. When he stretched his feet onto one of the gold coffee tables, Sky let out a small squeal and unleashed just a little of her pent-up fury.

No-one was as surprised as she herself, when the Queen re-entered the room. It must have been an hour or so, and she could so easily have left the situation to someone else to sort out, but the Queen had come up with a plan and determined to get to know the ordinary family she had always wanted.

Whatever had been said since she left, George seemed a little subdued. He stood up and bowed a little, as she came in. The Queen was rather touched, but saddened to realise how confronting all of this must have been for Sky. George started to mumble something about getting back to the hostel and the Queen held up her hand to quieten him. 'You won't be going back there. I've taken the liberty of having your belongings moved to alternative accommodation.' She nodded towards one of the charts. 'Just while we all take time to absorb this information.'

George looked worried. He quickly regressed to one of the many times and places where he seemed to be at fault, about to be punished for something he did not understand. 'Where am I going?' he asked, blankly, afraid of the answer to come.

'You'll be staying here for a while. If that's all right with you.'

'The palace? Buckingham Palace?' George said slowly. As the light gently returned to his eyes, something dimmed a little in the Queen's, as she resolved to keep narrowing the class divide, starting with her new family. She really was related to Sky. How wonderful. And now she had Laura too. Another distant cousin. Or something.

'For the time being, the staff will be informed merely that an apartment has been made available to members of the Minister's family. There will be plenty of space for you all to spend time together, whenever you so wish. There is no hurry for us to decide what information, if indeed any, we will share with our colleagues, compatriots or families - that is, family.' She warmed at her remark, paused and looked towards George, 'I trust the arrangement meets with your approval?' Unsure about the situation herself, and aware of how unintentionally starchy she could sound when trying to explain tricky matters, the Queen gave them all a small, and very genuine, smile. Laura smiled back happily and George nodded vigorously. Sky still looked rather stunned.

Meanwhile

Tom continued to divide his time between troubleshooting around the community pubs, overseeing the palace renovations and spending as much time as possible at home (or as little, according to the prevailing moods of his family).

Brett continued to revolutionise the tax, prison, legal, education and employment systems, in his own, quietly restrained, dignified, middle class way. Even as his assistants, the palace staff and numerous members of the public adopted him as their poster boy, he denied this virtual fan club and despaired at his chances of ending up with a nice little family like Tom's.

Whilst Sam tore apart and rewrote every little bit of annoying legislature he could lay his hands on, he continued to hate all forms of paperwork with a passion - but had never found anything quite so satisfying in his life. He had always known he would have to fight for recognition, despite realising his pacifist tendencies would never allow him to engage in physical altercations. Yet it had come as a shock to discover that the most productive way for him to release his inner fury had turned out to be through the innate gift he had for making officialdom understandable to all.

Sal was deeply committed to righting the wrongs of the health and social care systems and had been carrying on with the various plans she and Sky had devised. It was amazing how freely new ideas had sprung into their consciousness, given a little mutual encouragement. Sometimes they had more brainwaves than they needed or could cope with, even when there were two of them. So it was a lot to handle on her own, notwithstanding the input available to her from both their teams. But if anyone deserved a break it was Sky. Sal would never deny anyone a worthy break - except herself, obviously.

Andrina continued to make her mark in a big way: dealing with all the major players at the highest and lowest levels, changing the way the media was run and, ultimately, how the world would be governed. Considering the serious, and sometimes intimidating, presence which she and Sam adopted in their roles, it amused them no end to imagine they might run into people they knew, an observant member of the public or even one of the other ministers, when they were out paintballing, go-karting or generally being silly together. Just as friends, of course.

Little Birds

Despite the ongoing workflow and accomplishments, there had been a tangible air of disquiet for some time now, particularly in the rooms most often frequented by the ministers. Sal, especially, was finding it a struggle not to have Sky around, and there could be no doubt the palace rumour mill had reopened. The undercurrent was more focussed on concern than gossip these days, but the whispers which reached the ears of the Queen (usually via Alison) were still troubling. Other little birds had informed the Queen that Sky had not spent a great deal of time availing herself of the apartment where George had taken up residence, although it seemed some peace had been made and the relationship between George and Laura continued to blossom.

The knock on her office door could not have come soon enough, though the Queen was slightly taken aback to observe that Sky was accompanied by Alby. The Queen had been made aware of her chauffeur's role in the current 'situation' but she was not clear why he was standing in front of her now. She was more accustomed to exchanging pleasantries with the back of his head.

Sky produced a rather world-weary smile and asked the Queen if they might speak to her for a few minutes. The Queen guessed that might not be long enough for whatever they wanted to tell her, but she did not bank on Sky's recent experience of explaining the unexplainable.

'We thought it was only fair to let you know who Laura's father is, considering we're all, sort of, related now.' Sky looked a bit sheepish and the Queen sank to her chair in shock. Not incest, on top of everything else, surely? Just when she thought the family had pretty much run the gamut of every conceivable indiscretion. Sky and Alby observed the Queen with surprise, then turned to each other and suddenly twigged. Laura had been right, there were similarities in their looks. But not that many.

Finally, Sky and Alby found something amusing again. As they both began to smile, the Queen's expression changed to confusion, then mirth, until they all allowed themselves a quiet chuckle.

'What I mean to say is....' Sky looked to Alby and he nodded, '....we didn't break any palace rules or anything. We didn't have a relationship here....' (Her voice broke off, as she imagined Alby thinking, "or anywhere else, actually".) 'We only, er, got together, briefly, when he suddenly turned up in Australia....'

'You mean it worked?' the Queen almost shrieked with enthusiasm, causing confusion to spread across Sky's face and embarrassment to cover Alby's. The Queen observed that the poor boy still went red, even at his age.

Far be it from her to interfere in the lives of her subjects, or staff, but around forty years ago the Queen had concluded that a little light meddling would not go amiss in Alby's case. It would have been too much to buy him a round-the-world trip for loyal service, after just a few years, but to show him a certain postcard she had received and to remark upon the town from which it had been sent, did not seem too much of a contrivance to her. A generous bonus for his upcoming birthday had seemed quite reasonable too.

And now Alby remembered the postcard. And forgot he normally still tried to address the Queen by her official title. 'You showed me that postcard on purpose,' he ventured. 'When you asked who I thought S might be, you already knew....'

'Alby dear, I cannot in all honesty say that I actually knew who had posted it but I had a feeling that my conjecture may well have been accurate.' The Queen waffled in an effort to cover up her historical subterfuge.

And then it was Sky's turn to remember the postcard, vaguely. When she had first stopped off in Byron, and after a drunken evening with some fellow backpackers, she had returned to ruminating about whether the Queen had really given the order for her to be fired. Or sacked, as it was back then. As she was, back then. Sky had remembered when she first thought the Queen was really her friend. She had been so excited and overwhelmed and thought it must be too good to be true. And then, of course, it was. And she was out on her ear and her mum was having another go at her for being useless and, what else was it her mum had said? Oh yes, 'You're just like your dad. That bloody waste of space who's never paid a penny for you or to me or for anything. Why don't you just get out, like he did?' Too damaged by her own pain to acknowledge it was her mum's pain talking, Sky did as Maureen suggested. It was to be many years before she returned.

Feeling she had already lost her real mum, and wanting to test her royal surrogate somehow, after a few beers it had seemed like a good idea to fire off a cryptic postcard to the Queen. Sky had reasoned that a card signed with her full name might not get through, unusual as it was even in those hippier times, so she had settled on just an S. If the powers-that-be had chosen to force her out then they would not willingly enable the Queen to find her again. But Sky had not really thought it through, she had not included an address. She had more in common with her dad than she liked to admit.

Once it turned out they all knew a little more about how Laura had come into existence than they had previously realised, there was not much more to say, for the moment.

As Sky closed the door and walked away with Alby, he looked at her seriously and asked, 'do you remember what I told you about my arrival at the backpackers?' Sky regarded him intently and shook her head.

Alby bottled out. 'The bloke at the check-in asked my name, for the register, and when I said Alby Wright he said, "Sure yer will mate but what's yer name?" '

Sky was confused for a moment, then twigged as he started to smirk. She smiled too, glad to be back on old terms.

What Alby had really wanted Sky to remember was that he had flown all the way to the other side of the world, to find her, for his 21st birthday. And now he wanted to tell her that Laura was the latest and best 21st birthday present she could ever have given him.

Letting the Cats Out

As things settled down and those involved learned to accept their new family connections, it had to be agreed that it would be nigh on impossible to keep the general public in the dark indefinitely, never mind their nearest and (sometimes) dearest.

The Queen took the wise precaution of ensuring that Philip's various weapons had been removed from their private quarters, before dropping the bombshell. Granted, she could have approached the subject a little more gently, but Philip was hardly known for his tact and the Queen liked to have a little fun herself sometimes. So, in the end, it went something like this.... 'Remember the gentleman you referred to yesterday as "that scruffy oik who seems to have moved in"?' As usual, Philip was paying more attention to his newspaper than his wife, who just happened to be the most important woman in the country, to everyone else, so she felt no compulsion to employ more consideration than necessary. 'Well, he's a long lost cousin of mine so I've invited him and his family to stay for as long as they like.'

Philip promptly swore like a trooper, dropped his coffee in his lap, swore a lot more, kicked out at Jasper, lost his balance as the dog ran off, and ended up splayed across a large, decorative footstool, shaped like a swan. This only added to the Queen's enjoyment, as she recalled something her beloved father once told her. Neither he, nor she, had expected or wished to accede to the throne so, after he found himself in that unfortunate position, he did what he could to make her future task seem less onerous. As young Elizabeth had been feeding and chattering away to the swans on a beautiful summer's afternoon, beside one of the royal lakes, her father had knelt beside her, taken her hand in his and said, 'They'll all be yours one day, you know.'

A look of puzzlement had spread across her face as she asked, in awe, 'All the swans on this lake?'

She still remembered how Daddy's eyes had twinkled, and his lips curled up into a grin, as he told her, 'No, all the swans in the whole kingdom.'

Then her innocent reply, 'But what will I do with them all?'

Choosing to avoid her husband's stroppy mood and spend a little more time in pleasant reminiscing, the Queen had surreptitiously removed herself from the room and was musing on how the line of succession had never been written in stone. It seemed there was always the possibility that anything could happen. And who knew what might happen next.

With regard to Philip, she had to acknowledge that he had been badgering her for far too long to repeal the half-hearted Hunting Act. She knew just how to put a stop to that and she giggled quietly to herself as she imagined the scene which would ensue when she announced that she had finally taken his advice. She would have to move pretty sharp once she informed him that the act would be replaced with a real law, which would ban any 'sports' that involved terrifying, injuring or killing any living being.

Matters between Sky and George would not be sorted out quickly but they were making gradual progress. It would be easier once a few more people had been let in on the secret and, they reasoned, nobody else had the right to be shocked anywhere near as much as they all had been.

Unsurprisingly, things did not quite work out that way. James had seen it coming and, uncharacteristically, managed to inveigle a few days off, to avoid finding himself responsible for everyone around him, yet again. He really was getting a bit old for all this, he told himself sometimes. On his rare days off he would walk for miles along the river, contemplate retiring to a warmer country or travelling the world, then report back for duty and carry on as he always had. Having heard the latest news about Sky, from the Queen herself, James could not even admit to himself that he was just the slightest bit disappointed it was not he who had turned out to be a secret member of The Firm. Maybe he should have that DNA test after all.

It fell to Sky to take the initiative in explaining things to her closest colleagues, and inviting the other ministers to George's apartment seemed a good way to give them a small clue, before her announcement. The Queen had chosen not to divert attention by attending, but had sent Alison along as her representative.

When all the cats were finally out of the bag, Alison quietly remarked to Sal, 'I must say, the situation got a little bit bigger than I expected, when I first set out to surprise the Queen by finding that anonymous letter writer.' As taken aback as everyone else by the many turns of events, she did not know quite what else to say.

Sal could only respond, 'No kidding - it's pretty much blown our idea out of the water.'

'What was your idea?'

'Sky and I were going to take her charity shopping - in disguise, of course. She let it slip that it's on her bucket list.'

'Oh please do - she'd love that.'

Sal glanced over at Sky, not wanting to intrude on her new-found family, but Sky beckoned her over. Laura had just mentioned George's film and he had replied with feeling, 'I knew there must be a reason I'd survived it all,' so Sky was feeling warmer towards everyone.

'And this is the sister I never had,' she announced as she grabbed Sal's hand. You could have heard a pin drop - surely this was a relation too far?

It was. Sky continued, 'Not all the best relations are connected by blood and DNA and all that stuff, you know.' She would never know how those words, at that minute, touched Sal. Then Laura made it even better by pointing out that Sal's name could be spelt out using the initials of Sky, Alby and her, their daughter. It seemed they had the makings of one big happy family.

New men or not, Sam, Brett and Tom were huddled together in a corner, a little uncomfortable with all the deep emotions suddenly flying around. 'This is nuts, you couldn't make it up,' observed Sam.

'Well they do say truth is stranger than fiction,' replied Brett, equally out of his depth in this current sea of feelings.

As George passed by, Tom took the opportunity to engage him in conversation, hoping for a little more information about this instant family his fellow minister had produced. But all those years on the streets had made George a cautious man - very careful with what he said and who he trusted. 'You'll have to wait for the film,' he responded amiably, 'I've sworn James to secrecy until everyone gets to see it on the telly. Anyway, it's not quite finished yet.' With that, he headed off for his daily jacuzzi and the alcohol-free fizz he liked to keep on ice at all times. He would be pleased to report, to his new cousin/host, that he was taking to his new lifestyle like a duck to water, or to the palace born.

Andrina, rushed off her feet as ever, turned up just in time to offer a few congratulations. Being responsible for the screening of the programme that would tell George's story, and now reveal his newly discovered status to the world as diplomatically as possible, she had been privately briefed in advance of today's gathering. Anyway, in contrast to the other ministers, Sky's family situation was not the most shocking revelation to confront Andrina recently.

Charity Shopping

As the New Ministers continued to launch further schemes and overturn the laws instated by former governments, dissenters began to rear their heads again, in a final display of resistance. The knowledge that the New Ministers were expressing and acting on the wishes of the population, more honestly than the Old Guard had ever done, could not sway the outgoing establishment's inherent assumption that they knew what was best for the country. Or for themselves, at least. As all the new departments planned positive changes and campaigns which would benefit the man, woman and non-binary person on the street, the Old Guard plotted to regain the power they believed was rightfully theirs.

Meanwhile, encouraged by Alison, and to lighten the mood for Sky, Sal had forged ahead with plans to surprise the Queen and her new cousin with the long-awaited shopping trip. It might have been fun for Laura and Alison, and maybe even a few others, to join them, but that could have turned a simple outing into a security nightmare. As it was, plenty was going on in the country to divert people's attention away from something as mundane as a few older ladies wandering around looking for bargains.

It would have been too much of a giveaway to use one of the Queen's many cars and too much of a parking nightmare to use anyone else's. Therefore, Sal had decided the only sensible option would be to hail cabs on the street. They could have stuck to one cab and had the driver sit outside the shops with the meter running, but that would also have been likely to draw unwanted attention. Sometimes it was much easier to be poor and unknown.

When the day arrived, Alison relieved the Queen's regular lady-in-waiting of her duties and turned up at the Queen's bedroom door with her morning cup of tea, toast and a full disguise, guaranteed to effectively hide the identity of any wearer (according to the most reputable purveyors of such items). The Queen was thrilled, of course. Instantly regressing to the seventies, she only wished Alby could drive them all round in the yellow Capri. How simple life had been then, with the benefit of hindsight (and lack of insight). She eagerly slipped into her outfit and followed Sal's instructions on how to behave like an ordinary person. It had been some time since she attempted it and the Queen hoped she was not too rusty.

Sal had made the plan a little more exciting for Sky by not telling her anything about it, but finding a spurious reason to meet her at a place which, by a happy coincidence, was in a particularly good suburb for charity shops. It would draw less attention if only Sal was seen leaving the palace with a visitor and it would be amusing for Sky to realise who Sal had turned up with, then keep a straight face about it. To keep things simple, and safe, no-one else was to be informed or involved.

So far, so good. Sal had ventured out onto the road past the palace, hailed the most uninterested cabbie she could spot, and ushered the Queen in with minimal fuss. As they vacated the cab at the agreed meeting place, where Sky was waiting on the corner, she immediately realised the plan, beamed briefly, then waved a simple greeting to her friends, ready for an exciting day of charity shopping, never to be repeated.

As aficionados know, there is no way of telling which charity shops will have just what you are looking for on any given day. It is all very hit and miss. But Sal was so pleased she had chosen this area - fortunately the Queen had scored some delightful little china corgis in the first shop and some tartan thermal leggings in the second. It was not quite her own tartan but she decided to go wild and buy them anyway.

After Sky was unexpectedly confronted by a selection of genealogy research books, and seemed about to have hysterics, they decided to take a break and have a cup of coffee in a local cafe. The Queen did remark a little too loudly that she thought the milk might be orf but they seemed to get away with it.

Sal's only aim was to ensure that the Queen and Sky had an enjoyable day, so she was pleased to notice Sky light up when she spotted a small seventies guidebook to, of all places, Byron Bay. It had suddenly become a lot more special to her. Before Sal could get her purse out, the Queen was patting Sky's hand and saying, 'Please let me buy it for you, dear.'

As they emerged into the street, looking for a cab to hail to the next batch of charity shops, there was a flurry of excitement on the other side of the road, a couple of bright flashes and some sudden movement around them. As the shots rang out, the Queen dropped to the ground.

Time had stood still for a moment and Sky was relieved to note the screaming was not coming from her, nor Sal, nor the Queen. But the Queen lay pale and motionless, her arms loosely resting over her head.

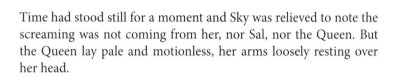

There was no other sound, save for the laboured breathing of a man lying off to the side of the Queen. Now Sky could see what had happened. The man was James. And he had taken a bullet for the Queen, as he had always vowed he would.

The hazy end to the shopping trip was becoming clearer to Sky. It was only a few days ago but it could have been a lifetime. Or five minutes. That's trauma for you. Now she remembered it well. She wished she did not, but a trigger is a trigger. She had heard the doctor say that she had to be sedated for her own good. Apparently it had been her screaming in the end.

Sky gradually became aware that she was in the palace apartment and that someone was holding a vigil by her bed. Her vision was a bit of a blur and the person had their head down, until Sky murmured something. As the head shot up in response, she saw the love in George's eyes, and with it, a new beginning for them.

Laura had been dozing in a chair in the corner, near her mum, and she called Sal in as soon as Sky showed signs of life. It did not take long for the three of them to connect the pieces of the puzzle.

Whilst not exactly relaxed about what had happened, Sal was able to hold it together enough to summarise the situation. And her first realisation was that they had taken an insane risk.

It was lucky that James had allowed himself those few days off: it had ensured he was on the ball to notice the warning signs of the hare-brained scheme. Whilst noting the possible dangers, he did not want to spoil a special day out for the Queen and he always lived in hope that nothing would go wrong. He knew there had been certain rumours but there always were.

Sky felt it was an unfortunate turn of phrase to say that James had lived in hope, until she realised only one person could have told that to Sal. The next surprise was how pleased she had been to realise he must be alive. Of course James would have been there. Any time the Queen had taken a stupid risk, he had always been there. And, sensibly, always wearing his vest. Whichever one had offered state of the art protection at the time. He had taken quite a jolt, but that was all.

The Queen, for her part, had apparently done what James had always drummed into her - if you hear shots or feel threatened: fall down, stay down and play dead. So it seemed they were both ok. Except someone had tried to kill the Queen.

The End of Civilization

Misleading the public was no light-hearted matter but then neither was an assassination attempt. Having found herself becoming dangerously enlightened with regard to some of the more nefarious activities of certain powerful organisations and world leaders, Andrina had made the call to take a leaf out of the communist rule book. To draw a veil over when to make a definitive statement on the extent to which the Head of State may or may not still be alive. It meant everyone needed to lay low for a while.

It went without saying that none of the New Ministers had any previous experience of this sort of situation. Andrina released a statement to inform the public that the Queen was 'resting and recovering' and that no further information would be provided for the time being. It seemed imperative that details were protected whilst the police and intelligence agencies concentrated all their efforts on discovering who was responsible for the blatant attack. Just when the country was finally becoming a safer and happier place for everyone, this incident had the potential to turn back time to the Dark Ages.

Sky and, particularly, Sal struggled not to blame themselves for this turn of events, reasoning that they had only planned a shopping trip, not intentionally attempted to bring about the end of civilization.

The ministers and their departments continued to forge ahead, albeit with a little less vigour and in a more subdued fashion than before. Fear is a powerful commander and life changes when a potential killer is on the loose.

It was hard to see how the clock could merely be turned back to the positive zeitgeist of the preceding months. Until, out of the blue, the police received a tip off which led them right to where they needed to be. And, this time, no Old Boys Club in the world was going to save those responsible for the damage that had been done. Some called high treason and demanded the death penalty be reinstated for those concerned. Tempting as it was, the New Ministers had resolved to take the high ground and refused to fall at the first challenge.

People began to acknowledge that the country was no more full of killers than it had ever been: one person had simply fired a gun and caused outrage amongst decent folk everywhere.

Andrina's apparent fearlessness against some of the darker characters on the world stage had made a great impression. If a shopkeeper's daughter could make such a stand then surely the most powerful international military and political leaders must have the guts to use their power for good. Time was running out for the planet and there could be no choice but to fight for it together. As Andrina would be reiterating in her next speech.

Changes

As charges were laid and cases put together, Sky returned to her duties. But she noticed something different about the palace: the Queen never seemed to be around anymore.

William was in attendance more often and one day he and Harry appeared together, walking and chatting in the grounds. They seemed relatively relaxed and at peace with the world. Privately they joked about how their grandmother had often posed the question of who might send her a telegram when she reached the great milestone of 100 years. And William talked about how he had loved the comradeship of the forces but regretted that, as an intended heir to the throne, he had not been permitted to take such an active role as his brother had been able to insist upon.

'Come on Will, you're way too soft to kill anyone.'

'Well maybe that's a good thing. What we really need to be doing now is reducing, and ultimately eliminating, the need for any armed services. We should be providing young people - and everybody - with the stability and contentment that leads to peace.'

'You really should have been a politician you know.'

'Nah.'

'Nah, you're right.'

'Too sincere?'

'Yep.'

'Cheers Bro. You know Granny's favourite phrase - what would Di....'

'....would Mum do?'

'Well what do you think she'd have done about the way we've been behaving?'

'She'd have knocked our bloody heads together.'

'Damn right she would. Figuratively speaking, of course. She would have been so happy to see us both settled down, providing her with grandchildren to fuss over. It would have broken her heart to see us at each other's throats.'

'Especially since it took an attack on The Boss to sort us out.'

Things seemed to be progressing well; the case against those who had plotted to kill the Queen was indisputable and Andrina felt less tense than she had for some time. Until the tabloid editor rang her private number with his suggestion for the next morning's headline.

Attempting to contain a vast wave of inner fury, speak through pursed lips and sound unruffled was a challenge. Which, as usual, Andrina managed to pull off. 'I have no idea where you are getting your information but, if you wish to look like an incompetent fool, please feel free to publish whatever you choose.' She paused, to listen to the irritating, whiny voice, belonging to the irritating, whiny man. 'If I were you, I would think very carefully about the repercussions which are likely to ensue, should you run with "The Queen is Dead" or words to that effect. Now I really am very busy and I have to go.'

Her heart was racing as she placed the phone carefully on her desk. It would be foolhardy of him to go ahead and publish but there was no guarantee he would not. Andrina doubted she could risk it for more than a day or so. If one editor had heard rumours, the others would not be far behind. And the situation would swiftly escalate to a level where none of them would care so much what was true as who could claim the story first. Not to mention how the assassination of the Queen would be just the excuse needed to mobilise the troops, or push the button, in any number of countries.

It was not the timing Andrina would have chosen but she knew she had to make some fast decisions. There was no time to waste on explaining to her confused assistant why she was cancelling all her appointments for the day. Andrina knew who she had to contact and what they needed to do. How she could arrange that urgently, without drawing unwanted attention, was more of an issue.

Headlines

After all the dramas of recent weeks, everyone was looking forward to getting together to watch the first episode of Who Do I Think I Am? It was one of Andrina's initial pet projects and was predicted to turn into quite an occasion. Particularly by the small number of individuals who were privy to the incendiary nature of the information to be revealed in the programme. It may have been a rash decision to present the Inner and Outer Circles with more information than they may be ready to handle, at the same time as it was made known to the general public and the world at large, but there seemed to be no going back on taking risks now.

Somewhere along the line it had been decided that it would be fun to have a 'pot luck' indoor picnic to accompany the viewing, in the spirit of one of the phenomenally successful community pub initiatives. So it was that the New Ministers, their assistants and various palace staff gathered together, with a light sprinkling of royalty, in one of the grander reception rooms of the palace.

They squeezed onto plush 17th century sofas with their vegan treats, placed their porcelain plates of poppadoms on mahogany coffee tables, or sat on Persian rugs, eating pizza straight from the box (some of the new trainees had not received the memo, apparently).

The chatter was lively as introductions were made, roles discussed and gossip caught up on. Gradually the talking quietened and the shushes increased as the ads ended and the country prepared to enjoy the start of a much-touted new series....

'We regret to advise that we are unable to show the advertised programme at this time....'

Groans of disappointment and confused glances were exchanged around the function room and the country.

....due to the pressing nature of the announcement which follows. Please stay tuned....'

The screen changed, a little less smoothly than is to be expected on a major tv channel, to a hazy view of greenery and water of some sort, in the background. It was almost as if the location was intended to remain secret. Which it was.

The camera panned around and the screen cleared, then focussed on the Queen, sitting next to Prince Philip. More casually dressed than they had ever been seen in public, they both wore relaxed smiles and seemed to have lost years. They could have passed for late eighties, at least.

'My husband and I,' she glanced at him affectionately, 'no - Philip and I would like to reassure you that we are still very much with you all, not just in spirit. I was tempted to say we're feeling quite "bright-eyed and bushy-tailed" but, at our age, we decided that might be.... what was it?'

'Pushing our luck?'

'Presumptuous.

Should any of you have suspicions that I, particularly, am in fact "no longer around", as I gather certain newspapers were about to announce, we discussed the best way to prove otherwise. Please note, however, that our chosen method is not intended to imply that we are being held hostage, nor are we seeking more of your hard-earned savings to bring us home safely. We are merely having a brief taste of freedom, whilst we still have the chance in this lifetime. Rest assured that I will be "back in business" again very soon. It's not quite the end of the line, nor time for my Quexit yet....'

At which point the view widened slightly, briefly showing a beautiful beach (which could have been just about anywhere) in the background.

A moment later the screen was dominated by the day's headlines, as the Queen and her husband held newspapers up in front of them. Philip struggled with a broadsheet, which announced in a slightly restrained typeface:

'Russia, China and the USA set to sign
universally supported agreement.'

The Queen, choosing again to exercise her common touch, had chosen one of the tabloids:

'WORLD PEACE IN OUR TIME
- UK Minister brokers historic pact.'

****

Thank you for reading my book.

It is not just a novel.

If you are feeling inspired and enthusiastic
about making the world a better place,
you might like to take up
one of the ideas I have included,
or start up one of the groups suggested.

If so, I would love to hear from you.

Wishing you happy days,

Jay

niftyuk@ yahoo.co.uk